# Contents

# Foreword

This book has been written for any individual who is considering undertaking a mentoring role with a secondary school student.

There is a danger that unless a number of organisational and implementation principles and requirements are recognised, this most valuable process will not achieve its potential – indeed in some cases it can cause more problems than it solves. In this book the author will draw from his extensive mentoring experience to provide suggestions and strategies that the reader can use to determine the status of their mentoring strategies and develop them to acceptable levels. He will also provide organisational guidelines that need to be followed if an accountable and productive mentoring programme is to be implemented.

In examining aspects of the implementation of such a programme, it may be useful to firstly consider a case study which illustrates the importance of developing self-esteem and resilience in students and how a failure to do so may have tragic consequences.

**Case Study: Franklin**

## This story reveals the tragedy of unhealthy self-esteem and low resilience.

Franklin brought to Secondary School a reputation fitting that of a juvenile delinquent from Juvenile Detention Centre. He'd been suspended from primary school more times than any student who had ever enrolled into a particular Secondary School. He had a lengthy record of shoplifting, he'd physically assaulted one of his primary teachers and through his reputation as a "fighter" he kept his peers in a constant state of fear. It was an automatic decision that the authorities came to in designating Franklin to join my class for the "academically slow and behaviourally difficult" students.

Seated at the back of the room, empty desks either side of him, Franklin introduced himself to me on day one of his secondary schooling by standing, staring me straight in the eye and saying:

"My name is Franklin. I hate school. I've never had a teacher I liked and I don't like the look of you Thompson!"

"Thompson! I can't read – I won't read in class, so don't ask me to read in class."

"Thompson! I can't do maths – I won't do maths, so don't ask me to do maths."

"Thompson! I can't write, I won't write, so don't ask me to write."

Just as I was recovering from this tirade, Franklin recommenced his "state of affairs" address.

"Hey, Thompson! What's the story in this school about smoking?"

"Well Franklin, if you get caught smoking at this school you are automatically suspended," I replied.

"That could be a problem Thompson. I've been smoking since I was seven and I need a packet of Rothmans a day to see me through."

Franklin continued:

"Hey, Thompson!"

My God, I thought, what now? Is this ever going to stop?

"Hey, Thompson, what's that old shed outside the window used for?"

"Well Franklin, that's an old storeroom that no one uses any longer."

"I'll tell you what I'll do for you, Thompson. When I need a smoke, I'm going out to that storeroom. Don't ask me what I'll be doing because I'll tell you that now – I'll be having

# Hey, Thompson

A ors

**Dev** **ience**
**s**

# How To Use This Book

This book has been written for mentors who are working to develop the self-esteem and resilience of a secondary school student. The author believes that all secondary school students will benefit from spending time in addressing self-esteem and resilience development needs. This is a very difficult task for a student to undertake alone. It is understood that it is not always possible for mentors to be found for secondary school students so teachers or parents can also introduce the activities and recommendations included in this book to the student.

It will be noted that the first person (e.g. "you") is used in association with many of the activities and tables of explanation. This is done so that once the activity has been introduced to the student by a mentor, parent or teacher, the student can work on their own through the activity and, on conclusion, discuss outcomes with the mentor. The more "personal" the students consider the activities to be, the more meaningful the disclosure they will share.

## To get optimum results from this book the following steps are recommended:

- ❑ The mentor should read through the Introduction to get a feel for the general focus of the book.

- ❑ Mentors should read through the information in Chapter 1 and enter into a general discussion about self-esteem with the student.

- ❑ The Thompson Self-Esteem Model should be discussed with the student.

- ❑ Students should be given the first two case studies to read in their own time.

- ❑ The students should then be encouraged to complete the *Student Performance Profiler*. Outcomes of this will highlight the chapters, activities and considerations that will be of immediate value to the student.

- ❑ After students have completed their *Student Performance Profile* they should be given the specific activities and case studies to work through quietly in their own time. It is important that the mentor ensures that the student understands the context in which the activity falls and the purpose of the activity.

Hey, Thompson! – A Manual for Mentors of Adolescents
Developing self-esteem and resilience in secondary school students.

©2009 Aber Education      Dedication: To John Franklin – the support never wavered.
Printed in Europe

The advice mentioned in this book is given in good faith. The author and the publishers and their agents cannot be held acountable for outcomes related to activities mentioned herein.

**ISBN: 978-1-84285-178-4**

Author: Lou Thompson
Cover Design: Shay Howard
**Published by:**
Aber Publishing
P.O. Box 225
Abergele
Conwy County LL18 9AY
Aber Publishing is a division of GLMP Ltd

a fag."In my years of secondary teaching and tertiary lecturing I have never had my teaching goals more clearly set out for me. With regard to Franklin:

* Don't ask him to read;
* Don't ask him to write;
* Don't ask him to do any maths;
* And for goodness sake don't ask him where he's going when he leaves the room.

True to form, for the first six weeks of his attendance in my class Franklin didn't read, write or do maths. He browsed through Phantom comics, frequently dozed off, forever smoked in the old storeroom and was truant two days each week.

An event then occurred which was to impact on my teaching for the rest of my career.

On this particular Friday I decided to tell the class the Maori legend of Hinemoa and Tutanekai. As I relayed the story I noticed from the corner of my eye that Franklin was taking, what was for him, an acute interest in the story. At the conclusion of the story I asked the class to write their version of the Hinemoa and Tutanekai story providing an original conclusion.

"Hey, Thompson!"

"It's O.K. Franklin," I replied. "Just read your comics. I don't expect you to write anything."

"Hey, Thompson! I won't write a story but I'll paint you my ending."

It is no exaggeration that at that moment I believed I was the greatest teacher in the Southern Hemisphere. The boy was going to actually do something productive for me. Was I a good teacher or what?

Thirty minutes before the end of school Franklin walked up to me and shared his work with me.

"Hey, Thompson! Have a look at this. This is how I believe that story should have ended."

Never before or since have I had such exemplary work presented to me by one of my students. The picture was painted in oils, using a pallet knife, with colours, texture and atmosphere that seemed to transport the observer back in time to a native bush setting. Franklin, in incredible detail, had painted the warrior Tutanekai with the spirit of Hinemoa just in front of him. Franklin's explanation:

"It didn't matter what the chief did to the couple, he would never be able to remove from them the spirit of love." It really took my breath away. Then I blew it! I called the attention of the class.

"Excuse me class – I would like to share Franklin's painting with you."

I will never forget the look Franklin gave me. It was a mixture of anger, disbelief and above all disappointment. He had intended that his painting was to be shared between himself and me, not something to be publicly shared with the class. He had tested the trustworthiness of our relationship and found it no different or better than any others he had attempted to form.

Two months later Franklin was to produce his second piece of art work for me. These were the years of the Vietnam War. My students had witnessed on television news the graphic reporting of the evacuation from the American Embassy in Saigon and the subsequent footage of a North Vietnamese officer shooting a South Vietnamese soldier. Following an hour of discussion on the Vietnam War with the class I asked them to write down their thoughts about it.

"Hey, Thompson! I'll do you a drawing."

Franklin's subsequent pencil sketch represented a profound and thought-provoking commentary of the Vietnam War. On the top right section of the paper Franklin had presented a stark, anatomically correct, photographic image of the brain. From the front of the brain, pointing down, Franklin drew a tap. Out of the mouth of the tap Franklin drew a ground to air missile exiting. Mid-left of the paper Franklin drew a lifelike image of the "Ho Chi Minh Trail Girl", frequently shown on TV – the young Vietnamese child, covered in napalm burns, running down a road. At the bottom of the paper Franklin drew the mushroom cloud associated with a nuclear explosion.

Franklin explained his drawing as follows:

> "Hey, Thompson! What that war is about is that people have been brainwashed by those in power. What's tapped out of that brain washing is stuff that kills. You know Thompson, what makes me really mad is that it's always the innocent people that get hurt. If they don't hurry up and end this war they'll have another Hiroshima."

Again I made a bad decision. This time I hung Franklin's Vietnam sketch on the wall of my classroom so we could all enjoy it and so he could see that I valued his work.

How wrong I was. Simply having a special talent is no guarantee that you value it or will develop it to its fullest. If, as Franklin had been, you've been subjected to significant negative feedback for a long period of time about aspects of your performance, it is easy, almost inevitable, that you will generalise this to a generic feeling of "I am a failure", and consequently be suspicious or embarrassed by praise.

Franklin never did another drawing for me. He left school the day he turned fifteen and got a job working as a labourer. Just after his sixteenth birthday he purchased a massive Kawasaki motorbike. On a Friday evening, having downed six bottles of beer, and trailed by two patched members of the "Sharks Bike Gang" Franklin cruised onto the Motorway. His task was simple. If he was going to be accepted into the Sharks he had to do "the ton", a hundred miles an hour. He accelerated the bike up to 100 miles per hour and gracefully glided around a corner headlong into a truck that had broken down.

Franklin died at the age of 16 years 3 months. He died never having actualised his potential nor experienced a quality lifestyle. Had his self-esteem been healthier and his resilience stronger this story might well have had a very different ending.

\*\*\*\*\*\*

Over the last 25 years I have shared my experience with Franklin with large numbers of educators, students, parents and community members from all over. In so doing I have received a vast number of explanations and suggestions about what lay at the basis of Franklin's demise. When I read and analyse these I always arrive at the same conclusion:

**Had Franklin's self-esteem been healthier and his resilience stronger, his story would have had a very different ending.**

These same people who offered their explanations of Franklin's demise frequently included suggested strategies and actions which they believed, had they been implemented, would have addressed the self-esteem and resilience needs that Franklin displayed.

The core of "Hey, Thompson!" is based around the explanations, suggestions and strategies that have been stimulated by the telling of the Franklin story. Often this feedback led me to further enquiry and new adventures in working with secondary school-aged students.

I now offer these suggestions, explanations, strategies and adventures to you and in so doing, believe that the death of Franklin was not as terrible a waste of human life as it may seem.

"Hey, Thompson!" is not a book that introduces new earth shattering educational breakthroughs but rather reaffirms many of the logical and practical things parents, educators and students have always known are important to the actualisation of potential during the adolescent years. What "Hey, Thompson!" does attempt to do is to place these experiences into the framework of healthy self-esteem and strong resilience.

# Introduction

## Introductory Comments

As we make our way into the new decade there is significant evidence of widespread concern about the current social and economic pressures that permeate all sectors of developed western society. These pressures are taking a toll on the quality of lifestyles of ever increasing numbers of people. For those in work, organisational downsizing and restructuring, a decrease in work as a lifetime career and an associated devaluing of job security and loyalty to an employing organisation instigate pressures and stresses. The impact can be detected in statistics available related to the burgeoning numbers of adults seeking stress management courses, mental health programmes and psychotherapy treatments.

In catering for the pressures that confront youth and adults in the new millennium, in the main we continue to adopt a "programme" approach. This approach emphasises that the many pressures and issues confronting people will be addressed by the implementation of psychotherapy programmes, professional development programmes, enrichment programmes, adventure programmes, challenge programmes, extension programmes, remedial programmes and so on. When the empirical data associated with the outcomes of such programmes are examined, the conclusion is that the enormous human endeavour and financial investment involved usually results in very small gains and successes.

In writing this book on mentoring I am acknowledging that the time is opportune to focus attention not on "programmes" as has traditionally been done, but to focus attention on "people" as the key source for making a difference. Naisbitt and Aburdene (1990) suggested that the most exciting breakthroughs of the 21st century will occur, not because of technology, but because of an expanding concept of what it means to be human. This book has been written to advance the role that mentoring has in this expanding concept of being human.

Many will have come across terms such as "the x-factor", "mental-toughness", "perseverance" and "attitude" when learning about heroes and role models. Very few people deny that these conditions are vital for people to actualise or realise the top 10% of their performance potential and are the factors that underpin displays of excellence. These factors are also essential for secondary school students if they are to actualise the top 10% of their learning potential and achieve outcomes of excellence. In this book we will consider these factors, referring to them as self-esteem and resilience status.

## Definitions

**Self-esteem** is related to the current "state of mind" a student has. It includes self-belief and the sense of having a focus or direction in life. It includes the goals and expectations that the student has.

***Resilience status*** is a measure of mental toughness. Resilience status is a reflection of the current state of self-esteem. It includes the level of confidence a student has in his or her ability to achieve their goals, despite setbacks. It also includes their ability to persevere and their ability to cope with crises.

The healthier the self-esteem, the greater the level of resilience and the greater the likelihood that the student will actualise their learning potential and, in turn, come closer to achieving outcomes of excellence.

Drawing on the ideas of a number of writers and researchers I have concluded that:

A **mentor** is a person who is able to project unconditional, positive acceptance of another person. The kind of acceptance and approval projected by the mentor is not contingent upon the person having to meet the mentor's expectations of what he or she should be. It simply depends on the person being alive.

**What Does Having a Healthy Self-esteem and Strong Resilience Mean for a Student?**

It has been found that students who have a healthy self-esteem and strong resilience:

- ❑ React calmly and constructively to mistakes, errors and disappointments;
- ❑ Overcome setbacks and adversities;
- ❑ Display confidence in their interpersonal relationships – their ability to make friends and maintain friendships;
- ❑ Have greater belief in their ability to achieve their goals;
- ❑ Persevere at striving for their goals in both the good and the bad times;
- ❑ Set themselves realistic goals;
- ❑ Are prepared to step outside their performance "comfort zone";
- ❑ Cope with negative feedback;
- ❑ Are prepared to take "acceptable risks", i.e. engage in tasks they haven't attempted before; tackle old tasks in novel ways; engage in tasks that there is a good chance they might fail at;
- ❑ Are more likely to actualise/use the top 10% of their performance potential;
- ❑ Are less likely to be inhibited in their performance by an underlying fear of failure;
- ❑ Respect their health and have a healthy body image;
- ❑ Are able to resolve conflicts positively;
- ❑ Are able to communicate their "real self" to others;
- ❑ Are able to communicate assertively.

**The Role of a Mentor**

Students may find that actualising their potential can, at times, be a lonely journey. At times they are likely to find themselves asking:

- ❑ Who can help me find my direction?
- ❑ Who is someone I can trust that I can share this with?
- ❑ Who do I know that can stand in my shoes and see things from my point of view?
- ❑ Who do I know that will really listen to me?
- ❑ Who will help me determine what my options are?
- ❑ Who do I know that accepts me unconditionally?

Whilst parents and teachers can fill the role in a number of the above situations they are not always available just when they are needed, and may sometimes be too close to the student to give objective advice.

I would like to suggest that if an effective student-mentor relationship can be established, then the challenge of students actualising their potential becomes a less lonely and less stressful journey. The most important role that a mentor can have for secondary school students is that of assisting them to identify the choices and options they have related to decisions they have to make. A mentor will assist a student to prioritise their options and turn these into meaningful goals. Related to this role is the role that a mentor can play in assisting a secondary school student to identify resources, agencies and strategies they might use in the pursuit of their performance goals. The trick is to make sure that students get a good mentor. In Chapter 2 of this book I discuss elements of being a good mentor and how the student-mentor relationship can most effectively help the student.

**The Student Profiler**

The self-esteem and resilience needs of secondary school students are diverse and unique to individual students. This book contains a large number of activities, surveys and checklists related to different aspects of self-esteem and resilience development. Students and their mentors should be selective in their use of this book. Some of the strategies, surveys, checklists and information are going to have higher priority than others.

The first challenge confronting the student and their mentor is to find a starting point. In Chapter 3 of this book I have included the Student Profiler, which will assist you to identify any areas of self-esteem or resilience development that could benefit from attention. It will also assist in identifying the sections of this book that will be of use in increasing self-esteem and resilience in the areas relevant to you.

### Case Study: The Jackson Street High School Story

The relationship between secondary school students and their significant others is crucial to healthy self-esteem and actualisation of potential, as was shown by the following experience:

## The Problem

The events of this story occurred during the 1980s when I was doing some self-esteem work at a co-educational secondary school. Although the students attending the school at this time were typical of many students in terms of their academic, social and sporting abilities many of the students did not see it this way. They perceived themselves as low academic and low sporting achievers and many of them turned this into a full blown self-fulfilling prophecy.

A number of the students came from a low socio-economic residential area, an area that had a bad public reputation. Frequently the newspaper or a local radio dj referred to a crime, an unsavoury incident or "social disgrace" associated with the community in which many of these children lived. Unfortunately this labelling by forces outside the community – labelling primarily based on stereotypes, rumour, gossip and misinformation – reflected a picture of the community that was far removed from the warm, friendly, and caring culture that actually existed. This took its toll on the students attending the School.

Many went to school expecting to fail – they believed that students who went to this school were losers, going nowhere.

THUS … The academic, sporting, art and music performance norms for this school could best be described as "comfort zone" level. The common attitude was: there's no point in pushing yourself, you're still going to fail.

Within this school the head of the Physical Education Department, Peter, was a high performance sportsman, having played county cricket and senior league football. Peter's family had lived in the area for a long time and were greatly respected by the members of this community. In his first two years at the school. Peter recognised that there was unbelievable sporting talent amongst many of the students, but the talent lay dormant and was wasting away.

Peter struggled to get students to change for physical education lessons, let alone form school swimming, athletic, cricket, football, basketball or netball teams to participate in secondary school sporting carnivals. He agonised over the lost opportunities for personal development, building of school spirit and the sense of belonging that these students were depriving themselves of by not engaging in team sporting pursuits.

The truth was that collectively this student population had slammed into a "self-esteem wall"; a wall that was preventing them from actualising their potential. The students had placed themselves in a "performance comfort zone", a playing field in which they deliberately removed any possibility of failure by setting themselves goals and expectations well below their capabilities.

In absolute desperation, one lunchtime, Peter sought me out:

"Hey, Thompson! What can I do to get these students out of their comfort-zones and through this self-esteem wall?"

My response to his cry for help was simple: "Peter, desperate situations require desperate measures. In situations like this you have to be assertive "Then you put in place the infrastructure and organisation that ensures the students' raw talents, combined with their desire, determination and commitment, guarantees they will succeed in meeting the challenge. Give them this real taste of working outside their "comfort zone" and gradually the self-esteem wall will crack and then crumble. Only then will the students' self-esteem status ensure that that comfort zone performance will become a thing of the past."

## The Impossible Dream

A fortnight went by. On a hot October lunchtime that all too familiar tap, tap, tap of the spoon on the saucer rang out in the staffroom – someone was about to make an announcement of relevance to all staff. Up stood Peter, a teacher considered by many of the teaching "old-timers" as someone being close to breaking point, someone who wouldn't last in the profession much longer. What Peter then proceeded to share with the staff left the old-timers in no doubt that their diagnosis was spot on.

"Fellow staff! I've been thinking about Thompson's self-esteem wall and his theory that in desperate times you have to grab students by the scruff of the neck and drag them through it. Well, boy, have I come up with a wall-breaking challenge.

Next October, to celebrate the school's 50th Jubilee, 12 teams of three student cyclists will, in a relay format, cycle for a total of 2500 kilometres."

You could hear a pin drop in the staffroom. Some of the old timers were all for calling the ambulance to cart the poor man away right then. Over the next fortnight Peter was unrelenting. On cue, five minutes into lunch, the tap, tap, tap rang out and amongst the staff groans of, "Oh no, not again," Peter would launch into, "Now about next year's Jubilee Challenge."

Eventually, the principal decided it was time for a decision on this optimistic plan.

## The Assembly

Harry, the principal, issued the following ultimatum to Peter:

"O.K. Peter, here's the deal. Tomorrow we have a full school assembly. At this you will address the students and call for 36 volunteers to cycle 2500 kilometres. If at the assembly you get just 50% of the numbers you require we will proceed with the Jubilee Challenge."

A collective sigh went around the staffroom. The principal's ultimatum would sink Peter's proposal and bring an end to this madness. The thought was that he'd be lucky to get five volunteers from this apathetic student population.

At the assembly the students were informed that Peter had a special announcement to make. Cynical smiles and sniggers emanated from the staff seated on stage. Peter stood and moved to the front of the stage. He was well-liked by the students so a hush quickly descended.

He began: "I need 36 students to volunteer to take three weeks out of school and by the way they'll need to cycle 2500 km. Are there any volunteers?"

With a roar of approval 800 hands went up. Peter had gazumped us. Whether we liked it or not there was now no backing out of the Jubilee Challenge.

## Preparing For The Challenge

Teams of cyclists drawn from Year 9 to 11 students had to be formed. Each team of cyclists, for insurance and "duty of care" requirements, needed to be supervised by a staff member. The staff member would be required to cycle with the students.

The. Jubilee Challenge, slowly at first, and then with growing speed and energy transformed from one man's dream to a whole community vision. Initially attracting small local community business and newspaper support, it gradually became the focus of local radio coverage. The Jubilee Challenge, for the first time in a long time, was putting our school in the public eye in a positive, proactive manner.

Overnight a transformation occurred in the students', parents' and community attitude towards the school. There were smiles and laughter amongst the students, a rare commodity at the school in the past, and a spring in the steps of many of the students. Even one of the cynical old-timers was heard to say:

"I don't believe it! All my Year 11 students handed in their homework, completed and on time. Every one of them, I don't believe it."

## Ominous Warnings

At school. there was a group of three Year 11 girls who had been referred to me for special counselling. They were on their final warning – if they offended one more time they would be expelled. A history of juvenile offending, a record of sexual promiscuity and numerous suspensions had earned these girls a reputation amongst the staff as the "students from hell"!

During a lunch break the "students from hell" carried out their own analysis of the Jubilee Challenge. This analysis lead them to the following conclusions:

* On the Cycle Relay girls would be outnumbered by guys 4:1. (Good odds for scoring!)
* Most of the guys on the Cycle Relay were Year 10 and 11 hunks. (This is looking better all the time.)
* The Cycle Relay began with a free weekend away. (burger bars, parties, parties. Yep, that seals it.)

The decision was made by "the girls from hell" – they would be Team 7 of the Cycle Relay. Showing initiative and the cunning of politicians they confronted Peter.

"Mr. P., Lou Thompson, our mentor, said that our self-esteem would be fixed up if we become Team 7 for the Cycle Relay."

Being a person who wore his heart on his sleeve, Peter couldn't resist this passionate plea from such troubled students.

"O.K. girls if that's what Mr. Thompson believes I'll go along with it. As from today you're officially Team 7 of the. Jubilee Challenge Cycle Relay."

The first I was to learn of this smouldering volcano was when Peter met me the next day with: "Hey, Thompson! You'll be proud of me. I've taken notice of what you said about building students' self-esteem and so have included "the girls from hell" as Team 7."

I thought I was hearing things.

"Why on earth would you jeopardise the entire project by doing that?" I asked crestfallen Peter who suddenly realised that he'd been had.

One by one, participating staff approached Peter with stories that had a common theme:

"Well Peter, I'm 100% behind you on this one but you give me Team 7 to supervise and I'm out of it."

It was at this time of potential staff mutiny that Peter called upon the wisdom and raw cunning that had allowed him to survive for so long as a P.E. teacher. A young, newly graduated, Home Economics teacher had been recently appointed to the school. Peter took her to lunch and presented her with:

"Boy, Nola do I have an offer for you that you'll find too good to refuse. I've considered all staff for the role of supervisor to Team 7 and decided that no one could do it as well as you."

Full of that magnificent idealism that new teachers bring to the profession, Nola's response to being given responsibility for Team 7 was:

"Neat. I don't know what they've done in the past and I don't need to know. We'll start with a clean slate and share this adventure together."

## The Cycle Relay

The Cycle Relay required each team to complete approximately 20 kilometres a day. The event began with a ceremony Initially all went well with smooth baton changes going from Team 1 through to Team 6. Each team completed their set distance in the designated time. Then it was time for the handover to Team 7.

There the three girls were, dressed in the briefest bikinis possible, accompanied by Nola decked out in suitable cycling attire looking every part the professional cyclist.

On their first ride the girls managed 4 kilometres and created absolute traffic chaos on the main highway out of town as drivers of car after car "rubber-necked" to take in the view of three bikini-clad cyclists meandering along the road. The relay officials monitoring the event believed that Nola covered close on 30 kilometres as she would advance a kilometre and then return to the girls to urge them on and provide them with support. On the second day of cycling the bikini pants were abandoned for the conventional cycle bottoms; the girls cycled 6 kilometres and Nola 21 kilometres. From then on each day new achievements were made. From Day 4 the term "the students from hell" was no longer heard, just "Team 7". By Day 5 Team 7 was right up there with the best performers, hitting their distances in the allocated times. Now achieving personal best performances was more important to them than any of the other hidden agendas they had previously had.

## The Remarkable Change

From my birds-eye view, (the passenger seat in the back-up van) I was privy to a phenomenon I had never before witnessed. I observed first-hand the development of a relationship between these girls and a significant other, their teacher/mentor, Nola. This relationship would eventually be responsible for removing forever the "students from hell" tag and nurturing the building of the girls' self-esteem and resilience to a level that would allow them to actualise their potential.

It was the simple things that seemed to make the greatest impact – Nola riding alongside one of the girls and putting a hand on her shoulder when she was struggling; Nola allowing one of the girls to give her a shove along when she was finding the going tough; the four of them laughing together at a shared joke; Nola listening patiently, listening with her eyes, letting the girls finish their stories. Nola never being too busy or tired to listen. Nola sitting around the evening campfire with the girls and displaying unconditional acceptance.

This relationship reached a peak approximately half-way through the relay. It was Team 7's responsibility to take the first relay leg out of this point. This involved a climb of the steepest most gut-wrenching hills of the entire relay. It was estimated that the climb of approximately 15 kilometres would take two hours to complete. At 7 am on the morning of the climb, in torrential rain, facing a 40 kilometres per hour headwind the girls, and their mate Nola, began the ride of their lives. All four were crying tears of pain after one hour of the ride. Often it was observed that the gale force winds were preventing them from making any progress. The four of them cried together, they shouted and screamed together, they cajoled, berated, pleaded and encouraged each other.

A local radio station had sent one of their announcers to comment on the relay that particular day. As the achievements of Team 7 began to unfold, the radio announcer reported to thousands of listeners that he was witnessing courage, determination, commitment and team spirit the likes of which he had never before witnessed. As car after car passed, their toots of support, their friendly waves, their cries of "Good on you Team 7, you can do it", gave strength to their legs and determination to their minds.

Three and a half hours after the struggle had begun they were within one kilometre of their target. Finally the last bend and the top of the hill. In front of them was a sight they will keep forever. For about one kilometre, lining either side of the road, was car after car that had stopped to show their recognition and acclaim for Team 7's achievement. Four abreast the girls cycled down this human corridor and about 50 metres from handing over the baton to the next team they stopped, turned around and looked at Peter and myself seated in the support van. As one person the three girls and their teacher raised their fists in a salute and we knew from that moment on the self-esteem wall had gone. Now the girls could get on with the business of actualising their various performance potentials.

# Chapter 1

# The Thompson Self-Esteem Model

## Contents

## Outcomes

### Readers will …

❑ Become familiar with key characteristics of the phenomena of self-esteem;

❑ Become familiar with the concepts of self-image and ideal image;

❑ Recognise the key processes involved in the development of self-esteem;

❑ Understand the concept of the "self-esteem wall";

❑ Be familiar with early warning indicators related to unhealthy self-esteem.

## 1.1 Important Information Mentors and Students Need to Know About Self-Esteem

A secondary school student's self-esteem is a complex phenomenon. They are not born with their self-esteem in place. They begin acquiring it from their early childhood.

❑ Self-esteem can be described as a "state of mind" which is made up of the attitudes, feelings, thoughts, values and beliefs held by the student about their skills and capabilities.

❑ It is formed through information the student absorbs from the key figures and other figures in their life, and from the student's own perception of their performance in comparison to others'.

❑ It can affect performance – good self-esteem enables good performance, as students feel confident trying new skills and reaching for their goals. Similarly, low self-esteem can prevent students from trying for goals in the belief that they are incapable of reaching them.

❑ It is a dynamic phenomenon in that it is forever changing. In most situations these changes are fairly small, ranging from small doubts about the ability to complete a task to a sense of well- being for having completed a task.

❑ However, occasionally events can occur that cause very significant changes to the state of a student's self-esteem. This may lead to distorted views of their performance. Overnight they can plunge to a feeling of desperation or absolute failure, or at the other extreme to a feeling of elation or "being on top of the world".

❑ The key to managing self-esteem and using it to assist a student to actualise their potential is to get as complete an understanding of it as possible. Only then can the early warning signs of unhealthy self-esteem be recognised, and action undertaken to improve self-esteem.

## 1.2 The Thompson Self-Esteem Model Explained

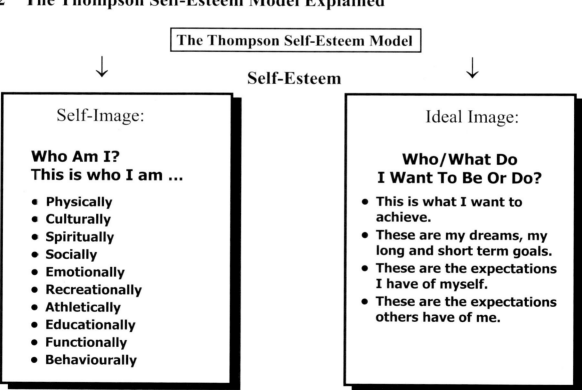

As discussed earlier in this chapter, self-esteem is the belief the student holds about their capabilities and inherent value. It can be seen that it is made up of the self view of who the student is (their self-image) and what they are capable of (their ideal image).

Thompson argues that the stronger and more informed a student's self-image is, then the stronger and more realistic their ideal image is, and accordingly the stronger and more resilient their self-esteem is likely to be.

## 1.2.1   The Self-Image

This represents collected the thoughts, impressions and knowledge of who the individual is, as shown in the model on Page 14. It includes the thoughts and knowledge they have about their physical appearance, their spirituality, their emotionality, their culture, their social competence, their intellectual capacity and their general functionality (what they can or cannot do).

Self-image is dynamic. New experiences, normal body changes, changes in home, family or school circumstances, new friendships, ill-health or an accident often cause an individual to add something to their self-image, to modify their thoughts about their self-image or to suddenly have doubts and insecurities about it. Self-image continues to change and develop throughout life.

**In the Thompson Self-Esteem Model, self-image is the launch pad for self-esteem.**

## 1.2.2   The Ideal Image

This represents the collected thoughts, ideas, knowledge and desires of who the individual wants to be and what they want to achieve in their life.

Ideal image incorporates the small daily short term goals individuals set themselves to the life dreams and aspirations they have.

Like self-image, ideal image is dynamic and ever changing. Past and new, successful and unsuccessful performance experiences, feedback from the "significant others" in life and changing family and social values and attitudes often cause students to change the goals and dreams that are part of their ideal image.

In the Thompson Self-Esteem Model ideal image is the target for self-esteem.

## 1.3   The Key Processes Involved In Developing Self-Esteem

If mentors are going to manage students' self-esteem and ensure that it allows them to actualise their performance potential, it is important for them to have an awareness and understanding of the key processes involved in self-esteem development.

Throughout students' lives many of the experiences, attitudes and awarenesses, and much of the knowledge that contributes to the building of self-esteem, result from self-discoveries. Every time students undertake a new adventure or challenge they gain new or extra information that they use to review their self-image and ideal image.

From these experiences they discover things they can do that previously they thought they couldn't. They also discover new likes and dislikes, new feelings, new attitudes, new values and new interests.

Each new adventure adds to the set of guidelines that students can use to evaluate who they are and what they want. The more self-discovery opportunities provided, the richer their self-esteem becomes.

From a very young age individuals have been receiving feedback from the significant others in their life. Often they used this feedback to add new thoughts, or change existing thoughts they have about their self-image. Frequently this feedback impacts on the performance expectations they set themselves, which are an integral part of the ideal image.

Studies have indicated that family members, teachers, friends, role models, employers, coaches and mentors are likely to represent students' significant others.

The influence of the feedback of these significant others will vary according to what aspect of the self- image or ideal image is under consideration, and the nature of the relationship they have with particular significant others.

## 1.4    The Self-Esteem Wall

Many students do not actualise their learning potential during their secondary school years because they have an unhealthy self-esteem.

For many students this unhealthy self-esteem takes the form of an internalised fear of failure that had its origins early in their primary schooling.

If students suffer from this fear of failure related to their school studies, it is probably the case that their family, teachers or friends are unaware that this is happening to them. It is likely that even the student themselves is unaware of just how negative an influence a fear of failure is having on learning performance.

Frequently this fear of failure is based upon a student having received some very hurtful feedback from a teacher, coach, family member or friend about a specific school performance that occurred in the past. Sometimes it happens because a student has a distorted or unrealistic evaluation of their past and current school learning performances.

For some students the fear of failure has its roots embedded in a damaged self-image. It could be that sometime during their secondary schooling, often in Year 10, they come to a conclusion something like the following description provided by Sonia, a Year 10 student:

*I am different from my peers. I don't look the same. I don't think the same. I don't learn the same. I don't have the same values and beliefs. This is unacceptable. I don't think the 'real me' can match it with other students at school. It is inevitable that I won't live up to the expectations of my family and my teachers and I'll fail. I might as well not even try.* (Sonia: 2002)

A number of students have internalised this fear of failure because of an unhealthy ideal image, which is dominated by the unrealistic expectations of others, inappropriate goals of their own or an absence of any goals or dreams.

The following comments by Frank, a Year 11 student, reflect this situation:

*I cannot meet the expectations others have of me. Too many people have put too many demands on my learning performance outcomes. The goals and dreams that are part of my ideal image are not my own but those of my family. These goals and dreams are meaningless to me; they're not mine; they're not what I really want to do or what I really want to be.* (Frank: 2002)

Somewhere in their final high school years this fear of failure – these uncertainties related to self-image or emptiness related to their ideal image – result in too many students reaching the following conclusions:

*I'm not going to make it. I can't satisfy the performance expectations and dreams others have of me. I'm not good enough to reach the study goals people say I should have reached in Years 10 - 11. I'm going to fail, I'm useless.* (Carol: 2002)

Too often when a student arrives at conclusions similar to those described above they slam into what can be termed a **self-esteem wall.** I have used this term because it seems to best describe the state of self-esteem many secondary school students have related to me when the above circumstances are encountered. The self-esteem wall has been described by students as follows:

*No matter how hard I try I can't get beyond this wall. Every time I step outside my comfort zone and attempt to break through this wall that's in front of the outcomes I have to achieve, I fail. I'll never make it. I'm not good enough; I don't think I have the necessary skills to reach my goals or satisfy the expectations of others. I might as well just go through the motions, do just enough to get by and, above all, avoid the embarrassment of failure.*

(Group of Year 11 student mentors)

The tragedy is that if the self-esteem wall remains in place for too long there's a strong possibility that the student will either:

❏     Give up and leave school prematurely or;

❏     Engage in inappropriate compensatory behaviour and/or unacceptable risk-taking behaviours.

## 1.5     Unacceptable Risk- Taking Behaviours

When students hit the self-esteem wall they frequently lose any sense of direction or focus in terms of their performance efforts. Frustrated and confused students who become stranded at the self-esteem wall quickly lose motivation and become stressed. Inevitably this state of affairs leads them to displaying behaviours for which they haven't fully considered the consequences. Some of these behaviours are inappropriate demands for attention and some are inappropriate expressions of emotions that the presence of the self-esteem wall has helped to generate. All such behaviours can be described as "unacceptable risk-taking" behaviours. These behaviours could include:

❏ Truancy;
❏ Engaging in bullying behaviours;

❏ Being the "class-clown";
❏ Displaying aggressive communication towards family members, friends, teachers and people in authority

❏ Running away from home;
❏ Hanging out with troublemakers;
❏ Getting involved with substance abuse
❏ Thinking about or attempting suicide.
❏ Running away from home;

❏ Joining gangs
❏ Getting involved with junior offending;
❏ Engaging in inappropriate sexual behaviour;
❏ Running away from home;

## 1.6     Early Warning Indicators Associated With the Self-Esteem Wall

In researching for this book I talked with over 500 secondary school students about self-esteem and especially the idea of the **self-esteem wall**. An outcome of these discussions was that the students were able to describe a large number of negative feelings, experiences and situations they had encountered that were either related to aspects of their self-image or aspects of their ideal image.

The problem was, that at the time these situations occurred, students were not aware of the impact they were having on their self-esteem or the potential of these situations to lead them into the self-esteem wall.

I have summarised these statements and arranged them into the categories of self-image and ideal image. They are presented in the context of them serving as early self-esteem wall warning indicators, i.e. if students are experiencing any of the indicators be warned that this can lead to them hitting the self-esteem wall, which has the effect of preventing them from actualising their performance potential.

I have cross-referenced these categories to the relevant domain of the Student Profiler, discussed in Chapter 3, which the student and mentor can examine in more detail. This will allow them to identify specific explanations and strategies that can be used to address related self-esteem needs.

## 1.7 Early Warning Indicators Related to Self-Image

The statements in the first table reflect doubts, uncertainties and fears students might have that are related to their self-image when they consider their ability to succeed with school study.

Students may often associate these statements with a deep-felt feeling that they are a failure at school. At times they are an indication that the student needs assistance to develop a specific learning or study skill. If a student finds that many of the situations in any of the following three checklists related to self-image apply to them they should be referred by their mentor to the appropriate domain of the **Student Profiler** included in Chapter 3 of this book. Having completed the relevant questionnaire, the student and mentor should review the associated menus of explanations and strategies.

---

**Activity 1: My Student Self — Me as a Learner (Related to Domain A of the STUDENT PROFILER) Indicate which of these statements seem to apply to you:**

- ❏ I never complete my homework.
- ❏ I never complete tasks set by my teachers.
- ❏ I am always in trouble with my teachers.
- ❏ I don't believe I am as smart or intelligent as the other students at school.
- ❏ I always take a long time to complete tasks
- ❏ I have never succeeded at anything at school set at school.
- ❏ I have no subjects I am any good at
- ❏ I get easily distracted when I'm studying.
- ❏ I never get my assignments completed on time.
- ❏ I always put off doing assignments and/or homework until the last minute.
- ❏ I can't remember names, dates, facts.
- ❏ I find it difficult to use the school library to help me with my study.
- ❏ I find it difficult to ask my teachers and tutors for assistance.
- ❏ I find it difficult to take notes during a lesson or lecture
- ❏ I get too nervous when I have to sit exams or tests.
- ❏ I never know what I have to do when given an assignment.
- ❏ I hate school.
- ❏ I feel really stressed when I'm asked to give an answer out loud in class.
- ❏ I'm dumb; nowhere near as bright as the others in my class.
- ❏ I'm useless at essay writing. I know the answers but I can't write them down.
- ❏ My teachers think I'm dumb.

---

The statements in the second table below reflect doubts, uncertainties or fears students might have related to their ability to make friends and their popularity with those they interact with. Sometimes they are an indication that students need assistance to develop a specific relationship skill.

## Activity 2: My Social Self — My Ability to Make Friends
## (Related to Domain B of the STUDENT PROFILER)

### Indicate which of these statements seem to apply to you:

- ❏ I don't find it easy to talk to mum or dad.
- ❏ I don't feel comfortable talking to any of my relatives.
- ❏ I don't make friends easily.
- ❏ I find it difficult to join in family celebrations.
- ❏ I am uncomfortable when I am in the company of someone in authority.
- ❏ I feel very shy when I am with other people.
- ❏ I prefer being on my own.
- ❏ I hate working in groups because I'm frightened I'll make a fool of myself.
- ❏ I feel uncomfortable when I go on an excursion with my family.
- ❏ I get embarrassed when I have to introduce someone to my parents.
- ❏ I don't like discussing my problems with my parents.
- ❏ I don't ask questions of my teacher because I'm frightened I'll be made to look stupid.
- ❏ I don't know how to introduce myself to others.
- ❏ I feel uncomfortable contributing to discussions when I am with my peers.
- ❏ I find it difficult to express my opinions when they are different from those previously expressed.
- ❏ I find it very difficult to relax when I'm with my peers.
- ❏ I don't have anyone I can call a close friend.
- ❏ I don't think people like being in my company.

The statements in the third table below reflect doubts, fears and uncertainties students might have about being able to communicate the "real them" to others. Sometimes they reflect doubts the student might have about being able to make him or herself understood by others. It could be that the responses to the statements reflect the student's need to develop specific communication skills.

## Activity 3: Myself As A Communicator — Communicating the Real Me to
## Others (Related to Domain C of the STUDENT PROFILER)

### Indicate which of these statements seem to apply to you:

- ❏ I find it difficult to explain things to other people.
- ❏ I find it difficult to write instructions for someone else to follow.
- ❏ I am useless at writing letters.
- ❏ I don't know how to show my feelings to others.
- ❏ No one understands me when I'm trying to tell them something important.
- ❏ I never share personal matters with anyone else.
- ❏ I don't know how to communicate personal matters to anyone else.
- ❏ I find it difficult to give directions to someone else.

❏ I am often frightened of saying no to someone or to disagreeing with him or her in case I upset them.

❏ I don't have the confidence to speak my mind if a situation requires it.

❏ I have trouble "tuning-in" to people when they are communicating something personal to me.

❏ I often find myself communicating aggressively to someone when I don't want to.

❏ I hate speaking in public.

❏ I have difficulty in displaying eye contact when talking with someone.

❏ I don't know have any confidence when asking questions.

## 1.8 Early Warning Indicators Related to Ideal Image

The following statements reflect doubts or uncertainties students might have about their ideal image, and about where their life is heading. Student responses might indicate that they have little sense of direction in their life, or that all their energies are being directed at meeting the expectations others have of them and trying to be the person others want them to be.

Student responses occasionally indicate that their performance endeavours are being driven by a perfectionist focus, i.e. they are trying to please all people all of the time, by always being the best or 100% correct.

If a student finds that many of the situations in any of the following two checklists related to ideal image apply to them they should be referred by their mentor to the appropriate domain of the *Student Profiler* included in Chapter 3 of this book. Having completed the relevant questionnaire the student, with their mentor, should review the associated menus of explanations and strategies.

---

### Activity 4: My Goals and Dreams – Who I Want to Be, What I Want to Do (Related to Domain F of the STUDENT PROFILER)

**Indicate which of these statements seem to apply to you:**

❏ I rush into learning tasks without first thinking about what the task requires me to do.

❏ I study mainly because that's what my parents want me to do.

❏ I don't have a clear goal for my studies.

❏ I never judge my performance outcomes against previous-best performances.

❏ I strive to achieve 100% for all learning tasks all the time.

❏ I always worry about how others will judge my learning outcomes.

❏ I have no idea why I am studying particular subjects.

❏ I have no particular focus or direction in my life.

❏ I expect to fail when I study.

❏ I expect to come near the bottom of the class in most areas of my study.

❏ I never set myself study goals.

❏ I don't care if I don't get a job when I leave school.

❏ I never worry about what I'll do when I leave school.

❏ My life is always about enjoying the moment and letting tomorrow take care of itself.

❏ I spend most of my life in a performance comfort zone.

❏ I wish I could change who I am.

---

❏ I go through the motions of living and have no sense of purpose.

❏ I am continually trying to please all people, all the time.

❏ I put all my hopes and efforts into achieving just one goal.

❏ I feel overwhelmed by the expectations placed on me by other people.

❏ I worry about not living up to my parents' expectations.

An important aspect of students' ideal image is the career aspirations they have and what sort of job, work or study they want to do.

The following statements reflect doubts and uncertainties related to students' post-secondary school future. Answers might indicate a lack of awareness of important skills or requirements related to this aspect of their ideal image.

## Activity 5:  My Career/Vocational Self
## (Related to Domain E of the STUDENT PROFILER)

### Indicate which of these statements seem to apply to you:

❏ I worry about being unemployed.

❏ I believe that a high wage is the most important thing a job should offer.

❏ I don't have the ability to engage in any post-secondary school study.

❏ Post-secondary school study is a waste of time for me.

❏ I don't expect to get a job when I leave school.

❏ I worry all the time about whether I'll get a job when I leave school.

❏ I don't care whether I get a job when I leave school.

❏ I worry about pleasing my parents with the sort of job I might get when I leave school.

❏ I have no idea what job skills I have.

❏ It'd be a waste of time for me to prepare a curriculum vitae.

❏ I don't know where to look for a good job.

❏ I wouldn't know where to start in terms of finding suitable post-secondary school study that is suitable for me.

❏ I just live for the day. I don't care about what happens when I leave school.

❏ I want to leave school the moment I can.

## 1.9   The Physical Self-Image

In recent years reported incidents of eating disorders, substance abuse and stress-related disorders amongst secondary school students have become common. Whilst unhealthy self-esteem is seldom the only contributing factor to such situations, few would disagree that in many of these cases an unhealthy self-image, especially an unhealthy physical self-image, is a contributing factor. Following are a number of suggestions related to physical self-image that all students should reflect on.

In her book *Developing Self-Esteem (1989)*, Anne Kotzman suggests that when a person has a habit of focusing on their mistakes and ignoring or trivialising their contribution to success, they should take off their dark glasses. It is suggested that this is very relevant when students reflect on their physical self. If they are influenced by the "perfect body image" which is frequently reflected on TV (and it is difficult for an adolescent, especially a female adolescent not to do so), this can cause them to have an unrealistic self-image which is dominated by their rejection of their physical self.

### 1.9.1 Activity 6: Discovering Why I Don't Like My Physical Self

This activity is one which the student needs to interact with someone they trust and respect.

It is imperative that they feel safe whilst they disclose information related to this issue. Obviously a mentor is an ideal person that they can share the information with. Together the student and mentor address the following questions:

1. What information can I give that describes me?
   - My weight
   - My height
   - My hair colour
   - My eye colour
   - My blood pressure
   - My skin colour
   - Any distinguishing features I have that identify me
   - My fitness status
   - My blood type
2. How much factual information do I have regarding each of the above areas?
3. How much of the information I have about the above areas is based on guess work? How can I get factual information about these areas?
4. Describe the physical appearance of:
   - Your best friend
   - Your sporting heroes
   - People you respect
   - People you don't like
   - Your favourite pop group

   Are there any patterns about the physical appearance of people you like or have as role models and those that you dislike?
5. What aspects of your physical self do you not like? Why do you think this is so?

## 1.9.2 Keeping track of highlights

It is suggested that if a student has a negative physical self-image, and this is preventing him or her from actualising their performance potential, then it is time for them to take some time out to review their life highlights. Terry Orlick, *(Embracing Your Potential, Human Kinetics (1998), New Zealand, P. 5)* suggests that when we open our vision and look for highlights, we begin to embrace the best things in life, generate joyfulness, and live each day more positively. The student should discuss the following suggestions offered by Orlick with his or her mentor:

- ☐ Look for beauty, meaning and simple joys that you experience. Tell your mentor about them nature and physical space.
- ☐ Keep your mind open to any physical experience that can bring you enjoyment.
- ☐ Embrace these magic moments.

## 1.9.3 Maintaining daily fitness

Many students who have a negative physical self-image are physically unfit. If they have a negative physical self-image they often neglect their body's requirement to be regularly fine-tuned. It is a generally accepted claim that the fitter someone is, the more likely it will be that they will actualise their performance potential. Further, the fitter they are, the better they are able to manage stress. In considering their fitness levels students should review the following three key areas with their mentor:

**A. Aerobic Fitness:** This is measured by recovery heart rate. To achieve this students need to ask the mentor to take the resting heart (pulse) rate before exercises are started.

- The idea is to undertake a series of activities that will get the heart rate up to about 150 bpm. Running at a constant pace for five minutes will normally raise the heart rate to this level.
- When students have finished running, the mentor should take the heart rate within one minute of stopping. Then, it is to be taken every one minute until the resting heart rate is reached.
- The shorter the time it takes to return to the resting heart rate, the fitter the student is.

**B. Strength:** Students can get one measure of their strength by determining their ability to do press-ups. For purposes of this test female students' press-ups are different from males'. Females press- ups are done by kneeling and crossing ankles, with arms placed shoulder width apart on the floor. It is important for females to keep the back flat and not to drop on their buttocks. When going down they should make sure that elbows are out from the body and not into the side.

- Male students should do their press-ups on the toes instead of on the knees.
- The fitter the student is, the more press-ups can be achieved.

**C. Flexibility:** This is the third aspect of fitness that students should monitor. It is measured by a hamstring/back stretch.

- The stretch is done sitting on the floor with legs straight out in front and feet pushed against a box. Leaning as far forward as possible students push a moving marker with the hands.
- This needs to be done in a smooth, controlled manner and not with a jerking motion.
- Normally flexibility is measured by numbers on the box – the further the marker is pushed, the higher the score that is achieved.
- Students should have three attempts and use their best result as their flexibility rating.

**D. Charting Student Fitness:** Monitoring students' progress towards fitness is an important component of this activity. As well as helping students get fit, this aspect of the exercise reinforces the concept of "personal best". For students who are inappropriately comparing the status of their physical self with that of others', using personal best performance monitoring in the way suggested can help to break any habit of using unrealistic expectations for this purpose. With the help of their mentor the student can record their performance fitness progress using charts like those on the next page.

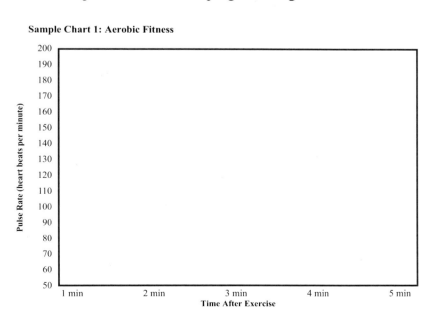

**Sample Chart 1: Aerobic Fitness**

**Sample Chart 2: Strength**

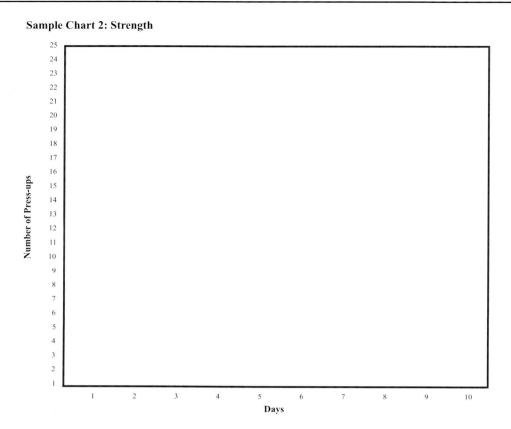

**Sample Chart 3: Flexibility**

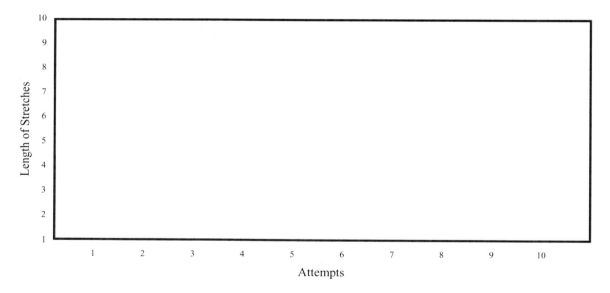

### 1.9.4   The student and substance abuse

An unfortunate occurrence amongst a number of students is their substance abuse behaviour. Many students who have hit the self-esteem wall, or who are experiencing a great deal of stress, turn to alcohol or drugs to compensate for the distressed state of mind they are experiencing. Given the physical, psychological, social and emotional pressures many students experience whilst engaging in the performance tasks required of them, they can inadvertently become "sitting ducks" to the dangers of substance abuse, especially alcohol. Whilst the dangers of alcohol abuse will be highlighted here much of the information, suggestions and activities provided also apply to any form of substance abuse, including drug-taking.

**Alcohol abuse: Enhancing student awareness**

The following information is a summary of factual information related to alcohol abuse. A mentor should ensure the student is made aware of this information but not be introduced to it in a manner that they might interpret as being an accusation. Rather, the mentor should ensure that the information is introduced in a manner that the student can accept as being part of the development of the self-awareness required for a healthy physical self-image. The mentor should inform students that such information will enable them to sort the facts from the myths associated with alcohol use.

General Facts About Alcohol

- When people talk about "alcohol" they are usually referring to drinks which contain varying amounts of pure alcohol.
- Alcoholic drinks have a restricted food value in the form of sugar (as in sweet wines) and carbohydrate (as in spirits and beer made from grain), but basically alcohol is a drug – that is, a substance which affects the workings of the mind and body
- Taken in moderation, alcohol can encourage the appetite and produces a feeling of well-being. This is because the alcohol stimulates the blood flow to the skin, which has the effect of making the drinker feel pleasantly warm.
- If heavy drinking is repeated over a period of time, changes can occur in one's personality. It is thought that these changes have a chemical basis and this can lead to the need to continue on with the drinking behaviour.
- A state known as dependency is reached when a person experiences an urgent desire for alcohol when a drink is delayed. In the early stages of heavy drinking the dependency tends to be psychological rather than physiological.
- Unfortunately, if the drinking becomes increasingly heavier, psychological dependence can give way to a physical dependence. As physical dependence grows, withdrawal will become more and more difficult and uncomfortable. Eventually, deprivation for any length of time will result in trembling, sweating and acute stress. The first drink will always relieve these feelings – until the next time.
- Alcohol tends to affect people in different ways. The same amount can turn one person into the "life and soul" of the party, bring out violent aggression in another, and send a third quietly to sleep.
- Contrary to what many people think, alcohol is not a stimulant but a depressant. As soon as it enters the blood stream, it begins to impair judgement, self-control and skill.
- Once an excessive drinker begins to suffer harm or to cause harm as a result of drinking, he or she can be classified as an alcoholic.
- Alcoholism can strike irrespective of age, socio-economic status, race, gender, amount of intelligence, aptitude or vocation.

**Warning signals**

The body develops a tolerance to alcohol and the danger lies in the fact that more drinks are soon needed to reproduce the original feeling of well-being. Specific signals a person should watch for when determining if alcohol consumption has become unmanageable are:

- An obvious obsession with alcohol, where a person can't relax or have fun without alcohol. They can't give it up or even restrict drinking to a reasonable level
- Alcohol consumption almost always leads to morally or physically unacceptable behaviour.
- Alcohol consumption is resulting in a sudden drop in performance standards.

**The physical effects of alcoholism**

The following physical consequences arise from alcohol abuse:

☐ Cirrhosis of the liver. There is no cure for this common disease associated with alcoholism.

☐ Peptic ulcers, kidney trouble and heart disease.

☐ Pins and needles in hands and feet.

☐ Attacks of trembling and sweating when alcohol is withdrawn.

☐ Loss of appetite, lethargy and weakness.

☐ Delirium tremens after withdrawal from drinking, accompanied by frightening hallucinations.

## 1.9.5 Strategies and suggestions for students who want to change their alcohol or drug use behaviours

☐ If a student is concerned about their alcohol or drug use behaviour they should contact their mentor, counsellor, doctor, parents or support person and disclose their worries and concerns.

☐ Students shouldn't listen to hearsay or gossip about addiction, alcoholism or effects of specific drugs, but should be encouraged to check the facts out with an expert. The mentor could help find such a person or resource.

☐ Students should determine where, when and with whom they are at their worst with alcohol or drugs.

☐ Students should take some time out to get in touch with their feelings and needs. They need to be honest about their feelings, both with themselves and with others. The mentor can assist in undertaking this task.

☐ Students need plenty of rest. If they are having difficulties with sleep they could consider the following:

• Setting themselves a regular time for going to bed, and not compromising it.

• Avoiding afternoon naps.

• Keeping in mind that it is better to go to bed earlier and get up earlier than the reverse if they wish to experience healthy sleep.

• Avoiding before-bedtime emotional arguments, excitement, and intense physical or mental activity.

• Making sure they have bed comfort – pillows, mattress and warmth.

• Ensuring that if they wake in the middle of the night they don't reward themselves by reading their favourite book, listening to their favourite music or watching a video.

• If there are things on their mind they have to remember the following day, they can briefly write the items down so that they can allow the mind to relax.

☐ Wherever possible students should use **meditation**, **relaxation** and **exercise** as substitutes for alcohol or drug use.

☐ Students could develop a regular meditation, prayer or relaxation practice to use for the beginning, during and conclusion of the day.

☐ Relaxation could be encouraged through a focused relaxation exercise or visualisation scenario.

☐ Students should monitor their diet very carefully by:

- Significantly reducing sugar, alcohol and caffeine from their diets.
- Eliminating coffee, chocolate, tea or alcohol before bedtime.
- Eating at regular times.
- Consuming warm milk or a banana, which contain the amino acid l-tryptophan, a natural relaxant and sleep inducer.

# Case Study: Rachel's Battle With The Self-Esteem Wall

Rachel had always done well with her school work. Her primary school reports were always exemplary and brought great pride to Rachel and her parents. Rachel's school successes continued into her first year of high school with an outstanding end-of-year report with high grades and positive comments from all her teachers.

In Year 9 things began to change for Rachel. Teachers frequently made reference to the demands of the forthcoming Year 11 and the exams and that preparation for these began now in Year 9. Rachel spent longer with her homework and gave up most lunchtimes to study in the library. Her summer holiday was spent at a study skills camp. She spent less time with her friends and gave up playing netball. For the first time her mum and dad began expressing concerns:

"Rachel, are you sure you are not pushing yourself too hard?"

"Rachel, why don't you have a break? You've been working so hard you deserve to take a couple of days off and just relax."

Rachel chose to ignore these suggestions and continued pushing herself to her study limits.

### Rachel's first encounter with the self-esteem wall

The final Year 9 exams were the first step towards Rachel's confrontation with the self-esteem wall. In spite of her enormous effort Rachel's overall results dropped by 5% to around a 75% average. Whilst such results would have been a reason for celebration for most students, Rachel reacted to them with great alarm, and interpreted them as an indication that she was failing at her school studies. Although this seems to be an exaggerated response, for someone like Rachel who has experienced years of high achievement, this rather slight fall in marks can be interpreted in such a negative manner.

### Damage to Rachel's self-image

Unbeknown to her parents, friends and teachers it was a very different Rachel that began her Year 10 studies. The disappointments of the final Year 9 exams dominated her thinking. Gone was the student who approached her studies confident that she would succeed in gaining satisfying results. Now Rachel's attitude was dominated by doubts – "Will I be able to do this?" – and an underlying fear that she might fail.

Rachel became very withdrawn, seldom interacting with her peers and never participating in out of school activities. She began losing weight, frequently had headaches and always seemed to be tired.

### The crash

On the day before second term exams, Rachel awoke with a sudden panic attack based around an all-encompassing belief that she would fail the forthcoming exams.

*"No matter how hard I try I will not be able to meet my expectations, the expectations of my teachers and those of my parents,"* she told herself.

It felt as though she had run at great speed into a brick wall. She felt sick, weak, defeated and incredibly depressed. She didn't even have the energy to get out of bed.

## Around the wall

A very concerned mum took Rachel to the family doctor, who was able to quickly diagnose all the symptoms related to serious stress. He informed Rachel that while he could provide certain medications to help her sleep, reduce the headaches and build up her strength, these were really only bandages. The real problem, the doctor told Rachel, was her current state of mind and the unrealistic expectations she was placing on herself. She needed to reset her performance expectations agenda so she could move around the self-esteem wall she was confronted with.

## Exclusivity time the answer

Two days after her visit to the doctor, Rachel's mum suggested that she and Rachel should go for a walk along the beach. It was just on dusk and Rachel and her mum sat on the beach and watched the magnificent sunset. Just before the sun disappeared Rachel's mum turned to her and said;

> *"The important things that happen in life often have a timetable and pathway all of their own; just like that beautiful sun disappearing into the ocean. You can't change that timetable and that pathway and if you try you will only become frustrated and miss out on the glorious uncertainties of the journey. You must let your studies take their own time and find their own pathway for you. If that means it will take you a bit longer, so be it – that just gives you more time to enjoy the glorious uncertainties of the journey."*

On numerous occasions after that sunset Rachel and her mum spent what they came to call their "exclusivity time" – just mum and Rachel on that beach. Little by little, Rachel began to set more realistic expectations for herself, and slowly the overwhelming fear of failure she had nursed for so long began to fade away. It was during the periods of exclusivity time with her mum that she would share doubts, concerns and anxieties. It was during these times she would sort out the options and choices she had.

## Postscript

Rachel went onto to study for her Bachelor of Education degree. Today Rachel teaches primary children.

# Chapter 2

# The Role of a Mentor

## Contents

## Outcomes

### Readers will ...

☐ Develop an understanding of the role of a mentor;

☐ Recognise the essential competencies a successful mentor should be able to demonstrate;

☐ Understand the unique features that characterise a successful mentoring relationship;

☐ Be familiar with key organisational requirements for a good mentoring relationship to occur.

## Introduction

In the introduction to this book it was suggested that the challenge of actualising potential can be a very lonely journey for a student. Having access to a mentor can make the journey towards actualising potential more manageable, fun and exciting for the student. A parent, teacher or a close friend can be this mentor but only if, firstly, they are prepared to establish a relationship with the student which is quite unique and different from normal parent, teacher or friendship relationships, and secondly, that they are satisfied they have adequate mastery of the essential competencies required for successful mentoring. To be effective, a mentor needs to be able to do more than "care about" or "love" the student.

In viewing the role of a mentor and what makes a successful mentor, this chapter will investigate some of these competencies and how they can be successfully applied.

## 2.1    What is a Mentor?

The term "mentoring" first appears in Greek mythology when Ulysses left his son, Telemachus, under the tutelage of his old friend Mentor. *(Carter & Lewis, 1994)* For a considerable time mentoring was a term associated with vocational training.

Mentoring is a relationship where a trusted adviser provides a less skilled or less experienced person with such things as career advice, encouragement, and help in developing specific competencies. *(Institute of Chartered Accountants, N.Z. Mentor Scheme, 1997)*

Whilst there are many definitions, the key characteristic that most writers agree on is that mentoring is based around a special kind of relationship. *(Cohen, 1995; Bennetts, 1999)* Consideration of what has been written about the mentoring relationship has lead me to the following definition of a mentor of secondary school students:

> *'A mentor is a person who is able to project unconditional positive acceptance of an individual. The kind of acceptance and approval projected by the mentor is not contingent upon the student having to meet the mentor's expectations of what they want the student to be or do. This kind of acceptance simply depends on the student being present.' (Thompson, 2001)*

## 2.2    The Mentoring Relationship

The key concept inherent in the above definition of a mentor is that of "unconditional positive acceptance of an individual". This is not an easy condition to establish and is one that is normally not part of a parenting or teaching relationship. As a father, I often find it very difficult to display unconditional acceptance to my children. Consider this typical statement:

*"I don't care if you think that I'm being unfair son. I do not give you permission to smoke cigarettes."*

This is a requirement, a rule, a non-negotiable condition if you like – there is no room for discussion, there are no choices or options related to this decision. Just because I've imposed this condition doesn't mean I'm a bad father – rather I am carrying out what I think is one of my parenting roles, setting and consistently modelling standards and values for my children.

Displaying unconditional acceptance requires some very special skills from a mentor. There are three fundamental skills mentors require if they are to establish effective mentoring relationships with secondary school students. These are:

### 2.2.1    Displaying respect

This involves the mentor displaying behaviours that convey to the student the message that they are worthwhile, unique and valuable. In simple terms this means helping the student to feel important and helping them realise that they are a valued person. At the centre of this requirement is the acknowledgement and respect of the inherent uniqueness of character that each person has. A mentor can display respect of the student through any of the following behaviours:

- ❏ Giving the student appropriate positive attention;
- ❏ Actively and accurately listening to the student;
- ❏ Showing the student that you have heard what they communicated;
- ❏ Giving the student "exclusivity time", i.e. time shared exclusively between you and the student when you are concentrating only on the presence of him or her;
- ❏ Introducing yourself to the student in a positive, friendly manner;
- ❏ Showing the student basic courtesies – offering them a chair, offering them a coffee, not interrupting them when they are communicating something to you;
- ❏ Asking the student non-threatening and interesting questions;
- ❏ Not making snap judgements or evaluations of the student.

### 2.2.2 *Displaying genuineness*

This involves the mentor displaying behaviours that convey to the student that the mentor is trustworthy and displaying openness to the student, not hiding behind roles or facades. In simple terms this means that the mentor comes across to the student as a "real person". They relate to the student from positions of correctness, truth, trust and honesty. A mentor can display genuineness to the student through any of the following behaviours:

❑ Talking to the student honestly about themselves;
❑ Displaying a degree of humbleness to the student;
❑ Responding naturally and unreservedly to the student's questions or comments;
❑ Sharing feelings with the student in a non-confrontational manner;
❑ Avoiding being defensive whilst interacting with the student;
❑ Displaying non-aggressive, non-threatening body language whilst communicating with the student;
❑ Not pretending to be someone or something else whilst interacting with the student;
❑ Admitting you don't know when you do not have an answer to a student's question.

### 2.2.3 *Displaying empathy*

This involves the mentor displaying behaviours that convey to the student the message that he or she can tune into the student's world as they perceive it – by standing in the student's shoes and seeing the world through their eyes. This empathy might be displayed to the student through any of the following behaviours:

❑ Reflecting back to the student feelings picked up from his/her communication – "You sound very happy"; " You sound very angry".
❑ Sharing related and similar experiences whilst avoiding saying, "I know exactly how you feel." The mentor probably doesn't.
❑ Paraphrasing the student's message, "You have just related that you are stressed out about your maths." Such responses indicate to the student that not only did the mentor listen, but that he or she heard accurately what was said.
❑ Smiling when the student smiles, frowning when they frown. This is engaging in "behavioural mirroring" of the student's non-verbal communication and sends them the message that the mentor is "tuned-in".

## 2.3 The Role of A Mentor

Cohen (1995) argues that mentors make a difference primarily because their mentoring behaviours enable them to transmit the essential quality of trust, which allows the student to honestly share and reflect upon their personal experiences. Building on the suggestions of Cohen (1995) it is suggested the role of a mentor in assisting students to enhance their self-esteem and build resilience includes any of the following:

❑ Facilitating discussions and conversations that assist the student to identify their options and choices related to situations causing them concern;
❑ Acting as a reflective listener that allows the student to test out their ideas, thoughts or decisions;
❑ Identifying resources, strategies or experiences the student can refer to for developing self-esteem and resilience;
❑ Acting as an advocate in identifying and actioning support services and agencies when required;
❑ Providing honest, reliable and relevant feedback that allows the student to make informed decisions about aspects of their self-esteem and resilience;

❏ Providing feedback that assists the student to formulate realistic, relevant and productive performance goals;

❏ Providing honest, reliable and relevant feedback that allows the student to monitor their progress towards their performance goals;

❏ Acting as a mediator in conflict-resolution situations involving the student.

## 2.4 Organisational Considerations for Implementing a Mentoring Programme

The following organisational considerations for implementing a mentoring programme for secondary students arise from a study of a pilot-mentoring programme I conducted during the late 1990's. This programme involved 300 mentors working with 400 students drawn from schools. The sample of students represented Years 9 to 13 and involved 235 female and 165 male students.

*(Thompson, L.J. 2000, A Review Of The Secondary School Mentoring Programme. Report delivered to the Tindall Education Foundation)*

### 2.4.1 Police checks

If anyone other than a student's parent is to take on the role of a mentor for a secondary school student they must undertake a standard police check. This is part of the process required to ensure the mentoring experience is safe. The police clearance should be shown to the student and his/her parents.

### 2.4.2 Mentor competencies

There are a number of specific mentor competencies that have been identified as essential for successful mentoring outcomes. These include:

❏ The ability to display reflective listening;

❏ The ability to communicate clearly;

❏ The ability to demonstrate appropriate non-verbal communication;

❏ The ability to demonstrate assertive communication;

❏ The ability to demonstrate unconditional acceptance;

❏ The ability to give focused, relevant, purposeful feedback;

❏ The ability to set goals and monitor performance outcomes;

❏ The ability to facilitate conflict resolution strategies;

❏ The ability to accept an advocacy role.

### 2.4.3 The mentoring setting

Students have reported that if they are to make the most of a mentoring relationship the contacts should be in out-of-school times at non-school venues. This helps to remove the risk of the students receiving mentoring being stigmatised by peers. Students reported the following as preferred places for contact with their mentors:

❏ A local coffee shop;

❏ The beach;

❏ The local community library;

❏ A community service organisation venue, e.g. Red Cross hall, St. John Ambulance rooms, drop-in student centres;

❏ A popular park or sporting venue.

To maintain safety it has been found that the mentor should initially meet the student at the student's home and then travel to the selected venue. Parents should always be informed of where the mentoring will occur and for what length of time, and the students should always be returned home immediately following the mentoring session.

Whilst the preceding settings, etc. are the ideal, and at the risk of contradiction it has been found that for practical and safety reasons and peace of mind that the mentoring is often best implemented in the school environment. If this is the case the mentoring sessions should be in a relaxed, comfortable setting.

### 2.4.4 The match-up

The matching of a mentor to a student needs to be handled very carefully. Given the importance of a quality relationship to the success of the mentoring initiative, time must be allowed for both the mentor and the student to determine if they are able to establish the appropriate kind of relationship. It is therefore suggested that a four-week trial time be used for the sole purpose of determining whether the appropriate relationship can be established. At the conclusion of the trial time either party – mentor or student – can terminate the relationship if they believe it is not appropriate for mentoring purposes.

Following is a list of activities that mentors have reported as being productive during the trial time:

- ❏ Informal conversations over coffee or a milkshake.
- ❏ Shared experiences, e.g. going to the movies, going to a game of football, netball or basketball,
- ❏ Going shopping.
- ❏ Watching a video.
- ❏ Playing board games – Monopoly®, chess, draughts, Scrabble®, etc.
- ❏ Playing cards.

The idea behind any activities engaged in during the four-week trial time is shared fun and stress-free interactions. It should not be a time when formal surveys or self-esteem and resilience strategies are implemented. This should occur only when both parties commit to engaging in a mentoring initiative.

### 2.4.5 How long, how often?

The frequency and time length of mentoring contacts will vary from student to student. Frequency of contact is more important than the time length of the contact. It has been found that a minimum of one weekly contact over a minimum period of six months has produced most effective outcomes. A contact can range from a brief phone call, text message or Internet chat to a planned meeting. The student's needs will determine the type and length of contact.

### 2.4.6 The mentoring safety net

As has been previously suggested the mentor's role is one of being a facilitator, mediator or advocate. This requires them to identify the range of support services and resources they might need to call upon should the student indicate they require them. To this end it has been found that a mentor needs to identify the location and contact procedures for the following support services:

- ❏ School guidance officer, psychologist;
- ❏ Career or vocational guidance officers;
- ❏ A proven sexual abuse agency;
- ❏ A proven legal aid advocate;
- ❏ Proven remedial teachers and subject teachers who are available for extra tuition if needed;
- ❏ A supportive general medical practitioner;
- ❏ A proven substance abuse agency;
- ❏ Learning resource centres.

## Case Study: Charlie M – Mentor Extraordinary Who was Charlie M?

I first met Charlie M whilst I was doing some work for a sports academy. He was a giant of a man, well over 190 cm and weighing about 110 kilos. Charlie M was a senior executive of a large multinational food company. He had played international rugby league and had also played rugby union at a national level. He was in his mid-forties when I met him, the proud dad of three talented adolescent children. Charlie M had volunteered to be a mentor for one year to one of the elite athletes attending this sports academy and I was responsible for supervising this mentoring initiative.

## Paul

Charlie M was matched to Paul, who had been identified as a potential golfing star of the future. Paul was an 18 year old boy, who came to the sports academy. He was an outstanding golfer and scholar and one of the most popular sports academy students. His family were very supportive of his endeavours and took a keen interest in his progress. After three months Paul was achieving top grades for his related study and was playing the best golf of his life. He and Charlie M hit it off from day one. It was obvious they enjoyed each others' company and found the mentoring relationship very rewarding. Occasionally Charlie M would invite Paul to his home for dinner or to join his family when they went off to watch a game of rugby.

## Surprise

On a Monday of the second last week of term Charlie M paid me a visit. I was most surprised with what he related to me.

"Lou, I'm very worried about Paul – something is not right with him. I can't put my finger on it but he is very stressed about something."

I was astonished with this comment as I had just finished reading through Paul's end of term report – straight As in all subjects and a glowing report from all his sport coaches. I shared this information with Charlie M who was aware of this excellent progress report, but nonetheless worried about the boy. Charlie M informed me he was going to pop down on the Saturday to have a chat with Paul's parents.

## Just in time

Charlie M arrived at Paul's home on Saturday morning and was invited to join the family for a meal. He was just about to begin his meal when he asked the whereabouts of Paul. His parents looked at each other querulously and his mum went to his bedroom to call him to the meal. No response – he wasn't in his room. Charlie M and the parents went outside and called for him. Again no reply. Next to the house was a large barn. Charlie M and the parents trotted across to it, opened the door and froze. On the top of a stack of hay, with a rope around his neck and ready to jump was Paul. Charlie M began quietly to talk to him, climbed the stack and for the next hour sat with him.

## Parents are often the last to know

What emerged from Charlie M's time with Paul that day was the fact that he hated being part of the sports academy. Whilst he enjoyed playing golf and mixing with the other students, for as long as he could remember he had had a desire to become involved in the fine arts, especially drama and dance. He believed his parents, relations, community members and friends all expected him to become a professional golfer and he was terrified that he would let them down if he quit, or worse think he was "gay" if he made his desires known to them.

## Thanks to Charlie M

This was not a case of unreasonable parent expectations, rather it was a case of communication break down. Once they became aware of Paul's plight his parents supported his entry into a higher education institution's Academy of Fine Arts and he proceeded to achieve outstanding results. Sometime after this event I asked Charlie what it was that alerted him to Paul's dilemma. His response, I believe, is the best illustration I can give of the consequences of a mentoring relationship based on unconditional acceptance:

*"There was no particular event that sparked my concerns – rather I just had a feeling that things were not as rosy as they appeared to others."*

# Chapter 3

# The Student Performance Profiler

## Contents

## Outcomes

### Readers will ...

☐ Be familiar with the purpose of the Student Performance Profiler;

☐ Be familiar with the composition of the Student Performance Profiler;

☐ Be familiar with the administration requirements of the Student Performance Profiler;

☐ Be able to score, record and interpret responses to the Student Performance Profiler;

☐ Be familiar with, and be able to apply the menus of explanations and strategies associated with the Student Performance Profiler.

## 3.1 Introducing the Student Performance Profiler

A major question facing a mentor and the student who together are going to embark on a journey of developing self-esteem and resilience is: *"Where do we begin?"*

A great deal of time can be wasted if the mentor and student systematically work through every activity and, every survey from start to finish in this book. The idea is for the student and their mentor to identify key need areas, prioritise these and identify the relevant sections of the book that will assist with addressing these needs. The ***Student Performance Profiler*** in this chapter has been provided to enable students and their mentor to carry out this process.

The profiler has been designed to allow students to review important areas related to their self-esteem and resilience. It allows them to identify current strengths and weaknesses related to these concepts. This in turn, ensures they are more informed when they come to setting goals that they can pursue that will enable them to actualise their performance potential. The profiler will provide the mentor with a framework within which they can work alongside the student in this endeavour.

## 3.2 The Composition of the Student Performance Profiler

The ***Student Performance Profiler*** requires students to rate themselves in six domains, each of which is divided into four sub-categories. The first four domains contain items related to self-image whilst the final two domains contain items related to ideal image and resilience. The domains are as follows:

### Domain A: Learning Abilities

Students' ratings in this domain reflect their current judgements, attitudes and thoughts related to their school performance and ability to learn. In this domain the ratings are recorded according to the following sub-categories:

1. **Awareness of learning strengths and weaknesses:**

   Are students familiar with these? Are they succeeding at school? Are they aware of their learning characteristics?

2. **Ability to set realistic learning goals:**

   Do students study just to please the family? Do they know how to set realistic learning goals? Do they know the difference between short term, medium term and long term learning goals? Are they able to monitor the progress they are making towards their learning goals? Do they build the idea of "personal-best" into the learning goals they set themselves?

3. **Strength of study skills:**

   Do students know what study skills are essential for them to be able to reach their learning potential? Which study skills do students need to improve? How well do they manage their study time?

4. **Attitude towards learning:**

   How much does the student care about his/her ability to learn? Is the value the student attaches to learning negatively influenced by his/her peers' attitudes? Is the student able to show commitment and/or desire towards achieving learning goals? Is the student's attitude towards learning dominated by a fear of failure?

### Domain B: Ability to Socialise

Students' ratings in this domain reflect their current judgements, attitudes and thoughts related to their ability to interact with other people, establish friendships and feel comfortable when they are with people. In this domain ratings are recorded according to the following sub-categories:

1. **The ability to form friendships:**

   Does the student have lots of friends and make new friends easily? Does he or she have close friends?

2. **The ability to interact with others:**

   Does the student find it easy to talk to parents? Is he/she comfortable at family gatherings? Can the student introduce him or herself to other people? Is he/she shy when with a group?

3. **The ability to be part of a group or team:**

   Is the student comfortable being part of a team or group? Does he/she know what is required to be a team member? Are they better working on their own?

4. **The ability to empathise with others:**

   Can the student tune in to the feelings of others? Is he/she comfortable in showing people enjoyment at being with them? Is the student able to show people that he/she is aware of their feelings? Can he/she show friends that they are trusted?

*Domain C: Communicating Self to Others*

Student ratings in this domain reflect their current judgements, attitudes and thoughts related to their ability to communicate accurately and purposefully to others. In this domain ratings are recorded according to the following sub-categories:

1. **The ability to communicate clearly and accurately:**

   Does the student communicate messages in a manner that others can understand? Does the student have the necessary skills to be able to communicate to others clearly and accurately? Does the student have difficulty in understanding or interpreting messages communicated to him/her?

2. **The ability to communicate genuineness:**

   Is the student comfortable communicating the idea of the "real me" to others? Is the student aware of the image that he/she communicates to others? Are they confident to express their views even though they might differ from the majority?

3. **The ability to use non-verbal communication:**

   Is the student comfortable in communicating his/her feelings to others? Do they experience difficulties in establishing eye contact with the people they are talking with? Do they know how to show people that they're interested in what they are saying?

4. **The ability to demonstrate leadership communication:**

   Is the student aware of what communication skills are required of a leader? Do they know how to chair a meeting? Can they communicate assertively?

*Domain D: Physical Self-Image*

Student ratings in this domain reflect their awareness of their physical characteristics and their acceptance of them. The awareness of health and lifestyle management responsibilities are also rated. In this domain ratings are recorded according to the following sub-categories:

1. **Awareness of physical characteristics:**

   Is the student aware of his/her optimum weight measurement? Are they aware of their key anatomical characteristics? How fit are they and are they aware of the physical developmental characteristics of someone of their age?

### 2. Acceptance of physical self:

Is the student comfortable with the way he/she looks? Would he/she like to change an aspect of their physical selves? Do they worry about the clothes they wear?

### 3. Awareness of health responsibilities:

Is the student aware of the importance of appropriate hygiene practices? Is he/she aware of the dangers of substance abuse? Is he/she aware of the value of a healthy diet? Is he/she aware of fitness levels?

### 4. Stress and lifestyle management:

Does the student ensure that he/she gets an appropriate amount of sleep? Is he/she able to relax? Can stress be managed? Does the student engage in quality leisure pursuits?

### *Domain E: Career Planning and Preparation*

Ratings in this domain reflect the current judgements, expectations, attitudes and thoughts related to a student's post-secondary school intentions. Ratings will reveal the state of preparedness for post-secondary school study or work and whether the student has given proper consideration to all options. In this domain ratings are summarised according to the following sub-categories:

### 1. Attitude towards work or post-secondary school study:

Are other things in the student's life more important than work or post-school study? What does the student think about being unemployed? Does he/she know what they want to get from a job?

### 2. Awareness of work preparation requirements:

Does the student know what they have to do to get a job? Do he/she know how to produce a curriculum vitae? How much does the student know about having to attend a job interview?

### 3. Awareness of post-secondary school study preparation requirements:

Is the student aware of the prerequisites for entry into the area of tertiary study he/she would like to undertake? Is he/she aware of the tertiary institution options available? Is he/she aware of the costs/fees related to undertaking post-secondary school study?

### 4. Ability to set realistic career/post-secondary school study goals:

Does the student know what kind of work or study he/she is capable of undertaking? Does the student know where his/her work or study interests and abilities lie? Does he/she have guidelines which can be used to determine how realistic the work or study choices are?

### *Domain F: Global Sense of Worth*

Student ratings in this domain will indicate whether the student has hit, or is in danger of hitting, a self-esteem wall. Students will get an indication of the strength of key components of their self-esteem. In this domain ratings are summarised according to the following sub-categories:

### 1. The status of the self-image:

How well does the student know him or herself? Does he/she have negative views about him or herself that are based on inappropriate feedback that has been received? Are there aspects of him or herself that he/she would like some information about?

### 2. Ability to set goals and have aspirations that provide a sense of direction:

Does the student devote all his/her energies at trying to meet the expectations others have of them? Is the student always trying to please the significant others in his/her life? Is most of the student's life spent in a performance comfort zone?

3. **Strength of the student's self-belief:**

   Does the student expect to fail at tasks he/she undertakes? Does he/she dwell too much on his/her weaknesses? Does he/she listen mainly to feedback that is critical of him/her?

4. **Sense of satisfaction with lifestyle:**

   Is the student able to get the right balance between work commitments and engaging in quality leisure activities? Is he/she able to manage stress? Are there things that worry him/her unnecessarily?

## 3.3 Interpreting and Using the Rating Outcomes of the Student Performance Profiler

Once students have completed working through the Student Performance Profiler their mentor should also rate the student on the same survey. This is one way the mentor can determine how close they are to viewing the student's world through the student's eyes. If they suspect unrealistic expectations are held by parents or teachers, the student and mentor can invite the parent or teacher to rate them on the same survey, thus determining if there are differences in perceptions of performance behaviours and where they might lie. Students should rate themselves again in about three months time to determine if any progress is being made towards performance behaviour goals they have set.

Once students and raters have responded to all the ***Student Performance Profiler*** items and have scored them using the scoring key provided, they should collate and record their outcomes on the ***Student Performance Profiler Outcomes Template*** that is provided (Page 55).

It is suggested that the student and their mentor can present the data recorded on the ***Outcome Template*** into a series of bar graphs. These might include an ***Overview Graph***, a ***Domain Graph*** and a ***Comparison Graph***. (Examples of these are detailed in the case study presented at the end of this chapter.)

- ❑ **An Overview Graph** will provide the mentor and student with an overview of the profile ratings. Raters mean scores for each domain are provided, where 1 = very negative rating and 5 = very positive rating. This bar graph will help students and their mentor to determine which general area(s) related to self-esteem and resilience development they would like to focus on.

- ❑ **A Domain Graph** will provide the student and mentor with a record of a domain's sub-category mean score ratings. The Domain Graph will help students and their mentors to pinpoint specific skills and/or attitudes that require attention if the student is to enhance their self-esteem and resilience. This will give further information regarding discrepancies between the mentor's and student's perceptions of the status of their current performance behaviours.

- ❑ **A Comparison Graph** will provide the student and mentor with a comparison for each of the domains between the first and second ratings. It will allow the student and mentor to monitor the progress the student is making in developing healthy self-esteem and strong resilience.

To develop a greater awareness of how to present and analyse outcomes from the Student Performance Profiler the student and their mentor should work through the case study example provided at the conclusion of this chapter.

# The Student Performance Profiler

Student Name: _____

Date: _____

## What is it?

The ***Student Performance Profiler*** is a "self-rating survey" that allows a student to rate themselves in important areas related to their self-esteem and resilience, so that they can identify and prioritise goals they wish to pursue to enhance their performance outcomes.

## Directions to students

❑ *It is a good idea to have your mentor within easy access to you as you complete the profile.*

❑ *You do not have to complete the entire profile in one sitting. You can complete it domain by domain. If you have limited time complete a domain and leave the rest of the profile until you have the time to do it.*

❑ *There are no right or wrong responses to the statements. All that is required is as honest a response as you can give.*

❑ *You need to read each item carefully before deciding what rating to enter. Sometimes the item is stated in a positive format and sometimes it is stated in a negative format. Check with your mentor that you understand this format before beginning.*

❑ *Try to avoid changing your original responses as your first responses are normally your most accurate.*

❑ *If you are not sure of the meaning of an item ask your mentor to clarify it for you.*

❑ *You have 5 rating options to choose from for each item. The rating options are:*

- **Strongly Agree:** If you tick this box it means that you are absolutely certain that the statement applies to you.
- **Agree:** If you tick this box it means that in most instances the statement applies to you.
- **Neutral:** If you tick this box it means that sometimes the statement applies to you and sometimes it doesn't.
- **Disagree:** If you tick this box it means that in most instances the statement does not apply to you.
- **Strongly Disagree:** If you tick this box it means that the statement would never apply to you.

| Items | Strongly Agree | Agree | Neutral | Disagree | Strongly Disagree |
|---|---|---|---|---|---|
| **Domain A: Learning Abilities** | | | | | |
| **Sub-category 1: Awareness** | | | | | |
| 1. I am aware of the school subjects I perform best at. | o | o | o | o | o |
| 2. My progress at school is slowed down by difficulties I have with reading and writing. | o | o | o | o | o |
| 3. I have learning skills that allow me to achieve results at school that make me proud. | o | o | o | o | o |
| 4. I don't know what is causing me to get school study results that I am unhappy with. | o | o | o | o | o |
| 5. I am achieving school study results that are close to the best I am capable of achieving. | o | o | o | o | o |
| 6. I am not achieving results at school that I am proud of. | o | o | o | o | o |

| Items | Ratings | | | | |
|---|---|---|---|---|---|
| **Domain A: Learning Abilities** | Strongly Agree | Agree | Neutral | Disagree | Strongly Disagree |

### Sub-category 2: Setting study goals

| | | | | | | |
|---|---|---|---|---|---|---|
| 1. | I judge my school success according to how pleased my parents are with my performance. | o | o | o | o | o |
| 2. | I set myself goals for study tasks I undertake at school. | o | o | o | o | o |
| 3. | I don't see any reason for setting myself study goals. | o | o | o | o | o |
| 4. | I know the difference between short term and long term study goals I set myself. | o | o | o | o | o |
| 5. | I don't know how to measure the progress I am making towards the study goals I set myself. | o | o | o | o | o |
| 6. | I use the idea of my "personal best" when judging how much progress towards my study goals I am making. | o | o | o | o | o |

### Sub-category 3: Study Skills

| | | | | | | |
|---|---|---|---|---|---|---|
| 1. | I get easily distracted when I'm studying. | o | o | o | o | o |
| 2. | I usually get my schoolwork finished on time. | o | o | o | o | o |
| 3. | I know how to make full use of the library or Internet | o | o | o | o | o |
| 4. | I don't ask my mentor or teacher for help when I'm having difficulties with my study. | o | o | o | o | o |
| 5. | I put off doing assignments until the last minute. | o | o | o | o | o |
| 6. | I find it difficult writing essay-type answers. | o | o | o | o | o |

### Sub-category 4: Learning Attitude

| | | | | | | |
|---|---|---|---|---|---|---|
| 1. | I enjoy being at school. | o | o | o | o | o |
| 2. | I am always worrying that I might fail or get a low mark at school. | o | o | o | o | o |
| 3. | It is important to me that I do as well as I can with my school studies. | o | o | o | o | o |
| 4. | I think going to school is a waste of time. | o | o | o | o | o |
| 5. | I understand that my school study performance is important for my future prospects. | o | o | o | o | o |
| 6. | I usually expect to fail when I hand in an assignment. | o | o | o | o | o |

### Domain B: Ability to Socialise
### Sub-category 1: Ability to form friendships

| | | | | | | |
|---|---|---|---|---|---|---|
| 1. | I have many friends that I keep in touch with. | o | o | o | o | o |
| 2. | I have some people that I can call close friends. | o | o | o | o | o |
| 3. | I don't need friends. | o | o | o | o | o |
| 4. | I find it difficult to make new friends. | o | o | o | o | o |
| 5. | I find it difficult to make new friends. | o | o | o | o | o |
| 6. | I know which of my friends I can trust. | o | o | o | o | o |
| 7. | I prefer being on my own. | o | o | o | o | o |

| Items | Ratings | | | | |
|---|---|---|---|---|---|
| **Domain B: Ability to Socialise (Cont.,)** | Strongly Agree | Agree | Neutral | Disagree | Strongly Disagree |

### Sub-category 2: Ability to interact with others

| | | | | | | |
|---|---|---|---|---|---|---|
| 1. | I find it easy to talk with mum and dad. | o | o | o | o | o |
| 2. | I don't like joining in family gatherings. | o | o | o | o | o |
| 3. | I am shy when I'm with other people. | o | o | o | o | o |
| 4. | I find it easy to introduce myself to other people. | o | o | o | o | o |
| 5. | I have difficulty in talking to people in authority, e.g. my teachers, my sports coach. | o | o | o | o | o |
| 6. | I find it easy to talk and mix with people from different cultural backgrounds | o | o | o | o | o |

### Sub-category 3: Being a team or group member

| | | | | | | |
|---|---|---|---|---|---|---|
| 1. | I can make new team or group members feel welcome. | o | o | o | o | o |
| 2. | I don't like being part of a team or group. | o | o | o | o | o |
| 3. | I am able to respect the decisions of the team or group leader. | o | o | o | o | o |
| 4. | I enjoy being part of a team or group that is undertaking a challenge. | o | o | o | o | o |
| 5. | I find it difficult to give support to other team or group members. | o | o | o | o | o |
| 6. | I find it difficult to listen to the views of team or group members I don't like. | o | o | o | o | o |

### Sub-category 4: Empathising with others

| | | | | | | |
|---|---|---|---|---|---|---|
| 1. | I am comfortable showing people that I enjoy being with them. | o | o | o | o | o |
| 2. | I find it difficult to make my friends feel relaxed when they are with me. | o | o | o | o | o |
| 3. | I am able to show my friends that I am aware of their feelings. | o | o | o | o | o |
| 4. | I find it difficult to show my friends that I can trust them. | o | o | o | o | o |
| 5. | I accept that people can have something important to offer even if I don't like aspects of their behaviour. | o | o | o | o | o |
| 6. | I don't like talking to people who are not my friends. | o | o | o | o | o |

### Domain C: Ability to Communicate
### Sub-category 1: Communicating with clarity

| | | | | | | |
|---|---|---|---|---|---|---|
| 1. | I find it easy to explain things to other people. | o | o | o | o | o |
| 2. | I have difficulty in writing messages to other people. | o | o | o | o | o |
| 3. | I experience no difficulties in understanding information I have to read at school. | o | o | o | o | o |
| 4. | I often have difficulty in finding the right words to use when I want to explain something. | o | o | o | o | o |

| Items | Ratings | | | | |
|---|---|---|---|---|---|
| **Domain C: Ability to Communicate (Cont.,)** | Strongly Agree | Agree | Neutral | Disagree | Strongly Disagree |
| 5. Normally I check that the information I am sharing with someone is accurate. | o | o | o | o | o |
| 6. I get embarrassed when I have to talk in front of others. | o | o | o | o | o |
| **Sub-category 2: Communicating honestly** | | | | | |
| 1. I find it difficult to say "No" to people I like. | o | o | o | o | o |
| 2. I can "speak my mind" when I have to. | o | o | o | o | o |
| 3. I keep my problems to myself. I find it difficult to share them with others. | o | o | o | o | o |
| 4. I enjoy arguing about a topic, in a positive way, with my friends. | o | o | o | o | o |
| 5. I'm frightened that I might hurt peoples' feelings when I'm talking with them. | o | o | o | o | o |
| 6. I am able to talk over most things with my parents. | o | o | o | o | o |
| **Sub-category 3: Ability to use non-verbal communication** | | | | | |
| 1. I don't experience difficulties in establishing eye contact with people I am talking with. | o | o | o | o | o |
| 2. I have little control over how I show my anger. | o | o | o | o | o |
| 3. I know how to show people I am interested in what they are saying. | o | o | o | o | o |
| 4. I often think people are showing anger to me when really they are not. | o | o | o | o | o |
| 5. I know how to show people I respect them. | o | o | o | o | o |
| 6. Often people say I am showing them rudeness when that's not what I'm meaning to do. | o | o | o | o | o |
| **Sub-category 4: Leadership communication** | | | | | |
| 1. I know how to run a meeting. | o | o | o | o | o |
| 2. I get stressed when asked to be a group leader or team captain. | o | o | o | o | o |
| 3. I am able to give my views strongly without causing people to feel uncomfortable. | o | o | o | o | o |
| 4. I enjoy being a team captain or the leader of a group. | o | o | o | o | o |
| 5. I usually have to "yell" to get people to do what I want them to do. | o | o | o | o | o |
| 6. I don't like having to make decisions for other people. | o | o | o | o | o |
| **Domain D: Physical Self-Image** | | | | | |
| **Sub-category 1: Awareness of my physical self-image** | | | | | |
| 1. I regularly check my weight. | o | o | o | o | o |
| 2. I am aware of my major body parts. | o | o | o | o | o |

| Items | Strongly Agree | Agree | Neutral | Disagree | Strongly Disagree |
|---|:---:|:---:|:---:|:---:|:---:|
| **Domain D: Physical Self-Image (Cont.,)** | | | | | |
| 3.  I do not know what my ideal weight should be. | o | o | o | o | o |
| 4.  I know what my normal blood pressure is. | o | o | o | o | o |
| 5.  I am not interested in knowing my fitness level. | o | o | o | o | o |
| 6.  I am unaware of the changes my body will undergo as I grow. | o | o | o | o | o |
| **Sub-category 2:  Acceptance of my physical self** | | | | | |
| 1.  I wish I could change the way I look. | o | o | o | o | o |
| 2.  My personality is just as important to me as the way I look. | o | o | o | o | o |
| 3.  I need expensive clothes for my physical self to be appreciated by other people. | o | o | o | o | o |
| 4.  I worry about what other people think of my body shape. | o | o | o | o | o |
| 5.  I am happy with the way I look. | o | o | o | o | o |
| 6.  I am comfortable with those aspects of my physical make up that make me different from others | o | o | o | o | o |
| **Sub-category 3:  Awareness of health responsibilities** | | | | | |
| 1.  I think it is important to shower or wash every day. | o | o | o | o | o |
| 2.  I am not concerned about the dangers associated with taking drugs. | o | o | o | o | o |
| 3.  I eat healthy food regularly. | o | o | o | o | o |
| 4.  I never seem to get a good night's sleep. | o | o | o | o | o |
| 5.  I exercise regularly each week. | o | o | o | o | o |
| 6.  I still smoke even though I know of the health dangers. | o | o | o | o | o |
| **Sub-category 4:  Stress and lifestyle management** | | | | | |
| 1.  I wake up feeling just as tired as when I went to bed. | o | o | o | o | o |
| 2.  I often miss meals because I am too busy. | o | o | o | o | o |
| 3.  I am able to relax and relieve my stress. | o | o | o | o | o |
| 4.  I am able to manage my time and don't feel constantly rushed. | o | o | o | o | o |
| 5.  I regularly engage in quality leisure activities. | o | o | o | o | o |
| 6.  I frequently lose my temper. | o | o | o | o | o |
| **Domain E: Career Planning and Preparation** | | | | | |
| **Sub-category 1:  Attitude towards work, post-secondary study** | | | | | |
| 1.  I worry about not being able to get a job when I leave school. | o | o | o | o | o |
| 2.  I accept that I have to give a great deal of thought to the sort of job I'm best suited for before I leave school. | o | o | o | o | o |
| 3.  I am not prepared to do more study after leaving school so that I can get the job I want. | o | o | o | o | o |

| Items | Ratings | | | | |
|---|---|---|---|---|---|
| **Domain E: Career Planning and Preparation (Cont.,)** | Strongly Agree | Agree | Neutral | Disagree | Strongly Disagree |
| 4. Getting a high wage is the most important thing I want from a job. | o | o | o | o | o |
| 5. I don't care if I'm unemployed when I leave school. | o | o | o | o | o |
| 6. I have confidence in my ability to get a good job when I leave school or complete my study. | o | o | o | o | o |
| **Sub-category 2: Awareness of work preparation requirements** | | | | | |
| 1. I am aware of the preparation I have to do to apply for the kind of jobs I want. | o | o | o | o | o |
| 2. I don't know how to prepare for a job interview. | o | o | o | o | o |
| 3. I have prepared a plan that I can follow when I'm looking for a job. | o | o | o | o | o |
| 4. I have not checked the prerequisites for the type of jobs I would like to get when I leave school. | o | o | o | o | o |
| 5. I have discussed with my school's career advisor the work and/or post secondary school study options available to me. | o | o | o | o | o |
| 6. I'm not interested in preparing for work or post-secondary school | o | o | o | o | o |
| **Sub-category 3: Awareness of post-secondary school study preparation requirements** | | | | | |
| 1. No matter what, I will not study again once I leave school. | o | o | o | o | o |
| 2. I am aware of the range of post-secondary school study options available to me. | o | o | o | o | o |
| 3. I don't believe that I'm intelligent enough to get involved in any post-secondary school study. | o | o | o | o | o |
| 4. I am looking forward to undertaking post-secondary school study that will help me get the job I want. | o | o | o | o | o |
| 5. I don't know what school qualifications I need to have so that I can get into a post-secondary school study programme. | o | o | o | o | o |
| 6. I believe I can succeed at the post secondary school study I want to undertake. | o | o | o | o | o |
| **Sub-category 4: Setting realistic work/post-secondary school study expectations** | | | | | |
| 1. I am unaware of the kind of jobs I am suited to doing. | o | o | o | o | o |
| 2. I don't want a job where I have to work my way up to senior positions. | o | o | o | o | o |
| 3. The only thing I want from a job is good money. | o | o | o | o | o |
| 4. I am aware that it takes time, and that I need to prove myself, before I can earn the sort of money I want. | o | o | o | o | o |

| Items | Ratings | | | | |
|---|---|---|---|---|---|
| **Domain E: Career Planning and Preparation (Cont.,)** | Strongly Agree | Agree | Neutral | Disagree | Strongly Disagree |
| 5.  I am aware of the post-secondary study options available to me that match my study strengths and interests. | o | o | o | o | o |
| 6.  I don't know the qualification I will need to be able to get the job I want. | o | o | o | o | o |
| **Domain F: Global Sense of Worth** | | | | | |
| **Sub-category 1:  Status of your self-image** | | | | | |
| 1.  I never think about who I am or what I am really like. | o | o | o | o | o |
| 2.  I am aware of my skills and abilities. | o | o | o | o | o |
| 3.  I am sensitive to what other people say about me. | o | o | o | o | o |
| 4.  I don't worry whether other people like the way I look. | o | o | o | o | o |
| 5.  I know who the real me is. | o | o | o | o | o |
| 6.  I wish I knew more about who I am. | o | o | o | o | o |
| **Sub-category 2:  Ability to set goals and have aspirations** | | | | | |
| 1.  I usually judge my successes against my previous personal best. | o | o | o | o | o |
| 2.  Most of what I try hard to achieve is aimed at pleasing others. | o | o | o | o | o |
| 3.  I frequently review my short term and long term goals. | o | o | o | o | o |
| 4.  I can tell the difference between feedback comments that are helpful and those that are negative. | o | o | o | o | o |
| 5.  I put all my energy into chasing one dream. | o | o | o | o | o |
| 6.  Making mistakes does not mean I have failed. | o | o | o | o | o |
| **Sub-category 3:  Strength of my self-belief** | | | | | |
| 1.  I feel I am in charge of where my life is heading. | o | o | o | o | o |
| 2.  I often think I'm not good enough to do the things I want to do. | o | o | o | o | o |
| 3.  I enjoy pushing myself hard when I go after my goals. | o | o | o | o | o |
| 4.  I don't tell anyone when I've made a mistake or got something wrong. | o | o | o | o | o |
| 5.  I think I have done well in my life so far. | o | o | o | o | o |
| 6.  I never feel satisfied with my performance outcomes. | o | o | o | o | o |
| **Sub-category 4:  Sense of satisfaction with my lifestyle** | | | | | |
| 1.  I enjoy being with my family and friends. | o | o | o | o | o |
| 2.  I worry about not knowing the direction my life is heading in. | o | o | o | o | o |
| 3.  I am able to relax and have fun. | o | o | o | o | o |
| 4.  I have a variety of leisure activities I participate in. | o | o | o | o | o |
| 5.  I often worry about things in my life over which I have no control. | o | o | o | o | o |
| 6.  I feel like I live my life to its fullest. | o | o | o | o | o |

## 3.4    Scoring Key for the Student Performance Profiler (1)

| Domain | Strongly Agree | Agree | Neutral | Disagree | Strongly Disagree |
|---|---|---|---|---|---|
| **A: Learning Abilities** | | | | | |
| **Sub-category 1** | | | | | |
| Item 1: | 5 | 4 | 3 | 2 | 1 |
| Item 2: | 1 | 2 | 3 | 4 | 5 |
| Item 3: | 5 | 4 | 3 | 2 | 1 |
| Item 4: | 1 | 2 | 3 | 4 | 5 |
| Item 5: | 5 | 4 | 3 | 2 | 1 |
| Item 6: | 1 | 2 | 3 | 4 | 5 |
| **Sub-category 2** | | | | | |
| Item 1: | 1 | 2 | 3 | 4 | 5 |
| Item 2: | 5 | 4 | 3 | 2 | 1 |
| Item 3: | 1 | 2 | 3 | 4 | 5 |
| Item 4: | 5 | 4 | 3 | 2 | 1 |
| Item 5: | 1 | 2 | 3 | 4 | 5 |
| Item 6: | 5 | 4 | 3 | 2 | 1 |
| **Sub-category 3** | | | | | |
| Item 1: | 1 | 2 | 3 | 4 | 5 |
| Item 2: | 5 | 4 | 3 | 2 | 1 |
| Item 3: | 5 | 4 | 3 | 2 | 1 |
| Item 4: | 1 | 2 | 3 | 4 | 5 |
| Item 5: | 1 | 2 | 3 | 4 | 5 |
| Item 6: | 1 | 2 | 3 | 4 | 5 |
| **Sub-category 4** | | | | | |
| Item 1: | 5 | 4 | 3 | 2 | 1 |
| Item 2: | 1 | 2 | 3 | 4 | 5 |
| Item 3: | 5 | 4 | 3 | 2 | 1 |
| Item 4: | 1 | 2 | 3 | 4 | 5 |
| Item 5: | 5 | 4 | 3 | 2 | 1 |
| Item 6: | 1 | 2 | 3 | 4 | 5 |

## Scoring Key for the Student Performance Profiler (2)

| Domain | Rating Score | | | | |
| --- | --- | --- | --- | --- | --- |
| | **Strongly Agree** | **Agree** | **Neutral** | **Disagree** | **Strongly Disagree** |
| **B: Ability to Socialise** **Sub-category 1** | | | | | |
| Item 1: | 5 | 4 | 3 | 2 | 1 |
| Item 2: | 5 | 4 | 3 | 2 | 1 |
| Item 3: | 1 | 2 | 3 | 4 | 5 |
| Item 4: | 1 | 2 | 3 | 4 | 5 |
| Item 5: | 5 | 4 | 3 | 2 | 1 |
| Item 6: | 1 | 2 | 3 | 4 | 5 |
| **Sub-category 2** | | | | | |
| Item 1: | 5 | 4 | 3 | 2 | 1 |
| Item 2: | 1 | 2 | 3 | 4 | 5 |
| Item 3: | 1 | 2 | 3 | 4 | 5 |
| Item 4: | 5 | 4 | 3 | 2 | 1 |
| Item 5: | 1 | 2 | 3 | 4 | 5 |
| Item 6: | 5 | 4 | 3 | 2 | 1 |
| **Sub-category 3** | | | | | |
| Item 1: | 5 | 4 | 3 | 2 | 1 |
| Item 2: | 1 | 2 | 3 | 4 | 5 |
| Item 3: | 5 | 4 | 3 | 2 | 1 |
| Item 4: | 5 | 4 | 3 | 2 | 1 |
| Item 5: | 1 | 2 | 3 | 4 | 5 |
| Item 6: | 1 | 2 | 3 | 4 | 5 |
| **Sub-category 4** | | | | | |
| Item 1: | 5 | 4 | 3 | 2 | 1 |
| Item 2: | 1 | 2 | 3 | 4 | 5 |
| Item 3: | 5 | 4 | 3 | 2 | 1 |
| Item 4: | 1 | 2 | 3 | 4 | 5 |
| Item 5: | 5 | 4 | 3 | 2 | 1 |
| Item 6: | 1 | 2 | 3 | 4 | 5 |

## Scoring Key for the Student Performance Profiler (3)

| Domain | Rating Score | | | | |
| --- | --- | --- | --- | --- | --- |
| | Strongly Agree | Agree | Neutral | Disagree | Strongly Disagree |
| **C: Ability to Communicate** | | | | | |
| **Sub-category 1** | | | | | |
| Item 1: | 5 | 4 | 3 | 2 | 1 |
| Item 2: | 1 | 2 | 3 | 4 | 5 |
| Item 3: | 5 | 4 | 3 | 2 | 1 |
| Item 4: | 1 | 2 | 3 | 4 | 5 |
| Item 5: | 5 | 4 | 3 | 2 | 1 |
| Item 6: | 1 | 2 | 3 | 4 | 5 |
| **Sub-category 2** | | | | | |
| Item 1: | 1 | 2 | 3 | 4 | 5 |
| Item 2: | 5 | 4 | 3 | 2 | 1 |
| Item 3: | 1 | 2 | 3 | 4 | 5 |
| Item 4: | 5 | 4 | 3 | 2 | 1 |
| Item 5: | 1 | 2 | 3 | 4 | 5 |
| Item 6: | 5 | 4 | 3 | 2 | 1 |
| **Sub-category 3** | | | | | |
| Item 1: | 5 | 4 | 3 | 2 | 1 |
| Item 2: | 1 | 2 | 3 | 4 | 5 |
| Item 3: | 5 | 4 | 3 | 2 | 1 |
| Item 4: | 1 | 2 | 3 | 4 | 5 |
| Item 5: | 5 | 4 | 3 | 2 | 1 |
| Item 6: | 1 | 2 | 3 | 4 | 5 |
| **Sub-category 4** | | | | | |
| Item 1: | 5 | 4 | 3 | 2 | 1 |
| Item 2: | 1 | 2 | 3 | 4 | 5 |
| Item 3: | 5 | 4 | 3 | 2 | 1 |
| Item 4: | 5 | 4 | 3 | 2 | 1 |
| Item 5: | 1 | 2 | 3 | 4 | 5 |
| Item 6: | 1 | 2 | 3 | 4 | 5 |

# Scoring Key for the Student Performance Profiler (4)

| Domain | Rating Score | | | | |
|---|---|---|---|---|---|
| | Strongly Agree | Agree | Neutral | Disagree | Strongly Disagree |
| **D: Physical Self-Image** **Sub-category 1** | | | | | |
| Item 1: | 5 | 4 | 3 | 2 | 1 |
| Item 2: | 5 | 4 | 3 | 2 | 1 |
| Item 3: | 1 | 2 | 3 | 4 | 5 |
| Item 4: | 5 | 4 | 3 | 2 | 1 |
| Item 5: | 1 | 2 | 3 | 4 | 5 |
| Item 6: | 1 | 2 | 3 | 4 | 5 |
| **Sub-category 2** | | | | | |
| Item 1: | 1 | 2 | 3 | 4 | 5 |
| Item 2: | 5 | 4 | 3 | 2 | 1 |
| Item 3: | 1 | 2 | 3 | 4 | 5 |
| Item 4: | 1 | 2 | 3 | 4 | 5 |
| Item 5: | 5 | 4 | 3 | 2 | 1 |
| Item 6: | 5 | 4 | 3 | 2 | 1 |
| **Sub-category 3** | | | | | |
| Item 1: | 5 | 4 | 3 | 2 | 1 |
| Item 2: | 1 | 2 | 3 | 4 | 5 |
| Item 3: | 5 | 4 | 3 | 2 | 1 |
| Item 4: | 1 | 2 | 3 | 4 | 5 |
| Item 5: | 5 | 4 | 3 | 2 | 1 |
| Item 6: | 1 | 2 | 3 | 4 | 5 |
| **Sub-category 4** | | | | | |
| Item 1: | 1 | 2 | 3 | 4 | 5 |
| Item 2: | 1 | 2 | 3 | 4 | 5 |
| Item 3: | 5 | 4 | 3 | 2 | 1 |
| Item 4: | 5 | 4 | 3 | 2 | 1 |
| Item 5: | 5 | 4 | 3 | 2 | 1 |
| Item 6: | 1 | 2 | 3 | 4 | 5 |

# Scoring Key for the Student Performance Profiler (5)

| Domain | Rating Score | | | | |
| --- | --- | --- | --- | --- | --- |
| | Strongly Agree | Agree | Neutral | Disagree | Strongly Disagree |
| **E: Career Planning** **Sub-category 1** | | | | | |
| Item 1: | 1 | 2 | 3 | 4 | 5 |
| Item 2: | 5 | 4 | 3 | 2 | 1 |
| Item 3: | 1 | 2 | 3 | 4 | 5 |
| Item 4: | 1 | 2 | 3 | 4 | 5 |
| Item 5: | 1 | 2 | 3 | 4 | 5 |
| Item 6: | 5 | 4 | 3 | 2 | 1 |
| **Sub-category 2** | | | | | |
| Item 1: | 5 | 4 | 3 | 2 | 1 |
| Item 2: | 1 | 2 | 3 | 4 | 5 |
| Item 3: | 5 | 4 | 3 | 2 | 1 |
| Item 4: | 1 | 2 | 3 | 4 | 5 |
| Item 5: | 5 | 4 | 3 | 2 | 1 |
| Item 6: | 1 | 2 | 3 | 4 | 5 |
| **Sub-category 3** | | | | | |
| Item 1: | 1 | 2 | 3 | 4 | 5 |
| Item 2: | 5 | 4 | 3 | 2 | 1 |
| Item 3: | 1 | 2 | 3 | 4 | 5 |
| Item 4: | 5 | 4 | 3 | 2 | 1 |
| Item 5: | 1 | 2 | 3 | 4 | 5 |
| Item 6: | 5 | 4 | 3 | 2 | 1 |
| **Sub-category 4** | | | | | |
| Item 1: | 1 | 2 | 3 | 4 | 5 |
| Item 2: | 1 | 2 | 3 | 4 | 5 |
| Item 4: | 5 | 4 | 3 | 2 | 1 |
| Item 3: | 5 | 4 | 3 | 2 | 1 |
| Item 5: | 5 | 4 | 3 | 2 | 1 |
| Item 6: | 1 | 2 | 3 | 4 | 5 |

## Scoring Key for the Student Performance Profiler (6)

| Domain | Strongly Agree | Agree | Neutral | Disagree | Strongly Disagree |
|---|---|---|---|---|---|
| **F: Global Sense of Worth** | | | | | |
| **Sub-category 1** | | | | | |
| Item 1: | 1 | 2 | 3 | 4 | 5 |
| Item 2: | 5 | 4 | 3 | 2 | 1 |
| Item 3: | 1 | 2 | 3 | 4 | 5 |
| Item 4: | 5 | 4 | 3 | 2 | 1 |
| Item 5: | 5 | 4 | 3 | 2 | 1 |
| Item 6: | 1 | 2 | 3 | 4 | 5 |
| **Sub-category 2** | | | | | |
| Item 1: | 5 | 4 | 3 | 2 | 1 |
| Item 2: | 1 | 2 | 3 | 4 | 5 |
| Item 3: | 5 | 4 | 3 | 2 | 1 |
| Item 4: | 5 | 4 | 3 | 2 | 1 |
| Item 5: | 1 | 2 | 3 | 4 | 5 |
| Item 6: | 5 | 4 | 3 | 2 | 1 |
| **Sub-category 3** | | | | | |
| Item 1: | 5 | 4 | 3 | 2 | 1 |
| Item 2: | 1 | 2 | 3 | 4 | 5 |
| Item 3: | 5 | 4 | 3 | 2 | 1 |
| Item 4: | 1 | 2 | 3 | 4 | 5 |
| Item 5: | 5 | 4 | 3 | 2 | 1 |
| Item 6: | 1 | 2 | 3 | 4 | 5 |
| **Sub-category 4** | | | | | |
| Item 1: | 5 | 4 | 3 | 2 | 1 |
| Item 2: | 1 | 2 | 3 | 4 | 5 |
| Item 3: | 5 | 4 | 3 | 2 | 1 |
| Item 4: | 5 | 4 | 3 | 2 | 1 |
| Item 5: | 1 | 2 | 3 | 4 | 5 |
| Item 6: | 5 | 4 | 3 | 2 | 1 |

## 3.6    Template for Collating and Recording Student Performance Profiler Outcomes

| **Domain Mean Score**<br>(Total Domain sub-category mean scores divided by 4.) | **Sub-category** | **Mean Score**<br>(6 rating scores for each sub-totalled and divided by 6.) |
|---|---|---|
| ***A. Learning Abilities:*** | 1. Awareness | |
| | Q.1 | _____ |
| | Q.2 | _____ |
| *N.B. Each rater – the student, the mentor and the third rater – should collate and record their responses on this template.* | Q.3 | _____ |
| | Q.4 | _____ |
| | Q.5 | _____ |
| | Q.6 | _____ |
| | Total | _____ |
| Divided by 6 = Sub-Category 1 mean score: | | |
| | 2. Setting study goals | |
| | Q.1 | _____ |
| | Q.2 | _____ |
| | Q.3 | _____ |
| | Q.4 | _____ |
| | Q.5 | _____ |
| | Q.6 | _____ |
| | Total | _____ |
| Divided by 6 = Sub-Category 2 mean score: | | |
| | 3. Study skills | |
| | Q.1 | _____ |
| | Q. 2 | _____ |
| | Q.3 | _____ |
| | Q.4 | _____ |
| | Q.5 | _____ |
| | Q.6 | _____ |
| | Total | _____ |
| Divided by 6 = Sub-Category 3 mean score: | | |
| | 4. Learning Attitude | |
| | Q.1 | _____ |
| | Q.2 | _____ |
| | Q.3 | _____ |
| | Q.4 | _____ |
| | Q.5 | _____ |
| | Q.6 | _____ |
| | Total | _____ |

Divided by 6 = Sub-Category 4 mean score:

Sub-Cat 1 mean score: _____    Sub-Cat 2 mean score: _____

Sub-Cat 3 mean score: _____    Sub-Cat 4 mean score: _____

Total: _____ Divided by 4 _____ = Domain A mean score: _____

| Domain Mean Score<br>(Total Domain sub-category mean scores divided by 4.) | Sub-category | Mean Score<br>(6 rating scores for each sub-totalled and divided by 6.) |
|---|---|---|
| **B. Ability to Socialise:** | 1. Ability to form friendships | |
| | Q.1 | _____ |
| | Q.2 | _____ |
| | Q.3 | _____ |
| | Q.4 | _____ |
| | Q.5 | _____ |
| | Q.6 | _____ |
| | Total | _____ |
| Divided by 6 = Sub-Category 1 mean score: | | |
| | 2. Ability to interact with others | |
| | Q.1 | _____ |
| | Q.2 | _____ |
| | Q.3 | _____ |
| | Q.4 | _____ |
| | Q.5 | _____ |
| | Q.6 | _____ |
| | Total | _____ |
| Divided by 6 = Sub-Category 2 mean score: | | |
| | 3. Being a team or group member | |
| | Q.1 | _____ |
| | Q.2 | _____ |
| | Q.3 | _____ |
| | Q.4 | _____ |
| | Q.5 | _____ |
| | Q.6 | _____ |
| | Total | _____ |
| Divided by 6 = Sub-Category 3 mean score: | | |
| | 4. Empathising with others | |
| | Q.1 | _____ |
| | Q.2 | _____ |
| | Q.3 | _____ |
| | Q.4 | _____ |
| | Q.5 | _____ |
| | Q.6 | _____ |
| | Total | _____ |
| Divided by 6 = Sub-Category 4 mean score: | | |

Sub-Cat 1 mean score: _____     Sub-Cat 2 mean score: _____

Sub-Cat 3 mean score: _____     Sub-Cat 4 mean score: _____

Total: _____ Divided by 4 _____ = Domain B mean score: _____

| **Domain Mean Score**<br>(Total Domain sub-category mean scores divided by 4.) | **Sub-category** | **Mean Score**<br>(6 rating scores for each sub-totalled and divided by 6.) |
|---|---|---|
| ***C. Ability to Communicate:*** | 1. Communicating with clarity | |
| | Q.1 | _____ |
| | Q.2 | _____ |
| | Q.3 | _____ |
| | Q.4 | _____ |
| | Q.5 | _____ |
| | Q.6 | _____ |
| | Total | _____ |
| Divided by 6 = Sub-Category 1 mean score: | | |
| | 2. Communicating honestly | |
| | Q.1 | _____ |
| | Q.2 | _____ |
| | Q.3 | _____ |
| | Q.4 | _____ |
| | Q.5 | _____ |
| | Q.6 | _____ |
| | Total | _____ |
| Divided by 6 = Sub-Category 2 mean score: | | |
| | 3. Ability to use non-verbal communication | |
| | Q.1 | _____ |
| | Q.2 | _____ |
| | Q.3 | _____ |
| | Q.4 | _____ |
| | Q.5 | _____ |
| | Q.6 | _____ |
| | Total | _____ |
| Divided by 6 = Sub-Category 3 mean score: | | |
| | 4. Leadership communication | |
| | Q.1 | _____ |
| | Q.2 | _____ |
| | Q.3 | _____ |
| | Q.4 | _____ |
| | Q.5 | _____ |
| | Q.6 | _____ |
| | Total | _____ |
| Divided by 6 = Sub-Category 4 mean score: | | |

Sub-Cat 1 mean score: _____     Sub-Cat 2 mean score: _____

Sub-Cat 3 mean score: _____     Sub-Cat 4 mean score: _____

Total: _____ Divided by 4 _____ = Domain C mean score: _____

| **Domain Mean Score** (Total Domain sub-category mean scores divided by 4.) | **Sub-category** | **Mean Score** (6 rating scores for each sub-totalled and divided by 6.) |
|---|---|---|
| **D. Physical Self-Image** | 1. Awareness of physical self-image | |
| | Q.1 | _____ |
| | Q.2 | _____ |
| | Q.3 | _____ |
| | Q.4 | _____ |
| | Q.5 | _____ |
| | Q.6 | _____ |
| | Total | _____ |
| Divided by 6 = Sub-Category 1 mean score: | | |
| | 2. Awareness of physical self | |
| | Q.1 | _____ |
| | Q.2 | _____ |
| | Q.3 | _____ |
| | Q.4 | _____ |
| | Q.5 | _____ |
| | Q.6 | _____ |
| | Total | _____ |
| Divided by 6 = Sub-Category 2 mean score: | | |
| | 3. Awareness of health responsibilities | |
| | Q.1 | _____ |
| | Q.2 | _____ |
| | Q.3 | _____ |
| | Q.4 | _____ |
| | Q.5 | _____ |
| | Q.6 | _____ |
| | Total | _____ |
| Divided by 6 = Sub-Category 3 mean score: | | |
| | 4. Stress and lifestyle management | |
| | Q.1 | _____ |
| | Q.2 | _____ |
| | Q.3 | _____ |
| | Q.4 | _____ |
| | Q.5 | _____ |
| | Q.6 | _____ |
| | Total | _____ |
| Divided by 6 = Sub-Category 4 mean score: | | |

Sub-Cat 1 mean score: _____     Sub-Cat 2 mean score: _____

Sub-Cat 3 mean score: _____     Sub-Cat 4 mean score: _____

Total: _____ Divided by 4 _____ = Domain D mean score: _____

| **Domain Mean Score**<br>(Total Domain sub-category mean scores<br>divided by 4.) | **Sub-category** | **Mean Score**<br>(6 rating scores for each<br>sub-totalled and divided by 6.) |
|---|---|---|
| ***E. Career Planning Awareness*** | 1. Attitude towards work/study | |
| | Q.1 | _____ |
| | Q.2 | _____ |
| | Q.3 | _____ |
| | Q.4 | _____ |
| | Q.5 | _____ |
| | Q.6 | _____ |
| | Total | _____ |
| Divided by 6 = Sub-Category 1 mean score: | | |
| | 2. Awareness of work preparation requirements | |
| | Q.1 | _____ |
| | Q.2 | _____ |
| | Q.3 | _____ |
| | Q.4 | _____ |
| | Q.5 | _____ |
| | Q.6 | _____ |
| | Total | _____ |
| Divided by 6 = Sub-Category 2 mean score: | | |
| | 3. Awareness of study preparation requirements | |
| | Q.1 | _____ |
| | Q.2 | _____ |
| | Q.3 | _____ |
| | Q.4 | _____ |
| | Q.5 | _____ |
| | Q.6 | _____ |
| | Total | _____ |
| Divided by 6 = Sub-Category 3 mean score: | | |
| | 4. Setting realistic study/work expectations | |
| | Q.1 | _____ |
| | Q.2 | _____ |
| | Q.3 | _____ |
| | Q.4 | _____ |
| | Q.5 | _____ |
| | Q.6 | _____ |
| | Total | _____ |
| Divided by 6 = Sub-Category 4 mean score: | | |

Sub-Cat 1 mean score: _____          Sub-Cat 2 mean score: _____

Sub-Cat 3 mean score: _____          Sub-Cat 4 mean score: _____

Total: _____ Divided by 4 _____ = Domain E mean score: _____

| **Domain Mean Score** (Total Domain sub-category mean scores divided by 4.) | **Sub-category** | **Mean Score** (6 rating scores for each sub-totalled and divided by 6.) |
|---|---|---|
| ***F. Global Self Worth*** | 1. Status of self-image | |
| | Q.1 | _____ |
| | Q.2 | _____ |
| | Q.3 | _____ |
| | Q.4 | _____ |
| | Q.5 | _____ |
| | Q.6 | _____ |
| | Total | _____ |
| Divided by 6 = Sub-Category 1 mean score: | | |
| | 2. Ability to set goals | |
| | Q.1 | _____ |
| | Q.2 | _____ |
| | Q.3 | _____ |
| | Q.4 | _____ |
| | Q.5 | _____ |
| | Q.6 | _____ |
| | Total | _____ |
| Divided by 6 = Sub-Category 2 mean score: | | |
| | 3. Strength of self-belief | |
| | Q.1 | _____ |
| | Q.2 | _____ |
| | Q.3 | _____ |
| | Q.4 | _____ |
| | Q.5 | _____ |
| | Q.6 | _____ |
| | Total | _____ |
| Divided by 6 = Sub-Category 3 mean score: | | |
| | 4. Sense of satisfaction | |
| | Q.1 | _____ |
| | Q.2 | _____ |
| | Q.3 | _____ |
| | Q.4 | _____ |
| | Q.5 | _____ |
| | Q.6 | _____ |
| | Total | _____ |
| Divided by 6 = Sub-Category 4 mean score: | | |

Sub-Cat 1 mean score: _____    Sub-Cat 2 mean score: _____

Sub-Cat 3 mean score: _____    Sub-Cat 4 mean score: _____

Total: _____ Divided by 4 _____ = Domain F mean score: _____

The collated results from this outcomes template can be used to create bar graphs to visually show an overview of the student's self-esteem and resilience, a domain breakdown and/or a comparison. Pages 75/6 has examples of bar graphs in use.

## 3.7   Student Performance Profiler Outcomes: Menu of Explanations

If the student has rated himself or herself lower than they expected on a particular sub-category and they would like to know what might be contributing to this unexpected rating they should consult the following menu of explanations. This is a list of what a number of so-called "experts" would suggest contributes to a lower rating. The student should discuss these possible explanations with their mentor. After examining the list the student might conclude that none of the provided explanations fits them. This is not uncommon. The explanation may be something small or something that is unique to the student's current situation. By eliminating the possible explanations in the following menu the student, through discussions with their mentor, is more likely to arrive at one that fits their particular situation.

### Domain A: Learning Abilities: Menu of Explanations

#### *Sub-Category 1: Awareness*
*A lower than expected rating might indicate:*

- You are judging your current performances against unrealistic expectations.
- You have had bad learning experiences in a previous class and, as a result, are unnecessarily putting yourself down.
- You have missed a period of schooling at a critical learning time.
- You are inappropriately comparing your learning performances against others in your class.
- You are placing no importance on learning and your current school study.
- Others are expecting too much of you in terms of your study achievements.
- You have a number of learning skills that need further building.
- You are using an inappropriate learning style in your studies.

#### *Sub-Category 2: Setting study goals*
*A lower than expected rating might indicate:*

- You are not attaching sufficient value to your study performance outcomes.
- You think that the people who are important to you are not interested in, or don't care about, your study performance outcomes.
- Certain people have told you that you are no good at your school work, that you're dumb, etc. and because of this you don't bother to set yourself study goals.
- You have never been shown how to set yourself meaningful study goals, or you don't know what part of your study for which you should be setting yourself goals.
- You have other things happening (sport, music, girlfriend/boyfriend) that are taking up all your energy and interest and are preventing you from setting yourself study goals.
- You are someone who is always trying to please others by getting things 100% right. As a result, you are overlooking the importance of "personal best" when you set goals.
- You are frightened of stepping outside your study performance comfort zone, i.e. having a go at tasks that you are likely to make mistakes with; trying out a study activity you have never done before; pushing yourself to use your top 10% of ability.

#### *Sub-Category 3: Strength of your study skills*
*A lower than expected rating might indicate:*

- You are unaware of the key study skills you require if you are going to achieve your study goals.
- You have developed a number of bad study habits that are having a bad influence on your study, e.g. putting things off to the last minute.
- At the moment you are mainly interested in non-study activities, e.g. sport, music, boyfriend/girlfriend, and as a result, your study skills are not as sharp as they should be.

# Student Performance Profiler Outcomes: Menu of Explanations (2)

- Your concentration span is not as strong as it should be when it comes to tackling study tasks.
- You are in too much of a hurry to complete a study task and, as a result, you are making unnecessary careless errors.
- You are having trouble organising yourself so that you can devote all your attention to the study task you should be working on.
- You are having difficulty in finding an appropriate space where you can fully concentrate on the study task you should be working on.
- You might be under the influence of a friend who is displaying inappropriate study skills.

### Sub-category 4: Your learning attitude
*A lower than expected score might indicate:*

- You might be too worried about failing at school. So strong is your fear of failing that you might always be holding something back when you tackle a study task.
- You might have had some bad experiences or disappointments related to study tasks you had previously undertaken and they might have affected your attitude towards learning.
- You might currently be involved in activities that you see as being more important than your school study, e.g. sport, music, boyfriend/girlfriend.
- You are studying mainly to please other people – parents, teachers, friends – and you don't have any study goals that you feel you "own".
- Your self-esteem might be low and you are lacking confidence in your ability to achieve satisfying study results.
- You are striving for study goals that are unrealistically high or low and this is having a bad effect on your learning attitude.

## Domain B: Ability to Socialise

### Sub-category 1: Ability to form friendships
*A lower than expected score might indicate:*

"You have low self-esteem that is stopping you from having the confidence to mix with others.
- You are too aggressive when communicating with others and this is stopping you from forming close friendships.
- You have a shy personality and this makes it difficult for you to make friends.
- You have been badly let down by friends in the past and are reluctant to make new friends.
- You don't show respect to others and this gives people the message that you don't want to mix with them.
- You are too interested in your own ambitions and dreams to make friends with others.
- You are trying to impress the people you mix with and they don't get to know the real you.

### Sub-category 2: Ability to interact (mix) with others
*A lower than expected score might indicate:*

- Any of the explanations offered for Sub-Category 1 of this domain.
- You are not listening appropriately to others and therefore sending them a message that you are not interested in them.
- You have not had many experiences of mixing with others and are unsure of what you have to do.
- You are a shy person and find it very difficult to mix with others.

- Your self-esteem is low and this results in you fearing that you might fail in front of others.
- You have had experiences at home or school where you felt that your views were laughed at and you felt "put down". Consequently you avoid situations where this might happen again.

## Student Performance Profiler Outcomes: Menu of Explanations (3)

### Sub-category 3: Being a team or group member
*A lower than expected score might indicate:*

- You have not had many experiences in performing as part of a team or group.
- You have had negative experiences of being a team or group member, e.g. you may have been incorrectly blamed for a team failure.
- You are a very independent person and don't enjoy having to rely on team or group members' contributions.
- You are preoccupied with satisfying your own needs or goals.
- You are unaware of the requirements to be an effective team or group member.
- You don't have the necessary listening skills to be an effective team or group member.

### Sub-category 4: Empathising with others
*A lower than expected score might indicate:*

- You are unaware of your emotional self – strong feelings you have and how you respond to them.
- You have been taught or encouraged to keep your feelings to yourself, or that showing your feelings to others is a sign of weakness.
- You are so committed to your own goals and needs that you seldom think about the needs or feelings of others.
- You have had a very bad experience that has caused you to keep your feelings to yourself.
- Your ability to empathise with certain people is negatively influenced by stereotypes and/or prejudices that you carry.
- Your self-esteem is such that you believe the feelings or concerns you have about other people are unimportant or not valued.
- You have some very strong emotions that you have difficulty controlling, e.g. anger, sadness, fears.

## Domain C: Ability to Communicate

### Sub-category 1: Communicating with clarity
*A lower than expected score might indicate:*

- You have not mastered the required reading skills.
- You have missed a great deal of school at critical times when reading or writing skills were being taught.
- You have not mastered the required writing skills.
- You rush your writing and reading and consequently make careless errors.
- You are not appropriately listening to instructions given to you.
- You have low self-esteem which causes you stress when you have to speak in front of others.
- You have a minor hearing or visual problem that is interfering with your ability to communicate accurately and clearly to others.
- English is your second language and you need to work on your reading, writing and speaking skills to achieve acceptable communication accuracy and clarity.
- You don't think through what you want to write or say before actually doing it.
- You don't spend enough time in preparing the messages you wish to write or say.

## Student Performance Profiler Outcomes: Menu of Explanations (4)

### Sub-category 2: Communicating honestly; Communicating the "real you"
*A lower than expected score might indicate:*

- You have low self-esteem that causes you to worry too much about upsetting other people.
- You are too concerned with trying to get people to like you.
- You crave attention and exaggerate things when communicating with others.
- You are a shy person and think the only way that people will like or notice you is by telling them things that you think they want to hear.
- You are too pushy and too preoccupied with being in the limelight when you are mixing with others.
- You are trying too hard to be like your hero or role model and not letting people see the real you.

### Sub-category 3: Ability to use non-verbal communication
*A lower than expected score might indicate:*

- You are unaware of what non-verbal communication is.
- You are unaware of the messages people read into the behaviours you display.
- You have developed a number of behavioural habits, like frowning, and are not always aware that you are displaying them.
- You are a poor listener and people interpret this as you not being interested in them.
- You don't have sufficient control over some of your feelings, (e.g. anger, fear, frustration) and this causes you to display inappropriate non-verbal behaviour.
- You have low self-esteem and people interpret this as you being negative towards them.

### Sub-category 4: Leadership communication
*A lower than expected score might indicate:*

- You have low self-esteem and think you aren't good enough to be a leader or captain.
- You have never had any experience of being a leader or captain and have no idea of what it involves.
- You don't know how to give instructions strongly without upsetting people.
- You don't know how to ask a team member to carry out a team task.
- You don't have the necessary speaking skills.
- You are too impatient to be a good team or group leader.
- You don't have the listening skills required for effective leadership.
- You have had bad experiences as a team member and this has left a poor impression on you.

## Domain D: Physical Self-Image

### Sub-category 1: Awareness of physical characteristics
*A lower than expected score might indicate:*

- You have low self-esteem and this causes you to ignore your own body.
- You are constantly overweight and this causes you to ignore the consequences of this.
- You are so preoccupied with your studies or other interests that you ignore the importance of being aware of your key anatomical characteristics.
- You have received misleading information from your significant others about your physical image.
- You have not been informed of the importance of key aspects of your fitness levels.
- You have a physical abnormality that takes too much of your attention.

# Student Performance Profiler Outcomes: Menu of Explanations (5)

### Sub-category 2: Acceptance of physical self
*A lower than expected score might indicate:*

- You have low self-esteem that is causing you to be overly concerned about your physical appearance.
- You have had a bad experience with a boy/girlfriend and blame it on your physical appearance.
- You are overly concerned about an aspect of your physical appearance which you believe is causing others to view you negatively.
- You have received negative feedback from someone important about your physical appearance.
- You might be trying too hard to look like one of your role models or the so-called perfect bodies advertised on TV.

### Sub-category 3: Awareness of health responsibilities
*A lower than expected score might indicate:*

- You are not aware of what good nutrition is.
- You mix with people who are heavy smokers, and/or heavy drug users, and this might have had a negative influence on you.
- You are unaware of the importance of fitness to your general health.
- You are unaware of the dangers to your health that smoking, drug taking or excessive alcohol consumption can pose.
- You are using smoking, drug taking and/or alcohol consumption as communication or social interaction props.
- You are unaware of the importance of good hygiene to your general health.
- You have developed inappropriate sleep habits.
- You are experiencing excessive stress and this is having a negative impact on your health.

### Sub-category 4: Stress and lifestyle management
*A lower than expected score might indicate:*

- You are experiencing difficulties in managing your emotions.
- You are a perfectionist trying to get things 100% correct, 100% of the time.
- You are not managing your time appropriately.
- You don't have sufficient access to, or engage in, quality leisure activities.
- You are unaware of the dangers of excessive stress to your health.
- You are unaware of the key contributors to unhealthy stress.
- You are trying to please too many people too much of the time.

## Domain E: Awareness of Career Planning

### Sub-category 1: Attitude towards work or post-secondary school study
*A lower than expected score might indicate:*

- The state of your self-esteem is such that you underestimate your ability to get work or engage in post-secondary school study.
- Other things in your life are dominating your interests and goals.
- You have had school experiences that have had a negative impact upon your attitude towards work or post-secondary school study.
- People with a poor attitude towards work or post-secondary school study have had a bad influence on you.

- You are not aware of the requirements associated with preparing for work or post-secondary school study.

## Student Performance Profiler Outcomes: Menu of Explanations (6)

- You are preoccupied with material things and have not given full consideration to all your options related to work or post-secondary school study.
- You see getting a job as a means of escaping from school.

### Sub-category 2: Awareness of work preparation requirements
*A lower than expected score might indicate:*

- You are preoccupied with non-work, non-study interests and activities.
- You are unaware of the need to prepare for work.
- You have a overly carefree attitude towards work.
- You are unfamiliar with the requirements of a curriculum vitae.
- You are unfamiliar with the preparatory requirements for a job interview.
- You are unaware of the role of your school's career advisor and the advantages of meeting with him/her.
- You don't know how to arrange a meeting with your school's career advisor.

### Sub-category 3: Awareness of post-secondary school study preparation requirements
*A lower than expected score might indicate:*

- You have had a number of bad experiences at school and this has given you a negative attitude towards doing further study.
- You have too narrow a view of learning and haven't given sufficient thought to the post-secondary school learning options available to you.
- Your desire for material things is leading you away from considering post-secondary school study options.
- You have low self-esteem that is causing you to doubt your ability to succeed at post-secondary school study.
- You are unaware of the post-secondary school qualifications some of your job options require.

### Sub-category 4: Ability to set realistic career/post-secondary school study goals
*A lower than expected score might indicate:*

- Other people, (parents, teachers, friends) are placing unrealistic work or study expectations on you.
- You are putting too much emphasis on making big money.
- You don't know how to set yourself realistic career or post-secondary school study goals.
- You are living too much for the moment and not giving sufficient thought to longer-term goals.
- You are considering getting a job simply as a means of escaping more study and not thinking about your longer-term prospects.

## Domain F: Global Sense of Worth

### Sub-category 1: The status of your self-image
*A lower than expected score might indicate:*

- You are taking too much notice of inappropriate feedback you are receiving from important people in your life.
- You have formed an inappropriate view of who you are, based on what you think you look like.
- You have felt rejected by certain friends and believe this has happened because of the way you look.

## Student Performance Profiler Outcomes: Menu of Explanations (7)

- You are trying too hard to be like certain of your friends or role models.
- You are a perfectionist, always trying to be the person you think others want you to be.
- You are dwelling too much on a specific physical characteristic you have and this is causing you to have an inappropriate self-image.

### Sub-category 2: Ability to set goals and have aspirations
*A lower than expected score might indicate:*

- You are driven by the expectations of others and don't see the need to set your own goals.
- You don't know how to set yourself goals.
- You are a perfectionist, directing your performance efforts almost totally towards pleasing others.
- You have low self-esteem and this is causing you to direct your performance efforts at avoiding failure.
- You are experiencing conflict in that your goals seem to clash with those your teachers or parents might have of you.
- You live for the moment and place no importance on setting yourself goals.
- You are not familiar with or understand the concept of personal best.

### Sub-category 3: Strength of self-belief
*A lower than expected score might indicate:*

- You are trying too hard to please others, to live up to the expectations they have of you.
- You are a perfectionist trying too hard to please too many people too much of the time.
- You dwell too much on the mistakes you make, or your relative areas of weaknesses.
- You haven't given sufficient time to identifying what your relative strength areas are.
- You are setting yourself unrealistic goals.
- You are not distinguishing between productive and non-productive feedback.

### Sub-category 4: Sense of satisfaction with lifestyle
*A lower than expected score might indicate:*

- You have too pessimistic (gloomy) an outlook on life.
- You are not managing stress adequately.
- You do not know how to relax.
- You do not have access to sufficient quality leisure opportunities.
- You are experiencing relationship problems that are causing you high stress.
- You are engaged in substance abuse, using alcohol or drugs as a way to hide from situations that are causing you stress.
- You have hit a self-esteem wall.
- People are placing unrealistic expectations upon you.

## 3.8  Following Up Student Performance Profiler Outcomes

**Menu of Strategies** If the student has rated himself or herself lower than they expected on a particular sub-category and, following discussions with their mentor, determine that he/she would like to enhance his/her development in this area, they should refer to the following Menu of Strategies. Many of the suggestions refer to specific activities included in later chapters of this book. The student and their mentor should review the strategies and activities to determine if they are appropriate to the needs identified by the profiler.

It is important to remember that no single activity will bring about significant improvements to the student's self-esteem and/or resilience needs. Students and their mentors should add activities and strategies they are aware of that are similar to those suggested in the *Menu of Strategies.*

*Remember: The more discussions between student, mentor, teachers and parents about self-esteem and resilience need areas identified, the more likely it will be that strategies and activities will be identified that bring positive outcomes for the student.*

## Domain A: Learning Abilities

### Sub-category 1: Awareness

- Ask your mentor to give you accurate and specific feedback regarding what he or she considers are the study skills you have that are strong and those you have that need working on.
- Complete The *Student Study Skill Survey* (P. 80; Activity 7). When you have completed it discuss your results with your mentor. This survey will help you to identify the study skills that are your strengths and those that you need to work at.
- Complete The *Learning Styles Survey* (P. 97; Activity 13). When you have finished it you should discuss your results with your mentor.
- Make a list of people that frequently make comments about your study achievements. Put a tick alongside those people whose comments you respect and value. Whenever you are in doubt you should check out your thoughts with the people you have ticked.
- Check the status of your current attitude towards learning. You can do this by completing the *Student Learning Attitude Survey* (P. 84; Activity 8).
- Take some time to list the things you enjoy studying and being involved with at school. This list will give you clues as to what your current learning strengths are.
- Review your self-image related to yourself as a learner. (P. 18; *Activity 1: My Student Self: Me As A Learner.*)

### Sub-category 2: Setting study goals

- Discuss with your mentor the concept of personal best and what this means in terms of you setting study goals. Read the information in Chapter 6 on personal best, (6.3, *The Importance of Personal Goals*).
- Observe some of your role models and see if you can determine what goals they might set themselves and how important these are to them.
- Read the information related to key considerations for effective goal setting in Chapter 6 of the book, (P. 130; *Effective Goal Setting*).
- Complete the goal setting activities in Chapter 6 of the book. (P. 30; *Activity 25: Distinguishing Between Short and Long Term Goals; P. 131; Activity 26: A Four Step Blue Print for Goal Setting.*)
- Work with your mentor to determine what your study options are and then practise turning these into study goals.
- Keep a daily diary and use it to practise setting daily short term goals. In your diary at the beginning of the day you should write a goal for that day. At the end of the day make a note which indicates how much progress you are making towards achieving that goal.

## Student Performance Profiler Outcomes: Menu of Strategies (2)

### Sub-category 3: Strength of study skills

- Complete the *Student Study Skill Survey,* (P. 80; *Activity 7*). Discuss your results with your mentor. This will assist you to develop an awareness of the study skills that are strong for you and those that you need to work on.
- If you are experiencing difficulties with essay writing skills, read through the section on essay writing in Chapter 4 of this book (P. 95). You could also ask your English teacher to provide

you with an essay writing guide that you can use with your mentor to improve your writing skills.

- Complete the *Student Learning Attitude Survey* contained in Chapter 4 of this book. (P. 84; *Activity 8.*) It might be that it is your attitude towards learning that is interfering with your study performance, rather than the status of your study skills. This survey will help you to determine this.
- Complete the *Student Learning Obstacle Survey* and discuss your results with your mentor. (P. 86; *Activity 9.*) This activity will help you to determine if outside influences are getting in the way of your study performance.
- Review your time-management skills to see if these are interfering with your study performance. Complete the activities in Chapter 3 related to developing your time management competency. (P. 91; *Activity 10: An Inventory of Time Wasters*; P. 96; Activity 11: *Carrying Out a Time Waster Audit.*) Discuss the outcomes of these activities with your mentor to determine if you need to work on this area.

### Sub-category 4: Learning attitude

- Complete the *Student Learning Obstacle Survey* (P. 86; *Activity 9*) and discuss your results with your mentor. This will reveal to you things that are having a negative impact on your attitude towards learning.
- Complete the *Student Learning Attitude Survey* (P. 84; *Activity 8*) and discuss your results with your mentor. Your results will indicate to you whether your attitude towards your study is sufficiently positive for you to actualise your learning potential.
- Select an area of school study and construct a learning success chart related to it. (P. 134; *Activity 27: Designing a Study Success Plan.*) This will help you to keep a positive attitude whilst you undertake your study towards the goals you have set yourself.

## Domain B: Ability to Socialise

### Sub-category 1: Ability to form friendships

- Examine and discuss the *Thompson Self-Esteem Model* with your mentor. (Chapter 1.) Determine if you have doubts or concerns about your self-image or ideal image. Ask yourself if you are approaching, or are at, the self-esteem wall. (Chapter 1 – *The Self-Esteem Wall.*)
- Check the early warning signs related to a negative self-image related to this aspect of your social self. (P. 19; *Activity 2: My Social Self: My ability to make friends.*)
- Check what kind of image you are presenting to the people you are mixing with. (P. 104; *Activity 15: Do You See Yourself As Others See You?*) Discuss your results with your mentor. This will give you a feel for the kind of image you are communicating to others.
- Familiarise yourself with the key interpersonal relationship skills that are required to form strong friendships. (P. 109; *Activity 16: The Interpersonal Relationship Survey.*) If you are unsure as to what these skills are, discuss them with your mentor.

## Student Performance Profiler Outcomes: Menu of Strategies (3)

- Discuss the meaning and importance of non-verbal communication behaviours with your mentor. (*P. 117; Distinguishing between verbal and non-verbal communication; Activity 19: Reading people's non-verbal communication behaviours; P. 117; Activity 20: Understanding the non-verbal messages associated with body language; P. 118; Activity 21: Clothes and situations; P. 119; Activity 22: Non-verbal communication practice scenarios.*) This is all about the messages you send to people through your "body language" and that often you are unaware that you are sending.

### Sub-category 2: Ability to interact (mix) with others

- Examine and discuss the *Thompson Self-Esteem Model* with your mentor. (Chapter 1.) Consider this in terms of whether something is causing you to lack confidence when mixing with other people. (P. 19; *Activity 2: My Social Self: My ability to make friends.*)
- Complete P. 113; *Activity 17: The Student Relationship Survey*. Discuss with your mentor people you have difficulty establishing relationships with and those that you find easiest to establish relationships with.
- Ask your mentor to observe you mixing with other people and invite them to give you feedback related to the behaviours you display when you are interacting with others.
- Find a book about body language, or see www.changingminds.org
- Keep a diary of your encounters with other people. Note those that you found it easy to mix with and those you found it difficult to mix with. See if any patterns emerge.
- Through discussions with your mentor get to know the aspects of the "real you" that you are comfortable or uncomfortable in sharing with other people.
- Through discussions with your mentor get to know the dangers of exaggeration and embellishment and the impact they may have on those you are communicating with.

### Sub-category 3: Being a team or group member

- If you are interested in sport, pick an elite sports team and follow their progress on TV. or in the newspaper. Keep asking, "What special abilities do these sportspeople display that contribute to them being so successful?" Discuss this with your mentor.
- Ask your mentor to observe you interacting with team or group members. Ask them to give you feedback about the appropriateness of the interaction behaviours you display.
- Review the communication you display when interacting in a group or team. Complete the *Sending and Receiving Behaviours Survey* (P. 115; *Activity 18*). Share your results with your mentor to determine if you have communication problems that need addressing.
- Strengthen your assertive communication. (Chapter 5, P. 123; *Developing Assertiveness;* P. 131; *What is assertive behaviour? P. 123; The advantages of assertive behaviour; P. 124; Code of Assertiveness Rights.*)
- Develop your conflict resolution and negotiation skills. (P. 142; *Conflict resolution strategies that help build resilience;* P. 144; Activity 30: *A student conflict-resolution strategy.*)

### Sub-category 4: Empathising with others

- Take some time-out to explore your feelings/emotions. What are the strongest feelings you experience? What triggers these feelings? How do you respond to these feelings? Engage in this self-exploration journey of your emotional self in the company of a trusted person.
- Check the strength of your listening skills to determine whether you are tuning into the feelings that lie behind the messages that people send you. (P. 121; *Important information related to listening skills*; P. 123; Activity 24: *Practice exercises to build student listening skills;* P. 122; Activity 23: *The effective listening quiz.*)
- Familiarise yourself with the concept of empathy and the behaviours associated with it. (P. 108: *The role of respect, genuineness and empathy in establishing relationships;* P. 108: *What behaviours can you use to show people respect, genuineness and empathy?*)

### Student Performance Profiler Outcomes: Menu of Strategies (4)

- Observe a range of people on TV and decide which you think are appropriate and inappropriate displays of feelings. Discuss your conclusions with your mentors/parents/teachers.
- If you feel uncomfortable when people display their feelings in front of you, think about the emotional behaviour that causes you most concern. Discuss this with your mentor to try and

determine what it is about this behaviour that causes concern to you.

**Domain C: Ability to Communicate**

*Sub-category 1: Communicating with clarity*

- If you have had difficulties with your reading or writing skills since primary school it is a good idea to have your hearing and vision checked by a doctor. Sometimes very minor visual or hearing problems can have a significant impact on your ability to read and write. Discuss this possibility with your mentor.
- If you have had problems with your reading and writing for a considerable time you should discuss with your mentor the possibility of getting a good tutor.
- Reflect on the current status of your self-esteem. Could it be that you have self-doubts that create for you a fear of talking in front of others? Check Chapter 1 of this book that discusses the impact that low self-esteem can have on your ability to communicate, (P. 19/20; *Activity 3: Myself as a communicator. Communicating the "real me" to others*).
- Complete the study skill checklist to determine if there are specific communication skills you need to work on, (P. 80; *Activity 7: The Student Study Skills Survey*).
- Complete the Learning Attitude Survey to determine if your attitude towards learning is interfering with your communication accuracy, (P. 84; *Activity 8: The Student Learning Attitude Survey*).

*Sub-category 2: Communicating honestly. Communicating the "real me"*

- Reflect on the current state of your self-esteem, especially the state of your self-image. How well do you know yourself? Do you value yourself? Review the information in Chapter 1 and then discuss the state of your self-image with your mentor, (Chapter 1, P. 15; *Your Self-Image; The key processes involved in developing self-esteem*; P. 19/20; Activity 3: *Myself as a communicator: Communicating the "real me" to others*).
- Practice describing the "real me" to your mentor. See if your descriptions of the "real me" match the descriptions of you provided by your mentor.
- Complete the activity related to reviewing the image you project to others, (P. 104; *Activity 15: Do You See Yourself As Others See You?*).
- With your mentor, observe well-known people and identify the behaviours they show that indicate the "real them".

*Sub-category 3: Ability to use non-verbal communication*

- Familiarise yourself with what non-verbal communication is. Chapter 5 contains information and activities about non-verbal communication. (P. 117: *Distinguishing between verbal and non-verbal communication*; P. 117; *Activity 19: Reading people's non-verbal communication behaviours*; P. 118; *Activity 20: Understanding the non-verbal messages associated with body language*; P. 119; *Activity 21: Clothes and situations*; P. 119; *Activity 22: Non-verbal communication practice scenarios.*)
- It can be fun to turn the sound off on your TV and try to read the messages a person is sending through their body language. This gives you practice in developing your ability to read body language. Advertisements provide you with an excellent source for this, in that you can write down what you think the key messages being communicated are and then turn the sound up when the advertisement reappears so you can check the accuracy of your observations.
- Ask your mentor to observe you mixing with other people and give you feedback on the non-verbal messages you were sending. If you disagree with their feedback it might be that you need to do more work on this.

# Student Performance Profiler Outcomes: Menu of Strategies (5)

- Ask your mentor to give you feedback regarding how well you control your emotions when you are mixing with others. If he or she informs you that you don't have good control of certain emotions you need to work with them in learning how to manage these behaviours.
- Listening is a vital component of non-verbal communication and your listening skills might need some working at. Chapter 5 has information and activities that will help you develop effective listening skills. (P. 120; *Listening Skills: The secret to being understood and to understanding others' behaviour;* P. 121; *Important information related to listening skills;* P. 121; *Attending, Following, Accepting;* P. 123; *Activity 24: Practice exercises to build secondary school student listening skills;* P. 122; *Activity 23: The secondary school student effective listening quiz.*)

### Sub-category 4: Ability to demonstrate leadership communication

- Observe well-known sports captains leading their teams. Make a note of the behaviours they display that you think makes them effective leaders.
- Review Chapter 1 on self-esteem and ask yourself whether a lack of self-belief is causing you to doubt your ability to carry out leadership duties. Discuss your conclusions about this with your mentor.
- Review the section on assertiveness. Discuss with your mentor your current ability to appropriately display assertiveness. (Chapter 5; Pp. 105-127: *What is assertive behaviour? The advantages of assertive behaviour; The difficulties associated with assertive behaviour; The concept of the "I" statement; The student's code of assertiveness rights.*)
- When offered an opportunity to be a team or group leader take it even if initially you feel uncomfortable or anxious about the task. Ask your mentor to provide you with feedback regarding your leadership competencies.

## Domain D: Physical Self-Image

### Sub-category 1: Awareness of physical characteristics

- Arrange a meeting with your family doctor, or perhaps staff from your school's student services office, to get information about the areas of your anatomy that you don't fully understand.
- Arrange a meeting with your physical education teacher, sports coach or family doctor to determine your current fitness level and what you need to do to get yourself up to a recommended fitness level.
- Review the information in Chapter 2 and ask yourself whether your self-image and self-belief is as healthy as it should be; (Chapter 1; P. 15 on: *The self-image; The key processes involved in developing self-esteem; The self-esteem wall.*)
- Have a discussion with your mentor or family doctor about the body changes you will experience in the near future and what impact these changes will have on you.

### Sub-category 2: Acceptance of physical self

- Review the information in Chapter 1 and ask whether your self-image and self-belief is as healthy as it should be. (Chapter 1; P. 14 on: *The Thompson Self-Esteem Model Explained; Your self-image; Your self-esteem; The self-esteem wall; Early warning indicators for the self-esteem wall; Early warning indicators related to self-image.*)
- Try describing your physical self to your mentor. Determine if he or she agrees with the image you describe. If not it might be that you have formed an inappropriate view of some aspect of your physical self.
- Try describing your physical self to a mentor. If you feel embarrassed about doing this you might be too sensitive about your physical self.

- Make a list of the parts of your body that you feel proud about and those that you feel sensitive or negative about. What causes these feelings?

## Student Performance Profiler Outcomes: Menu of Strategies (6)

### Sub-category 3: Awareness of health responsibilities

- Discuss the dangers of smoking or substance abuse with your mentor.
- Discuss your normal eating habits with your mentor or family doctor to determine how healthy your diet is.
- Review the information in Chapter 7 on stress management and discuss your conclusions with your mentor. (Chapter 7, P. 152 on; *Key facts and concepts related to stress*; P. 153; *Activity 34: Identifying stress warnings*; P. 154; *Activity 35: Relaxation strategies*.)
- Keep a diary of your sleep patterns to determine if you have developed inappropriate sleep habits.

### Sub-category 4: Stress and lifestyle management

- Discuss the dangers associated with smoking or substance abuse with your mentor or family doctor.
- Review the information in Chapter 7 on stress management and discuss your conclusions with your mentor. (Chapter 7; P. 152 on; *Key facts and concepts related to stress; P. 153; Activity 34: Identifying stress warnings; P. 154; Activity 35: Relaxation strategies*.)
- Discuss your diet with your mentor or family doctor. Check that it is appropriately balanced.
- Review the section on time management in this book. Complete the associated activities. Discuss the outcomes with your mentor. (Chapter 5; *Developing time management competency; P. 90; Activity 10: An Inventory of Time Wasters; P. 91; Activity 11: Carrying Out a Time Waster Audit.*)
- Make a list of quality leisure activities available to you. Determine those that you would like to engage in. If you are currently not engaged in any quality leisure activities discuss the possibilities with your mentor.

## Domain E: Awareness of Career Planning

### Sub-category 1: Attitude towards work or post-secondary school study

- Find time to talk with your mentor about work and post-secondary school study. Above all, you need to identify your options.
- Read through the information in this book about ideal image. (Chapter 6, P. 130; *Effective goal setting – the key to a strong ideal image; P. 130; Key considerations for effective goal setting; P. 130; Activity 25: Distinguishing between short and long term goals; P. 131; Activity 26: A Four Step Blue Print for Goal Setting; P. 137; Activity 28: What Do I Want From a Job?*) Discuss your performance on these activities with your mentor.
- Meet with someone you know who has recently left school and got a job, or entered into post-secondary school study. Find out what it was like for them. Do they have tips for you about things to do and/or not to do?
- Find out what is meant by the term "having a good work ethic". Discuss this with your mentor. Where do you stand in terms of a work ethic?

### Sub-category 2: Awareness of work preparation requirements

- Work with your mentor in developing your curriculum vitae. (P. 138; *Activity 29: Developing Job Seeking Skill Awareness.*)
- Work with your mentor to identify where you can look for jobs.

- Work with your mentor to make a list of job opportunities. From these make a list of work options that interest you. Discuss your options with your mentor or careers advisor so that you can prioritise them.
- Ask your mentor to assist you in making an appointment to visit your school careers advisor.
- Work with your mentor/parents/career advisor to prepare for a job interview.

## Student Performance Profiler Outcomes: Menu of Strategies (7)

### Sub-category 3: Awareness of post-secondary school study preparation requirements

- Arrange with your mentor to get the prospectus from a variety of tertiary institutions or post-secondary school study organisations. Review these identifying study courses that interest you. Discuss these with your mentor so that you can make a list of your post-secondary school options.
- Read through the information about establishing your goals in Chapter 6 of this book. Apply this information to establishing your post-secondary school study priorities.
- Work with your mentor in familiarising yourself with the entry requirements of the post-secondary school study courses you are interested in.
- With your mentor or parents visit a range of the post-secondary study institutions you are interested in to get a feel for what they are like.
- Contact your school's career advisor to determine when there are tertiary institution or training organisation open days.

### Sub-category 4: Ability to set realistic career/post-secondary school study goals

- Read through Chapter 6 of this book and complete the activities. (P. 130 on: *Effective goal setting – the key to a strong ideal image; Key considerations for effective goal setting; P. 130; Activity 25: Distinguishing between short and long term goals; P. 131; Activity 26: A Four Step Blue Print for Goal Setting.*) Work with your mentor in applying these principles to setting yourself realistic career or post-secondary school study goals.
- Make a list of all work options or post-secondary school study options you think are available to you. Work with your mentor in prioritising your list, putting the most desired choices at the top.
- Review the outcomes you desire from a job. Discuss these with your mentor and use them as a reality rating check. Complete Chapter 6, P. 137; *Activity 28: What Do I Want From a Job?* Discuss the associated questions with your mentor.
- Talk with people who are currently working in jobs you are interested in, or studying in post-secondary courses you are interested in. Ask them to give feedback about the requirements for the job or study. This will help you to determine their suitability for you.

## Domain F: Global Sense of Worth Sub-category 1: The status of self-image

- Read through the information in this book related to the relationship between self-image and self-esteem (Chapter 1). Discuss your understandings of the importance of self-image with your mentor.
- Attend a reputable fitness centre and work with a qualified instructor. The aim here is to get to know your body, your physical characteristics, attributes and capabilities.
- Discuss the importance of positive feedback with your mentor. (Chapter 1, P. 15; *The key processes involved in developing self-esteem.*)
- In your diary describe the "Real Me". What physical characteristics, personality traits, interests, beliefs, abilities, etc. contribute to your uniqueness?
- Ask someone to describe the image you project to him or her. Is this the "real you"? If not, why not?

- Check the various early warning indicators related to negative self-image included in Chapter 1. (P. 18; *Early warning indicators related to self-image.*)

## Student Performance Profiler Outcomes: Menu of Strategies (8)

### Sub-category 2: Ability to set goals and have aspirations

- Discuss the concept of "personal best" with your mentor. (P. 90; *The Importance of Personal Best.*) Set yourself a goal that focuses on achieving a personal best outcome.
- Read through Chapter 6 which introduces you to strategies you can use to set yourself realistic goals. (P. 130; *Key considerations for effective goal setting;* P. 130; *Activity 25: Distinguishing between short and long term goals;* P. 131; *Activity 26: A Four Step Blue Print for Goal Setting;* P. 90; *The Importance of Personal Best.*) Use these strategies to set yourself performance goals related to "need areas" you have identified.
- Meet with recent school leavers you know and get them to share with you their approach to setting goals whilst at school and their approach to setting goals now that they have left school.
- Discuss with your mentor approaches you can use to monitor the progress you are making towards the goals you have set yourself.

### Sub-category 3: Strength of self-belief

- Read through, and discuss with your mentor, the information on resilience. (P. 142; *Explaining resilience;* P. 123; *Developing assertiveness.*)
- Find a number of out-of-school challenges, experiences or adventures that will force you to undertake new and novel activities that test such attributes as perseverance, endurance, pride, etc. (walking, camping, white water rafting, climbing, abseiling, fine-art experiences, etc.) Participation in such adventures will help you to develop resolve, resilience and self-belief.
- Keep a personal diary in which you record your "personal best" performances, achievements you are proud of, or things you've accomplished that give you a sense of satisfaction.
- Discuss with your mentor the expectations they and others have of you. Where there are differences between the expectations others have of you and your own expectations, find out what lies behind these differences and what you can do about it.
- Discuss with your mentor the specific **Student Performance Profiler** sub-category indicators where your ratings differ from others' ratings of you. Try and find out what they see differently from you.
- Discuss with your mentor the dangers of being a perfectionist and, if you think this applies to you, what you can do about it.

### Sub-category 4: Sense of satisfaction with lifestyle

- Review the current status of your self-esteem. Read through the information in Chapter 1, (P. 14 on: *The Thompson Self-Esteem Model Explained; The self-esteem wall; Early warning indicators associated with the self-esteem wall*).
- Read through the information in Chapter 7 on stress. Discuss with your mentor the situations that cause you stress and get from him or her strategies you can use to manage these. (P. 152 on: *Key facts and concepts related to stress;* P. 153; *Activity 34: Identifying Stress Warnings;* P. 154; *Activity 35; Relaxation Strategy.*)
- Create your own inventory of quality leisure activities. If you cannot identify such activities, discuss this with your mentor.
- If you have an overwhelming sense of helplessness and hopelessness discuss this with your mentor. Such feelings are an important indicator that you are experiencing high stress. Your mentor will assist you to find a specialist counsellor you should consult with.

## Ken – A Case Study Background

The following three tables represent outcomes of the Student Performance Profiler related to a student called Ken. Following is some key background information related to Ken:

Age: 16 years 4 months.

School Year Level: Year 12

Family History: Dad a lawyer, mum a teacher. Has a sister who is 1 year 6 months older. She is studying medicine at university.

Interests: Plays cricket and football in his school's top team. Ken is a very good surfer and an excellent swimmer.

Social Background: Ken is very popular at school and is a school prefect. He had been going steady with a girl for about a year. Recently they split up and the girl is now going steady with Ken's best friend.

School Performance: Up until this year Ken has always got good marks for most of his subjects, with an average of about 70%. This year Ken has been struggling with his schoolwork. His marks have dropped to an average of 54% and he is increasingly behind with his assignments. His parents and teachers are worried he is going to do badly in his final exams.

Emotional State: Ken has lost confidence in himself. He's worried that he is going to disappoint his parents and teachers. He isn't enjoying his sport. At the moment he has no sense of direction, he doesn't feel as though he's going anywhere with his life. He feels very anxious, stressed out.

## Ken's Student Performance Profiler Outcomes

|   | Domain Mean Scores | | |   | Sub-Category Mean Scores | | |
|---|---|---|---|---|---|---|---|
|   | Ken | Mentor | Parent |   | Ken | Mentor | Parent |
| A |   |   |   | 1 | 3.2 | 3.6 | 3.4 |
|   |   |   |   | 2 | 2.6 | 2.4 | 2.3 |
|   |   |   |   | 3 | 3.1 | 3.3 | 3.2 |
|   | 3.1 | 3.2 | 3.1 | 4 | 3.5 | 3.6 | 3.5 |
| B |   |   |   | 1 | 3.9 | 3.8 | 3.9 |
|   |   |   |   | 2 | 3.6 | 3.7 | 3.7 |
|   |   |   |   | 3 | 2.1 | 2.9 | 3.3 |
|   | 3.2 | 3.4 | 3.5 | 4 | 3.2 | 3.3 | 3.2 |
| C |   |   |   | 1 | 3.9 | 4 | 3.8 |
|   |   |   |   | 2 | 4.1 | 4.3 | 4.1 |
|   |   |   |   | 3 | 2.9 | 3.6 | 3.4 |
|   | 3.3 | 3.7 | 3.5 | 4 | 2.4 | 2.9 | 3 |
| D |   |   |   | 1 | 2.1 | 2.3 | 2.2 |
|   |   |   |   | 2 | 1.9 | 1.8 | 2 |
|   |   |   |   | 3 | 3 | 2.6 | 2.4 |
|   | 2.2 | 2.1 | 2.1 | 4 | 1.9 | 1.8 | 2 |

| Domain Mean Scores | | | Sub-Category Mean Scores | | | |
|---|---|---|---|---|---|---|
| Ken | Mentor | Parent | | Ken | Mentor | Parent |
| **E** | | | 1 | 2.9 | 1.8 | 1.7 |
| | | | 2 | 2 | 1.8 | 1.6 |
| | | | 3 | 1.9 | 1.7 | 1.6 |
| 2.2 | 1.7 | 1.6 | 4 | 2 | 1.5 | 1.6 |
| **F** | | | 1 | 2 | 2.2 | 2.3 |
| | | | 2 | 2.4 | 2.4 | 2.5 |
| | | | 3 | 2.3 | 2.3 | 2.6 |
| 2.2 | 2.3 | 2.4 | 4 | 2.2 | 2.5 | 2.5 |

## Overview Graph: Table One: Ken – Student Performance Profile
## Domain Mean Scores: Ken, Mentor, Parents

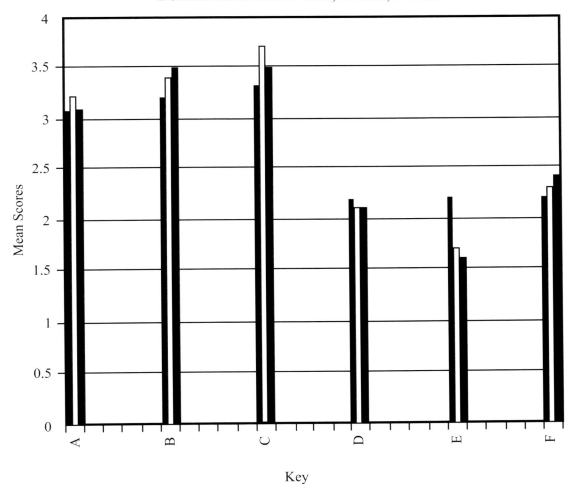

### Key

Black bar = Ken's mean scores    Grey bar = Parent's mean scores    White bar = Mentor's mean scores

| | | | |
|---|---|---|---|
| Domain A: | Learning Abilities | Domain B: | Ability to Socialise |
| Domain C: | Ability to Communicate | Domain D: | Physical Self-Image |
| Domain E: | Career Planning Awareness | Domain F: | Global Self Worth |

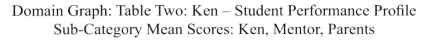

## Domain Graph: Table Two: Ken – Student Performance Profile
### Sub-Category Mean Scores: Ken, Mentor, Parents

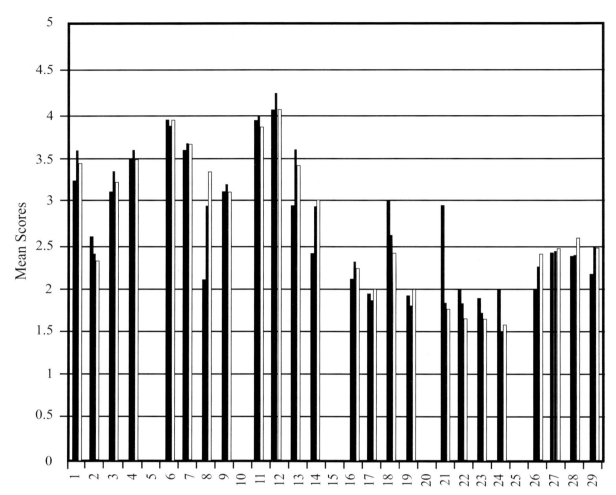

Sub-Categories

### Key

Gray bar = Ken's mean sub-category ratings   Black bar = Mentor's mean sub-category ratings
White bar = Parent's mean sub-category ratings

| Domain A sub-categories: | 1 = Awareness, 2 = Study goals, 3 = Study skills, 4 = Learning attitudes |
|---|---|
| Domain B sub-categories: | 6 = Friendships, 7 = Interacting with others, 8 = Team member, 9 = Empathising |
| Domain C sub-categories: | 11 = Clarity, 12 = Honesty, 13 = Non-verbal communication, 14 = Leadership |
| Domain D sub-categories: | 16 = Physical awareness, 17 = Acceptance, 18 = Health responsibilities, 19 = Stress and lifestyle management |
| Domain E sub-categories: | 21 = Attitude, 22 = Awareness of career requirements, 23 = Awareness of study requirements, 24 = Setting career goals |
| Domain F sub-categories: | 26 = Self-image, 27 = Sense of direction, 28 = Self-belief, 29 = Sense of satisfaction |

## Ken – A Case Study (cont.)

### *Questions*

The mentor and student should discuss the information supplied about Ken's current situation. The mentor should endeavour to clarify the meaning of the information provided in the tables. Together the mentor and student should then respond to the following questions:

1. How would you describe the current status of Ken's self-esteem?
2. Which performance domains and specific sub-categories require some attention?
3. Where do the most significant discrepancies between Ken's, his mentor's and his parents' ratings occur? What might explain this?
4. What explanations could be attributed to Ken's need areas?
5. State three goals Ken might set himself, related to his performance development?
6. How might Ken use his mentor in pursuit of his goals?
7. Select strategies that Ken might use to develop his performance ability?
8. What do you think are Ken's major performance strengths?

# Self-Esteem and Learning Performance

**Related to Domain A of the Student Performance Profiler**

## Contents

## Outcomes

**Readers will ...**

❒ Be more familiar with the relationship between a student's self-esteem and learning performance;

❒ Be aware of a strategy for identifying a student's learning performance strengths and weaknesses;

❒ Be aware of a strategy for determining the strength of students' study skills;

❒ Be familiar with strategies for setting realistic and purposeful learning performance goals;

❒ Be aware of the importance of students' learning styles and performance outcomes;

❒ Be familiar with the self-discipline and attitudes students require to realise their learning potential;

❒ Be aware of potential obstacles that can interfere with students' learning performance outcomes;

❒ Be better placed to enhance the aspect of students' self-esteem that is related to learning performance.

## 4.1  Self-Esteem and Its Relationship to Learning Performance

Perhaps the area of self-esteem that causes secondary school students most concern, is their perception of themselves as a learner. This reaches a crescendo just before their final school year and final exams. If a student enters this year full of doubt and concerns about themselves as a learner and their ability to achieve their learning performance outcomes, they are in for a very difficult ride.

If this is the case it is unlikely that the student will have either a positive outlook towards their study (self-esteem), or the mental toughness to cope with any hurdles they might encounter in this year of study (resilience).

The greater the awareness students have of themselves as learners, the more likely it will be that they will build a strong self-esteem and resilience foundation. This foundation will greatly enhance their ability to cope with the trials and tribulations of studying at secondary school. It will also increase the likelihood that their final school year learning outcomes will result in them having the satisfaction of actualising their learning potential and this, in turn, will allow them to look forward to their post-secondary school future with optimism and confidence.

## 4.2  Identifying Study Skills

The following survey has been designed for students to use to identify their relative strengths and weaknesses in the study skill areas previously described. There is no recommended score that students should achieve. Students are to answer the questions as honestly as they can. After the results have been scored and analysed students and mentors can determine which areas, if any, need to be worked on.

### 4.2.1  Activity 7 - The Student Study Skill Survey

*Indicate which of the statements seem to apply to you:*

If the statement **always** applies to you tick ...           ☐     *Always*
If the statement **occasionally** applies to you tick ...    ☐     *Sometimes*
If the statement **never** applies to you tick ...             ☐     *Never*
If you're **not sure** or **don't understand** the statement tick ...  ☐  *Don't know*

| THE STATEMENTS | Always | Sometimes | Never | Don't know |
|---|:---:|:---:|:---:|:---:|
| *A. MOTIVATION* | | | | |
| 1.  Do you know why you are studying a subject? | ☐ | ☐ | ☐ | ☐ |
| 2.  Do you set yourself study goals? | ☐ | ☐ | ☐ | ☐ |
| 3.  Do you study just to please others? | ☐ | ☐ | ☐ | ☐ |
| 4.  Do you enjoy studying? | ☐ | ☐ | ☐ | ☐ |
| 5.  Are you studying to avoid being bottom of the class? | ☐ | ☐ | ☐ | ☐ |
| 6.  Are you interested in the subjects you are studying? | ☐ | ☐ | ☐ | ☐ |
| *B. ORGANISATION* | | | | |
| 7.  Do you set yourself a weekly study/homework timetable? | ☐ | ☐ | ☐ | ☐ |
| 8.  Do you hand your assignments in on time? | ☐ | ☐ | ☐ | ☐ |
| 9.  Do you begin to study and find that you don't have all the resources necessary to do the task? | ☐ | ☐ | ☐ | ☐ |

| THE STATEMENTS | Always | Sometimes | Never | Don't know |
|---|:---:|:---:|:---:|:---:|
| 10. Do you put off doing assignments until the last minute? | ☐ | ☐ | ☐ | ☐ |
| 11. Do you have a study space where you feel comfortable and are not distracted when working at learning tasks? | ☐ | ☐ | ☐ | ☐ |
| 12. Do you diary your daily study tasks at the beginning of each day? | ☐ | ☐ | ☐ | ☐ |

**The following activities and strategies will help students to gain maximum awareness of themselves as learners. They could be incorporated into remedial programmes where study skills or learning obstacles problems have been identified.**

C. *MEMORY*

| | Always | Sometimes | Never | Don't know |
|---|:---:|:---:|:---:|:---:|
| 13. Do you find it hard to remember dates, names & facts? | ☐ | ☐ | ☐ | ☐ |
| 14. Do you try to remember every fact you hear? | ☐ | ☐ | ☐ | ☐ |
| 15. Do you make an effort to check that you understand the information you have to remember? | ☐ | ☐ | ☐ | ☐ |
| 16. Do you break down large pieces of information that you have to learn into smaller units? | ☐ | ☐ | ☐ | ☐ |
| 17. Do you consistently revise information you have to learn? | ☐ | ☐ | ☐ | ☐ |
| 18. Do you use games or tricks to help you to remember information like dates and formulas? | ☐ | ☐ | ☐ | ☐ |

D. *USING RESOURCES*

| | Always | Sometimes | Never | Don't know |
|---|:---:|:---:|:---:|:---:|
| 19. Do you know how to make best use of the library? | ☐ | ☐ | ☐ | ☐ |
| 20. Do you use the library when researching for an assignment? | ☐ | ☐ | ☐ | ☐ |
| 21. Do you use the Internet when researching for an assignment? | ☐ | ☐ | ☐ | ☐ |
| 22. Are you able to use word processing to assist you in presenting assignments or keeping study records? | ☐ | ☐ | ☐ | ☐ |
| 23. If you are having difficulty with an assignment do you have an "out of school" person you can turn to for help? | ☐ | ☐ | ☐ | ☐ |
| 24. Do you use a dictionary when tackling assignments? | ☐ | ☐ | ☐ | ☐ |

E. *EFFECTIVE LISTENING*

| | Always | Sometimes | Never | Don't know |
|---|:---:|:---:|:---:|:---:|
| 25. Do you listen for key ideas when the teacher is talking? | ☐ | ☐ | ☐ | ☐ |

| THE STATEMENTS | Always | Sometimes | Never | Don't know |
|---|---|---|---|---|
| 26. Do you use paraphrasing (repeating what someone has said to you) to check that you have correctly heard the message? | ☐ | ☐ | ☐ | ☐ |
| 27. Can you read the feelings behind a person's words? | ☐ | ☐ | ☐ | ☐ |
| 28. Do you take notes while your teacher is talking? | ☐ | ☐ | ☐ | ☐ |
| 29. Are you able to keep appropriate eye contact with someone who is talking to you? | ☐ | ☐ | ☐ | ☐ |
| 30. Are you easily distracted when someone is talking to you? | ☐ | ☐ | ☐ | ☐ |

### F. NOTE TAKING

| | Always | Sometimes | Never | Don't know |
|---|---|---|---|---|
| 31. Do you listen for key ideas when taking notes from the teacher's lessons? | ☐ | ☐ | ☐ | ☐ |
| 32. Do you rewrite your rough notes, organising them according to sub-headings, numbering or lettering? | ☐ | ☐ | ☐ | ☐ |
| 33. Do you use diagrams, illustrations or graphs as a form of note taking? | ☐ | ☐ | ☐ | ☐ |
| 34. Do you make sure you organise your notes at the end of each day? | ☐ | ☐ | ☐ | ☐ |
| 35. Have you developed your own shorthand for note taking? | ☐ | ☐ | ☐ | ☐ |
| 36. Do you find that when you go to use your study notes you can't read them? | ☐ | ☐ | ☐ | ☐ |

### G. ESSAY WRITING

| | Always | Sometimes | Never | Don't know |
|---|---|---|---|---|
| 37. Before you begin to write an essay do you take the time to produce a plan? | ☐ | ☐ | ☐ | ☐ |
| 38. Do you make plenty of spelling mistakes when you write an essay? | ☐ | ☐ | ☐ | ☐ |
| 39. Do your essays always contain a conclusion? | ☐ | ☐ | ☐ | ☐ |
| 40. Do your essays have an introductory paragraph? | ☐ | ☐ | ☐ | ☐ |
| 41. Do you proofread your essays? | ☐ | ☐ | ☐ | ☐ |
| 42. Do you clarify what it is you have to write about before you begin your essay? | ☐ | ☐ | ☐ | ☐ |

### H. READING

| | Always | Sometimes | Never | Don't know |
|---|---|---|---|---|
| 43. Do you try and read every word of every chapter of a text book? | ☐ | ☐ | ☐ | ☐ |
| 44. Can you skim read? | ☐ | ☐ | ☐ | ☐ |

| THE STATEMENTS | Always | Sometimes | Never | Don't know |
|---|:---:|:---:|:---:|:---:|
| **45.** Do you make full use of the table of contents and bibliographies of books you read for reference? | ☐ | ☐ | ☐ | ☐ |
| **46.** Do you have to follow words you are reading with your finger? | ☐ | ☐ | ☐ | ☐ |
| **47.** Do you often find that you can read the words but not understand the meaning of what you have read? | ☐ | ☐ | ☐ | ☐ |
| **48.** Are you easily distracted when reading? | ☐ | ☐ | ☐ | ☐ |

## *I. PREPARING FOR EXAMS*

| | Always | Sometimes | Never | Don't know |
|---|:---:|:---:|:---:|:---:|
| **49.** Do you make sure you are familiar with the topics and subjects that you are going to be examined on? | ☐ | ☐ | ☐ | ☐ |
| **50.** Do you make up an exam preparation revision timetable for yourself? | ☐ | ☐ | ☐ | ☐ |
| **51.** Do you check beforehand the format of the exam? | ☐ | ☐ | ☐ | ☐ |
| **52.** Do you rework your study notes for exams? | | | | |
| **53.** Do you study for hours without taking a break? | ☐ | ☐ | ☐ | ☐ |
| **54.** Do you read the whole exam paper through before deciding which questions to answer and in what order? | ☐ | ☐ | ☐ | ☐ |

## *J. MANAGING STRESS*

| | Always | Sometimes | Never | Don't know |
|---|:---:|:---:|:---:|:---:|
| **55.** Do you get so worried or nervous before exams that you feel ill? | ☐ | ☐ | ☐ | ☐ |
| **56.** Do you constantly feel uptight? | ☐ | ☐ | ☐ | ☐ |
| **57.** Do you get so worried about your study that you have difficulty sleeping? | ☐ | ☐ | ☐ | ☐ |
| **58.** Do you have someone you can share your concerns and worries with? | ☐ | ☐ | ☐ | ☐ |
| **59.** Are you able to stop yourself feeling miserable? | ☐ | ☐ | ☐ | ☐ |
| **60.** Do you keep a balance between study and leisure? | ☐ | ☐ | ☐ | ☐ |

### 4.2.2 *Scoring and recording responses to the study skills survey*

Responses to the the following questions are to be scored as in Table A below:

1, 2, 4, 6, 7, 8, 11, 12, 15, 16, 17, 18, 19, 20, 21,

22, 23, 24, 25, 26, 27, 29, 31, 32, 33, 34, 35, 37, 39, 40

41, 42, 44, 45, 49, 50, 51, 52, 54, 58, 59, 60

| TABLE A | ALWAYS | = | 10 |
| | SOMETIMES | = | 5 |
| | NEVER | = | 0 |
| | DON'T KNOW | = | 1 |

Responses to the the following questions are to be scored as in Table B below:

3,    5,    9,    10,    13,    14,    28,    30,    36,    38,    43,    46,    47,    48,    53,
55,    56,    57

| TABLE B | ALWAYS | = | 0 |
| | SOMETIMES | = | 5 |
| | NEVER | = | 10 |
| | DON'T KNOW | = | 1 |

### 4.2.3   Recording results

- Using the above key, calculate the total score for each study skill category.
- Determine the mean score for each study skill category. (Divide the category total by 6.)
- Plot study skill category mean scores on a bar graph. The vertical axis should represent the category mean scores whilst the horizontal axis should represent the 10 study skill categories.

### 4.2.4   Following up the study skills survey

If students identified a study skill area that they would like to further develop to assist them to realise their learning potential, discuss it with them. The idea is to arrange a collection of strategies that students can use to build up this study skill. The strategies and activities on the following pages might be of use to the mentor and their student for strengthening study skills. They are organised to follow the study skill areas as presented in the survey.

## 4.3   Developing a Positive Attitude Towards Learning

The following expression may be familiar to students:

*"The difference between winning and losing is the top 10%."*

This expression is referring to the mental attitude brought to a performance. An individual can have all the ability or skills in the world but if they do not believe in themselves, their ability to succeed at the task, or their level of commitment to the task, then it is unlikely that they will achieve an outcome that reflects their potential.

The following Learning Attitude Survey will provide students with information on questions such as:

- *Am I "failure-oriented" when it comes to studying or undertaking a learning task?*
- *Is my ability to actualise my learning potential negatively influenced by a negative attitude towards learning?*
- *Is my motivational level high enough for me to realise my learning potential?*

### 4.3.1   Activity 8: The Student Learning Attitude Survey

*Instructions*

- *For each question tick either True or False, whichever is the appropriate response for you.*
- *Respond to each question quickly and don't try and analyse it. The first reaction you have*
- *to the question is the one that is required.*
- *Remember there are no "right" or "wrong" answers. This is simply a survey of your current thoughts related to the questions.*

| QUESTIONS | TRUE | FALSE |
|---|---|---|
| 1. I am prepared to do a lot of revision and out-of-school study related to the assignments and exams I'm required to complete at school. | ☐ | ☐ |
| 2. Studying is a very unpleasant task for me. | ☐ | ☐ |
| 3. I expect to fail the exams I sit at school. | ☐ | ☐ |
| 4. I enjoy doing school assignments. | ☐ | ☐ |
| 5. Exams don't overly stress me. | ☐ | ☐ |
| 6. I always worry whether I am intelligent enough to succeed with my studies. | ☐ | ☐ |
| 7. If I am having trouble completing a school assignment I just give up on it. | ☐ | ☐ |
| 8. I take great pride in the assignments I do at school. | ☐ | ☐ |
| 9. I just don't care about my schoolwork. | ☐ | ☐ |
| 10. I don't mind having my learning mistakes pointed out to me by my teachers. | ☐ | ☐ |
| 11. I hate school and can't wait until I leave. | ☐ | ☐ |
| 12. I have no trouble in asking for help if I am having trouble with an assignment. | ☐ | ☐ |
| 13. I am always trying to please my family by getting good results at school. | ☐ | ☐ |
| 14. Completing an assignment on time gives me a great sense of satisfaction and happiness. | ☐ | ☐ |
| 15. When I get a mark for an assignment that is lower than what I expected I feel as though I'm a failure. | ☐ | ☐ |
| 16. I am able to set myself realistic study goals. | ☐ | ☐ |
| 17. I enjoy being presented with study challenges. | ☐ | ☐ |
| 18. I don't believe that I'm as intelligent as my classmates. | ☐ | ☐ |
| 19. I am a failure when it comes to sitting exams. | ☐ | ☐ |
| 20. I am interested in the subjects I study at school. | ☐ | ☐ |

### 4.3.2 Scoring for the Student Learning Attitude Survey

| Question | True | False | Question | True | False |
|---|---|---|---|---|---|
| 1: | 5 | 0 | 2: | 0 | 5 |
| 3: | 0 | 5 | 4: | 5 | 0 |
| 5: | 5 | 0 | 6: | 0 | 5 |
| 7: | 0 | 5 | 8: | 5 | 0 |
| 9: | 0 | 5 | 10: | 5 | 0 |
| 11: | 0 | 5 | 12: | 5 | 0 |
| 13: | 0 | 5 | 14: | 5 | 0 |
| 15: | 0 | 5 | 16: | 5 | 0 |
| 17: | 5 | 0 | 18: | 0 | 5 |
| 19: | 0 | 5 | 20: | 5 | 0 |

## 4.3.3 Interpreting the Student Learning Attitude Survey scores

Students total up their scores and reflect on the score in terms of the following classifications:

| Score Range | Classification |
|---|---|
| 15 to 20 | A very positive attitude towards learning. |

| | |
|---|---|
| | Realistic study expectations. |
| | Enjoys studying and is interested in the things he/she is studying. |
| 10 to 14 | A positive attitude towards learning. Perhaps performance expectations or study habits need reviewing. |
| 5 to 9 | A negative attitude towards learning. |
| | The student does not enjoy learning. |
| 1 to 4 | A very negative attitude towards learning. |
| | The student is "failure-oriented" and believes they are incapable of achieving acceptable study outcomes. |

### 4.3.4    Follow up and strategies

If their *Learning Attitude Survey* results are lower than expected it is suggested that students need to think about the things that have contributed to their attitude. They might ask their mentor to help them identify these factors.

## 4.4    Identifying Student Learning Obstacles

The saying "not being able to see the woods for the trees" is most appropriate when students reflect on what might be contributing to a negative learning attitude, or a learning performance that is less than satisfactory for them. The answer can be right in front of them but they can't see it because they are overwhelmed by their situation.

This activity will help the mentor to determine if there are existing serious obstacles preventing the student from realising their learning potential.

**Remember!** *Obstacles to learning have little to do with who you are but rather what you do or not do when tackling a learning task.*

### 4.4.1    *Activity 9: Student Learning Obstacles Survey*

Check yourself on the following common obstacles to learning:

| OBSTACLE A | YES | NO |
|---|---|---|
| **Lack of Study Discipline** *Self-discipline is an old-fashioned concept but lack of it when you are studying can be devastating on your performance outcomes.* | | |
| 1. I procrastinate – I leave everything to the last moment. | ☐ | ☐ |
| 2. I don't concentrate – I doodle, daydream, doze off. | ☐ | ☐ |
| 3. I don't study on a regular basis. I only study when I really have to. | ☐ | ☐ |
| 4. I regularly revise my study notes. | ☐ | ☐ |
| 5. I often can't be bothered making study notes. | ☐ | ☐ |
| 6. I never organise my study time. | ☐ | ☐ |
| **OBSTACLE B** | **YES** | **NO** |
| **Lack of Planning** *Learning must be planned and monitored. This is a key value that underpins positive learning.* | | |
| 1. I have goals, aims and a sense of direction for my study. | ☐ | ☐ |
| 2. I don't know what I want to achieve through my study. | ☐ | ☐ |
| 3. I set myself realistic expectations for study tasks. | ☐ | ☐ |

| OBSTACLE B | YES | NO |
|---|---|---|
| 4.  I never match my study resources (time, effort, etc.) to my study endeavours. | ☐ | ☐ |
| 5.  I never allow myself sufficient time to achieve my study goals. | ☐ | ☐ |
| 6.  I have no way of knowing whether I'm making satisfactory progress towards my study goals. | ☐ | ☐ |

| OBSTACLE C | YES | NO |
|---|---|---|

### Lack of Time Management

A widely accepted study consideration is:
*It's not how hard you work but how smart you work that brings positive learning outcomes. This implies that you need to consider how you will get maximum results from the time you invest in your study.*

| | YES | NO |
|---|---|---|
| 1.  I have no idea where my study time goes. | ☐ | ☐ |
| 2.  I know what my common time wasters and distracters are. | ☐ | ☐ |
| 3.  I leave everything to the last minute, constantly finding excuses avoid finishing a study task. to | ☐ | ☐ |
| 4.  I make sure I take time out from my study to engage in quality leisure activities. | ☐ | ☐ |
| 5.  I feel guilty because I never seem to catch up on unfinished work. | ☐ | ☐ |
| 6.  I feel as though I never finish study tasks that I begin. | ☐ | ☐ |

| OBSTACLE D | YES | NO |
|---|---|---|

### Lack of Self-Esteem Related To Myself As A Learner

*A healthy learning self-esteem means that you have sufficient belief in yourself to achieve the learning goals you set yourself. If you are preoccupied with avoiding failure and not getting things wrong when you are studying, you do not have a healthy learning self-esteem.*

| | YES | NO |
|---|---|---|
| 1.  I know what my learning strengths and weaknesses are. | ☐ | ☐ |
| 2.  I have no learning abilities that I am proud of. | ☐ | ☐ |
| 3.  I see myself as a learning failure. | ☐ | ☐ |
| 4.  I never ask for help when I am having problems with my study. | ☐ | ☐ |
| 5.  I tell people I understand things when I really don't, so that people won't think I'm stupid. | ☐ | ☐ |
| 6.  I never try different ways of learning things. | ☐ | ☐ |

### 4.4.2   Scoring for the Student Learning Obstacles Survey

*Obstacle A: Lack of Study Discipline*

| 1. Yes: = 0 | 2. Yes: = 0 | 3. Yes: = 0 |
|---|---|---|
| No: = 5 | No: = 5 | No: = 5 |
| 4. Yes: = 5 | 5. Yes: = 0 | 6. Yes: = 0 |
| No: = 0 | No: = 5 | No: = 5 |

*Obstacle B: Lack of Planning*

| 1. Yes: = 5 | 2. Yes: = 0 | 3. Yes: = 5 |
|---|---|---|
| No: = 0 | No: = 5 | No: = 0 |
| 4. Yes: = 0 | 5. Yes: = 0 | 6. Yes: = 0 |
| No: = 5 | No: = 5 | No: = 5 |

*Obstacle C: Lack of Time Management*

| 1. | Yes: | = | 0 | 2. | Yes: | = | 5 | 3. | Yes: | = | 0 |
|---|---|---|---|---|---|---|---|---|---|---|---|
| | No: | = | 5 | | No: | = | 0 | | No: | = | 5 |
| 4. | Yes: | = | 5 | 5. | Yes: | = | 0 | 6. | Yes: | = | 0 |
| | No: | = | 0 | | No: | = | 5 | | No: | = | 5 |

*Obstacle D: Lack of Self-Esteem*

| 1. | Yes: | = | 5 | 2. | Yes: | = | 0 | 3. | Yes: | = | 0 |
|---|---|---|---|---|---|---|---|---|---|---|---|
| | No: | = | 0 | | No: | = | 5 | | No: | = | 5 |
| 4. | Yes: | = | 0 | 5. | Yes: | = | 0 | 6. | Yes: | = | 0 |
| | No: | = | 5 | | No: | = | 5 | | No: | = | 5 |

### 4.4.3 Interpretation of the Student Learning Obstacles Survey

The following scale should be used to determine the meaning of the *Learning Obstacle Survey*. Result:

| Score: | Meaning: |
|---|---|
| 100 to 120 | Student engages in obstacle free learning. |
| 80 to 99 | Student's learning is relatively obstacle free. |
| 50 to 79 | There are learning obstacles that the student needs to attend to. |
| 0 to 49 | There are serious learning obstacles that the student needs to attend to. |

### 4.4.4 Follow up and strategies

If the mentor or student have identified that the student has learning obstacles that need addressing, discussion should take place with the teacher or mentor. Working together, a strategic plan designed to eradicate the obstacles should be developed. The following section details elements that could be incorporated into such a plan.

## 4.5 Strategies for Strengthening Study Skills

No matter how much learning ability students possess, or how strong the desire they have to succeed at their study is, unless they have access to proven study skills it will be difficult for them to realise their learning performance potential. A number of educators have agreed that if a student is to realise their learning performance potential they need to have the study skills detailed in this section:

### 4.5.1 Motivation

A student needs to have a desire to learn. They need to have a reason for learning and to know why they are studying a particular subject. The most powerful motivation for a student to engage in learning is to achieve a personal best outcome, whatever that might be for them. To use this form of motivation they need to know the difference between their "comfort zone" learning performance and "top 10% zone" performance. For students to engage on what might be the most demanding and challenging journey of their lives without a sense of direction, a focus or target, is like trying to climb Mt. Everest without knowing where the top is and the best path to take to get there.

Kim Hughes, a famous Australian cricketer related the following to me:

*"When I went to secondary school I was driven by the following thought:*
*If I am going to become one of the world's greatest cricketers I need a fire in my belly that matches the cricket skills I've got. Just as I have to daily improve my cricket skills, so I have to work daily at my motivational skills.*
*If I don't, the fire goes out and I'll spend my time in my performance comfort zone."*

### Sources of Motivation

If students are to better manage their motivation related to learning performance they need to have a sound understanding of the process of motivation. The following are important facts related to motivation that students should become familiar with:

- ❑ There are two forms of motivation that students need to be aware of – **intrinsic motivation** and **extrinsic motivation**. Intrinsic motivation refers to a motive that keeps a student involved in a task because of the nature of the task itself. The task might something very unusual and arouse the student's curiosity. It could be challenging and appeal to the student's competitive nature or desire to experience adventure. It could be humorous and appeal to the student's sense of humour. Studies have shown that students who are intrinsically motivated are more likely to persist with it and more willing to try different strategies to achieve their goals. (McInerney & McInerney, 2002) Extrinsic motivation refers to the offering of incentives or rewards for successful task performance. Barry & King (1993) suggest that, if the material a secondary school student is required to learn is regarded as being intrinsically valuable by the student, then we should not risk undermining that intrinsic motivation through the introduction of rewards or incentives. Extrinsic motivation, rewards and incentives should be kept to those situations involving students whose motivational level to a particular task is low.

- ❑ There is a theory (**attribution theory**) that claims that an individual's reasons for success and failure influence their future motivation. Secondary school students try to explain and interpret their successes and failures in terms of causes. Students might ask questions such as "Why did I fail the exam?" or "Why did I get such a poor mark?". It is more likely that students will ask these types of questions after failure rather than after success. In answering these questions students come to attribute their successes and failures to various causes, some of which are controlled by the student while others lie outside the student's control. If the student comes up with an acceptable explanation, their motivation for future endeavours in this area is enhanced. If they can't come up with an acceptable explanation their motivation for future endeavours in this area decreases.

The following activities and strategies have been shown to be successful in developing secondary school students' motivation:

## Strategies mentors can use to enhance the motivation of secondary school students

Many of these strategies are based on suggestions presented by Barry, K. and King, L. (1993) *Beginning Teaching* 2nd Edition (*Social Science Press, Pp. 443-461*) and McInerney D.M. and McInerney, V. (2002) *Educational Psychology, Constructing Learning* 3rd Edition (*Pearson Educational,. Pp. 208-242*).

- ❑ Mentors need to encourage students' awareness of the link between effort and outcome, i.e. that students' motivation is increased when they recognise successful outcomes that have resulted from increased effort on their part.

- ❑ Mentors need to provide students with feedback that reinforces effort and outcome linkages. Mentors can support the notion that students' efforts will eventually bring knowledge or mastery through persistence and this will result in them actualising their potential.

- ❑ Mentors can minimise student performance anxiety by stressing the message that learning tasks, assignments, etc. are learning experiences rat

- ❑ Mentors need to provide students with feedback that reinforces effort and outcome linkages. Mentors can support the notion that students' efforts will eventually bring knowledge or mastery through persistence and this will result in them actualising their potential.

- ❑ Mentors can minimise student performance anxiety by stressing the message that learning tasks, assignments, etc. are learning experiences rather than performance occasions at which you either fail or succeed. Mentors can reinforce the message that "it's O.K. to make mistakes" or "get things wrong" as long as the student can learn from this situation.

❏ Mentors can reinforce the following messages with their students:
  • When undertaking a learning task expect success and work towards this;
  • Never feel anxious about asking for feedback from their teachers on their learning progress;
  • Be curious – ask questions about what they are doing and why;
  • If they are uncomfortable or confused about a learning task they are undertaking, they should express these concerns to their teacher.

❏ Mentors can reinforce the following messages with their students:
  • When undertaking a learning task expect success and work towards this;
  • Never feel anxious about asking for feedback from their teachers on their learning progress;
  • Be curious – ask questions about what they are doing and why;
  • If they are uncomfortable or confused about a learning task they are undertaking, they should express these concerns to their teacher.

### *Motivational Awareness Activity (McInerney & McInerney (2002) p. 212)*

The student should observe a range of television advertisements which are directed at adolescents. They should:
  • List the kinds of motivation demonstrated in the advertisement;
  • Decide what kind of motivation (intrinsic or extrinsic) seems to be used most;
  • Decide which advertisement they found most motivating in terms of the influence it had on them. Why was this advertisement so influential?

### *The Importance of "Personal Best"*

A worrying feature of current student performance endeavours is that they are directed at pleasing other people and not towards any personal achievement goals students have set themselves. The following student comments are all too common:

To experience maximum learning achievement satisfaction students must find learning goals that are meaningful to them and are directed at achieving their "personal best" outcome.

### *What do we mean by "personal best" performance?*

A "personal best" performance occurs when a current performance attains a higher, better outcome than any previous attempts at the task. The outcome might be only marginally better but this does not matter. However looked at, a mark of 4/10 is better than a mark of 3/10. 4/10 tells a student that he/she is making progress towards a goal of attaining 7/10. It also tells them that whatever they are doing to attain the goal of 7/10 is working. They are moving in the right direction.

### *4.5.2  Organisation*

Bad organisational habits will always cost students valuable study time. The everyday demands on a secondary school student are numerous and it is as though everyone has a claim on their time – family, teachers, sports coaches, friends and so on. If students have not established an effective and practical study timetable for themselves, too many distractions will interfere with their study.
  Good organisation means:

  • *Have I got all the books I need?*
  • *Have I had something to eat or drink before beginning my study?*
  • *Have I done my telephoning before beginning my study?*
  • *Have I checked what's required of me before beginning my study?*

### *Developing Time Management Competency*

*"Time is life. It is irreversible and irreplaceable. To waste your time is to waste your life, but to master your time is to master your life and make the most of it."* – Lakelin (1973)

Poor time management can cause stress for many students and interfere with their learning performance. Managing their time more effectively might require students to make changes to their study habits – habits that are ingrained and fit very comfortably with the student. Some students waste time because it is satisfying for them to do so.

Time management is first and foremost about self-discipline. Students need to accept that there are no easy strategies for correcting inappropriate time management practices.

**Activity 10 – An Inventory of Time Wasters:** How aware are you of your time wastage? Often students are unaware that they are engaging in behaviours or activities that are time wasting. By completing the following inventory you should become more aware of these time wasting behaviours.

| TIME WASTER | STUDENT RESPONSE | |
| --- | --- | --- |
| | YES | NO |
| 1. Procrastination: putting off work until the last moment | ☐ | ☐ |
| 2. Lack of priorities: Doing your assignments on a first come basis without working out the time requirements of each assignment. | ☐ | ☐ |
| 3. Telephone interruptions: The phone controls you – you don't control it. | ☐ | ☐ |
| 4. Attempting too much at one time: Working at several assignments at one time resulting in finishing none of them on time. | ☐ | ☐ |
| 5. Socialising: Engaging in frequent chit-chat and meetings with your friends who constantly interrupt your study sessions. | ☐ | ☐ |
| 6. Too much time engaged in leisure activities: Study always comes second to these pursuits. | ☐ | ☐ |
| 7. Failure to listen to instructions: This often means you waste a great deal of time by beginning your assignment only to find you have to restart | ☐ | ☐ |
| 8. Inability to say "No". Saying yes to your friends just to please them or keep on side with them can result in you spending all your time pleasing others | ☐ | ☐ |
| 9. Coffee breaks: Forever interrupting your study with a coffee break? Why not take a thermos to your study room? | ☐ | ☐ |

*Once the student has completed this survey the outcomes can be discussed with the mentor. Any time waster they have ticked "yes" for has the potential to disrupt their study. Mentors/teachers can now explain strategies to challnege the above situation.*

## Activity 11 - Carrying Out a Time Waster Self-Audit

We take time so much for granted that often we are wasting it without realising we are doing so. It is not unusual for a student to experience stress when completing an assignment and to conclude that the stress is caused because the task is too difficult, when in fact it is because they haven't given themselves enough time to complete the task.

If you think this could be you it would be useful for you to carry out the following time waster self-audit.

## What to do:

Keep the following *Time Waster Self-Audit Log Sheet* for two days. Break your day up into 60 minute blocks. (You will need to rule up more spaces for yourself.)

- You need to keep the log sheet in an easily accessible place so that activities can be logged as they occur.
- Everything should be recorded including: Attending classes; training; homework; hanging out with friends; coffee breaks; watching TV; surfing the net; phone calls; socialising; playing sport; having a meal; sleeping; after school cultural activity.

LOG SHEET FOR _____ (Name)

DATE/S: _____

| From: | To: | Minutes: | DESCRIPTION OF ACTIVITY: |
|-------|-----|----------|--------------------------|
| | | | |
| | | | |
| | | | |
| | | | |
| | | | |
| | | | |
| | | | |
| | | | |
| | | | |
| | | | |
| | | | |
| | | | |
| | | | |
| | | | |
| | | | |
| | | | |

### 4.5.3   Memory

A study skill many students take for granted is their use of memory. What students need to accept is that when someone tells them that they have a poor memory, or when they conclude that they can't remember things it really means that they are using inappropriate learning strategies.

*Memory requires students to:*

- *Listen to information, directions or instructions accurately and appropriately;*
- *Ensure that they are not trying to learn too much at one time;*
- *Determine what their most effective learning style is;*
- *Determine what their most effective means of recording information is. It might not be just writing down the information – perhaps they could try using Mind-Maps, tape recorders, using more graphics or creating their own shorthand.*

### 4.5.4   Using study resources

Too often students undertake a learning task without having accessed the appropriate resources. Students should always check whether they have made appropriate use of the school library, the Internet or the text book issued, before tackling the assigned learning task. A challenge for mentors is to be continually on the look out for resources that might assist students to realise their learning performance potential, e.g. new software, new books, new magazines or new videos.

There are a number of essential considerations about the use of the library that students should be aware of. These include:

- *The term Learning Resource Centre (LRC) is often used today instead of library. This term is designed to reflect the fact that the centre (library) has a whole range of learning resources, not just books;*
- *The services a library offers (accessing equipment, borrowing facilities, inter-library loans, direct information, Internet services);*
- *The library layout;*
- *The sections of the library;*
- *The catalogue system.*

### 4.5.5   Effective listening

Often students' ability to use the top 10% of their learning performance potential is hindered by difficulties they experience in concentrating or paying attention during class. If this is the case it is likely that the specific skill the student needs to work on is their ability to listen effectively.

Effective listening requires students to:

- *Identify the key words of the speaker;*
- *Tune into the meanings behind the speaker's words;*
- *Paraphrase, (talk back what the speaker has said) to ensure that they have captured the meaning of the speaker's message.*

The following suggestions made by Anne Kotzman *(Kotzman, A. (1989) Listen To Me, Listen To You Penguin Books Pp. 5-69)*, are worth considering by the student and his/her mentor:

**Attending Skills:** These are essential if the student is to accurately, concisely and meaningfully understand information, directions and instructions given by teachers or instructors. Attending skills involve the student paying physical and psychological attention to the person who is talking, listening with the whole body and modifying the environment in ways that reduces distractions. This requires the student to:

- Attend to immediate needs: If it is apparent that someone is about to deliver information or instructions it is important that potential interfering needs that could disrupt this process are reduced, e.g. hunger, thirst, toilet requirements, body temperature and so on.
- Maintain the appropriate eye contact: Looking at the speaker softly most of the time expresses interest, attention, involvement and the desire to listen. Eyes wandering around a room indicate that attention is elsewhere. At the other extreme, focusing too intently, staring fixedly or in a way that seems to probe, can be very unnerving and distracting for the speaker.
- Maintain attentive posture: A posture of involvement is important for appropriate attending. This can involve the listener being: relaxed and alert; leaning slightly towards the speaker; concentrating, but not menacing; facing the other person squarely; maintaining an "open" position; and being at a comfortable and appropriate distance from the speaker.
- Maintain psychological attention: This means the listener has to tune in to the speaker, being aware of their non-verbal communication, posture, expression, tension level, energy level, mannerisms, eye contact and general demeanour.

### Activity 12 – Attending Skills Practice

*(Anne Kotzman, 1989, Pp. 66-67)*

### Instructions

1. This activity can be done with your mentor. Pick a topic to talk about – anything will do but it needs to be a reasonably simple and open topic, e.g. something you saw on last night's TV news; a weekend sports encounter; a good movie you have seen.

2. Decide who will be the speaker and who will be the listener.
3. In each of the following activities the speaker is to talk to the listener for about a minute.
4. The roles should then be reversed so each person can play both roles for every activity.
5. Discuss how each of you felt before moving on to the next activity.
6. Be aware of how your feelings are affected, like neck strain, heart rate, etc.

### *The Activities*

- **Non-attending:** Speaker talks, listener deliberately does not attend – is silent, fiddles, looks away, leans back, folds arms.
- **Non-attending:** Continue the conversation, this time sitting about two metres apart. Try different distances to see how it feels
- **Non-attending:** Sit back to back. Try to carry on a conversation.
- **Attending without responding:** Face the other person squarely; attend carefully but make no response. What sort of response did you want? How did you feel without it?
- **Attending from unequal positions:** Let the speaker kneel on the floor and then stand up. Try having a conversation. Note the physical strain as well as the feelings of both people.
- **Attending at eye level:** Repeat the above exercise with both kneeling down at a comfortable distance apart and with eyes at approximately the same level. Discuss the different feelings accompanying these two exercises.
- **Attending but responding with movements only:** Attend well but do not respond verbally. Use head nods, facial expression, hand movements.
- **Attending using simple encouraging words only:** Follow the above but occasionally respond with expressions of encouragement like "uh-huh", "mmm", etc.
- **Attending fully,** responding as completely as you want to.

### *Conclusion*

When you have completed these activities discuss the exercise as a whole. What did you discover about attending and non-attending from both the listener's and the speaker's experience?

### *4.5.6   Note taking*

Often students' learning performance is hindered because they are using inappropriate note taking strategies:

- *Are they trying to write down too much information?*
- *Are they not identifying the key points that need to be recorded?*
- *Are their notes so badly organised that they can't make sense of them when they come to study them for a test or exam?*

Students can use the following checklist to improve the quality of their note taking:

**Note Taking Checklist: Techniques for effective note taking of a lesson**

As you take notes during the lesson:

- ❏ Use headings and sub-headings;
- ❏ Use your own words;
- ❏ Listen for a while, then summarise the main idea;
- ❏ Don't try and transcribe verbatim;
- ❏ Highlight important points;
- ❏ Don't bother with illustrations and examples;
- ❏ Develop your own shorthand for commonly used terms;
- ❏ Use arrows to make links, if you think a later point belongs under an earlier heading;

❏ Leave lots of white space between points;

❏ Use point form, but make sure it contains enough grammar to make sense of them later.

### 4.5.7 Essay writing – Guidelines to assist students with their essay writing

*Reference: The Academic Essay, Dr Derek Soles. (Studymates)*

As previously mentioned one of the most difficult study skills for a student to master is essay writing. A great deal of student learning outcome performance at secondary school is judged through their written essays. Soles, in discussing this aspect of study highlighted the following suggestions and in trials 93% of students achieved top grades after using Soles methods.It is absolutely essential that mentors refrain from judging students' learning potential or ability to achieve study outcomes on the basis of their ability to write essays.

### The Essay Writing Process

It is suggested that following this process will help students to break down the writing of an essay into smaller manageable tasks. In summary …

1. Select a suitable topic or question.
2. Analyse and interpret the question. Mind map everything you know on the topic and highlight gaps in your knowledge
3. Make a plan to focus research. Fill in the gaps mentioned in 2
4. Find relevant sources of information and quote/reference from them
5. Do the reading, i.e. read a textbook or reference book to find the required information and make notes of key points.
6. Make a plan for writing the body of the essay.
7. Write the body of the essay. DO NOT COPY FROM BOOKS, WRITE IN YOUR OWN WORDS.
8. Write the conclusion and introduction.
9. Proofread the essay. *Does it make sense? Are there any spelling mistakes? Are there any punctuation mistakes? Is the grammar O.K.?*
10. Present the final essay copy on time.

### 4.5.8 Reading

Many educators argue that students' ability to read appropriately is the major study skill requirement for actualising their learning potential. Mentors need to realise that there are numerous forms of reading, e.g.

- *Reading for pleasure;*
- *Research reading;*
- *Reading for information;*
- *Reading for explanations;*
- *Reading for directions;*
- *Reading for rules and regulations;*
- *Reading for people's opinions;*
- *Reading to find support for arguments.*

The point that students need to grasp is that each type of reading requires a different style and a different approach. For example if a student needs to read a reference book to find an important piece of information and they apply the same approach to this as if they were going to read a novel for pleasure, not only would they waste a great deal of their precious time but there would be a good chance that they wouldn't find what they were looking for.

Following are some techniques that the student could employ when developing study reading skills:

### *Reading Faster*

There are times when reading faster is an advantage. Fast reading allows the student to:

- ❑ Read a greater amount of material in a limited amount of time;
- ❑ Concentrate intently on the passage being read;
- ❑ Grasp "the big picture" more easily.

### *Activities For Increasing Reading Speed*

De Porter (1992) (*Quantum Learning: Unleashing The Genius In You, Dell Publishing, P. 252*) provides the following suggestions that can help students increase the speed of their reading:

- ❑ Contrary to popular opinion she advocates that the student should use his/her finger as a pointer to establishing new reading habits. Instead of moving the finger along under each word De Porter suggests that the student quickly whiz it along the line forcing their eyes to follow. The student shouldn't allow him/herself to drop back or re-read and they should increase the "whiz" as they become faster.
- ❑ Another method is to divide each line into three, and to focus on each third of the line at a time. Again, the student shouldn't stop or re-read.
- ❑ Like any skill this will take practice and moments of frustration. However it is worth the effort when students consider how many hours they will spend studying over the next few years.

### *4.5.9 Exam preparation*

Students might be a little like many other people studying – they do O.K. with set assignments and class activities but when it comes to formal exams they just go to pieces. Many secondary school students have related how their continuous assessment mark of 80% has crashed to a final mark of 60% because of how badly they did in their exams.

Students must not believe that getting a poor exam mark means that they are a learning failure or do not have the potential to achieve the learning outcomes they desire.

Students should always remember that all a poor exam mark is telling them is that, in using this particular form of communication, they were not able to communicate to someone else their real knowledge, understandings and experiences about the subject being examined.

Be that as it may, the fact is that the longer students stay at school the more exams and formal tests they will be required to undertake. To give themselves the best chance of displaying their learning potential in an exam or formal test there are a number of techniques, strategies, organisational requirements and routines they can learn. Students should discuss these with their teachers or mentor.

### *Exam Preparation Suggestions for Students: Understanding and Applying Test Techniques*

- ❑ Before you begin, work out how much time you have to spend on each question and allocate your time accordingly.
- ❑ Read every question carefully.
- ❑ Use your memory techniques to recall information.
- ❑ Answer the questions first that you are confident you have the answers for.
- ❑ Have a scrap piece of paper handy on which you can jot down ideas as they come to you, even if you are in the middle of answering another question.
- ❑ Leave time at the end so that you can proofread your answers.
- ❑ If you find yourself running out of time make sure you put down the key points regarding the question you won't have time to fully answer. You can use note form if necessary – if you put nothing down you can only score 0 marks.

***Developing a positive attitude towards exams***

❑ Use self-talk, e.g. say to yourself before beginning the exam something like: *"I've put heaps of time into studying for this exam; I know most of the material we had to learn. What I don't know I can use my common sense to work out. Bring it on!"*

❑ Acknowledge any nervousness you might experience and tell yourself that this is natural and that this nervousness will ensure you perform to your potential in the exam. If you tell yourself and others that you get stressed out and have performance anxiety when doing exams, then this is exactly what will happen.

### 4.5.11   Managing Stress

Recently I mentored a number of secondary school-aged high performance international sportspeople, and found that, very often, the difference between their delivering a "comfort zone" performance and a "top 10%" performance was related to how well they were able to manage their stress during a given performance.

The same is true for secondary school students when it comes to them realising their learning potential.

The way in which they manage their stress for a particular learning task being undertaken will have a considerable bearing on the amount of learning potential that they realise for that task. If they consider that they have difficulties in managing their stress they should refer to the suggestions related to stress management reported in Chapter 7 of this book.

## 4.6   Identifying and Making The Most of Preferred Learning Style

A difficulty that many students face with their study is that they are not approaching the learning task in a manner that allows them to make maximum use of their preferred learning style. We don't all learn in the same manner, e.g.

❑ Some students are primarily visual learners, i.e. they understand and recall information they see.

❑ Some students are primarily auditory learners, i.e. they understand recall information they hear.

❑ Some students are primarily tactile and kinaesthetic learners, i.e. they best understand and recall information they can sense and whilst they are moving and getting a feel for its shape, texture, etc.

❑ Some students are primarily divergent thinkers, i.e. they are creative, they think "outside the box" and they enjoy engaging in unusual, novel and strange learning activities. They enjoy and feel challenged when engaged in music, art, carving, acting, dance, etc.

❑ Some students are primarily convergent thinkers, i.e. they are problem solvers and enjoy working according to rules and formulas. They enjoy mathematical and scientific learning activities, solving puzzles and being engaged in research projects.

❑ Some students are primarily investigators, i.e. they learn best when they have to examine all the clues and then come to the answer.

The important challenge for mentors and students is to find out what the preferred and most productive learning style is. Once this has been determined students should seek opportunities to apply the learning style and find ways to make maximum use of it.

Perhaps the following activity could be used as a first step in this direction. Students could have a go at this survey and then discuss the outcomes with their teacher or mentor.

### 4.6.1  Activity 13: The Learning Styles Survey

*(Adapted from Bernice McCarthy's 4-Mat Learning Styles)*

Tick the question response that best describes you. There are no correct answers so answer them as honestly as possible:

1. *When giving information in class do you prefer the teacher to ...*
   - ☐ a) Tell you the information in class and then give you a questionnaire to answer?
   - ☐ b) Tell you the information and then have a group discussion?
   - ☐ c) Tell you the information and then get you to do an activity using the new information?
   - ☐ d) Give you a questionnaire first, with the written information so you can find your own answers?

2. *When given a written assignment by your teacher, would you ask ...*
   - ☐ a) What do you want me to write?
   - ☐ b) How are we to do this assignment?
   - ☐ c) What will happen if I don't pass this assignment?
   - ☐ d) Why do we need to do this assignment?

3. *When you have to attend class at 8.45 am Monday morning, do you ...*
   - ☐ a) Look forward to what you might learn this day?
   - ☐ b) Turn up late just to see if you can get away with it?
   - ☐ c) Hope there will be loads of opportunities for you to talk in class?
   - ☐ d) Hope that there will be heaps of fun activities?

4. *When in class do you really dislike ...*
   - ☐ a) Having to obey the rules?
   - ☐ b) Listening to the teacher talking to the whole class?
   - ☐ c) Not being able to have discussions in during class?
   - ☐ d) Wasting time in group discussions?

5. *The teacher is going to let you out early from class.*
   - ☐ a) Would you prefer to stay and do some written assignments?
   - ☐ b) Would you prefer to stay in the classroom and perhaps play a game?
   - ☐ c) Would you rather stay and work on a real life situation to test/try out things you have covered in class.
   - ☐ d) Would you prefer to stay and talk about what you've learned in class?

6. *As part of your assessment you have to make a presentation to the class. Before deciding on what to present do you prefer ...*
   - ☐ a) To discuss all aspects thoroughly with your friends?
   - ☐ b) To experiment with lots of different ideas?
   - ☐ c) To have lots of choice on how you can do the presentation?
   - ☐ d) To have clear directions from your teacher about what is expected?

7. *For some classes there is an attendance rule. The rule is that you must attend at least 80% of the time. Do you ask ...*
   - ☐ a) Why do we have this rule?
   - ☐ b) What are the details of the rule?
   - ☐ c) What if I don't comply?
   - ☐ d) How will it help me if I follow the rule?

**8.** *In a learning/study situation are your strengths in ...*
- ☐ a) Following instructions exactly in order to produce what is being asked for?
- ☐ b) Being an active student in discussing what is needed?
- ☐ c) Finding solutions to problems?
- ☐ d) Producing practical work for practical assignments.

**9.** *When told you are going on a school excursion would you ...*
- ☐ a) Ask "What will happen if I don't go on the outing?"
- ☐ b) Ask "What do I need to know before going on the outing?"
- ☐ c) Ask "Why do I need to go?"
- ☐ d) Ask "How are we getting there?"

**10.** *When you are studying at home do you ...*
- ☐ a) Like to study in different places, e.g. lying on the floor, sitting outside in the sun?
- ☐ b) Keep getting distracted and tend to put off your study?
- ☐ c) Always learn best when working with other people, so you can chat about your learning?
- ☐ d) Sit in a chair at a desk or table, preferably in a quiet area?

**11.** *When studying for exams do you ...*
- ☐ a) Find out exactly what you need to learn and learn only that?
- ☐ b) Spend a lot of time learning as much as you can about the study subject?
- ☐ c) Get bored quickly and want to chat on the phone or watch TV?
- ☐ d) Not bother to study and hope that you have learnt enough in class time?

**12.** *In class group discussions do you ...*
- ☐ a) Feel that it is a waste of time and prefer to hear information straight from the teacher?
- ☐ b) Really enjoy the opportunity to chat and discuss the topic or work to be done?
- ☐ c) Like to see what happens rather than contribute to the group?
- ☐ d) Get bored because you want to do something on your own?

**13.** *In your leisure time do you prefer to ...*
- ☐ a) Do something physically active?
- ☐ b) Read a book?
- ☐ c) Chat with friends?
- ☐ d) Do something different?

### 4.6.2 Scoring Of The Learning Styles Survey

| Q.1: | | | | Q.2: | | | | Q.3: | | | |
|---|---|---|---|---|---|---|---|---|---|---|---|
| | a) | = | 1 | | a) | = | 2 | | a) | = | 2 |
| | b) | = | 2 | | b) | = | 3 | | b) | = | 4 |
| | c) | = | 3 | | c) | = | 4 | | c) | = | 1 |
| | d) | = | 4 | | d) | = | 1 | | d) | = | 3 |
| Q.4: | a) | = | 4 | Q.5: | a) | = | 2 | Q.6: | a) | = | 1 |
| | b) | = | 3 | | b) | = | 4 | | b) | = | 4 |
| | c) | = | 1 | | c) | = | 3 | | c) | = | 3 |
| | d) | = | 2 | | d) | = | 1 | | d) | = | 2 |
| Q.7: | a) | = | 1 | Q.8: | a) | = | 2 | Q.9: | a) | = | 4 |
| | b) | = | 2 | | b) | = | 1 | | b) | = | 2 |
| | c) | = | 4 | | c) | = | 4 | | c) | = | 1 |
| | d) | = | 3 | | d) | = | 3 | | d) | = | 3 |

| Q.10: | a) | = | 3 | Q.11: | a) | = | 2 | Q.12: | a) | = | 2 |
| | b) | = | 4 | | b) | = | 3 | | b) | = | 1 |
| | c) | = | 1 | | c) | = | 1 | | c) | = | 4 |
| | d) | = | 2 | | d) | = | 4 | | d) | = | 3 |
| Q.13: | a) | = | 3 | Q.14: | a) | = | 4 | Q.15: | a) | = | 2 |
| | b) | = | 2 | | b) | = | 2 | | b) | = | 3 |
| | c) | = | 1 | | c) | = | 1 | | c) | = | 1 |
| | d) | = | 4 | | d) | = | 3 | | d) | = | 4 |

## 4.6.3   Calculating the learning style

- Students count up the number of 1's, 2's, 3's and 4's they have given themselves.
- The number they have the highest count for is their current dominant learning style.
- The number they have the lowest count for is their current least favoured learning style.
- It is possible to have two dominant learning styles.

## 4.6.4   Explanations of dominant learning style

*1's Dominant Result: The "Why/Why Not" Learning Style*

If this is your favoured learning style it indicates the following characteristics are typical of you:

- You learn best when you are aware of, and comfortable with, the reasons for studying a particular subject. Learning things by rote is not for you.
- You enjoy learning when the primary purpose of the study is to either prove or disprove something.
- You like learning that involves carrying out experiments and discovering unexpected truths.
- You enjoy learning where the emphasis is on solving problems or a mystery.

*2's Dominant Result: The "What" Learning Style*

If this is your favoured learning style it indicates the following characteristics are typical of you:

- You learn best when provided with clear and detailed instructions related to the tasks to be undertaken or learning to be encountered.
- You work well at learning tasks that require you to follow set rules, formulas or equations.
- You feel a strong sense of achievement when you complete a task by getting the correct answer.
- You work best at tasks that have clear structure and a well-defined beginning and end. You need to know all task requirements prior to beginning it.
- Group/team work is not your preferred option – you are at your best when tackling an independent assignment.

*3's Dominant Result: The "How" Learning Style*

If this is your favoured learning style it indicates the following characteristics are typical of you:

- You enjoy discovering how things work and why things happen.
- You enjoy unravelling mysteries.
- You enjoy freedom in a learning activity, not being tied to strict task rules or requirements.
- You enjoy being creative and doing things in a "new" way or in an unusual way.
- Brainstorming in a group when it's directed at solving a mystery or coming up with novel explanations is enjoyable for you.
- You are comfortable in presenting your solutions, answers and explanations in non-conventional ways; not just being tied to pen and paper reports.

- You favour "doing" rather than just thinking or reading.
- You tend to stick at a learning task until you have solved the problem, or provided what you think is the correct answer.

*4's Dominant Result: The "What If ...?" Learning Style*

If this is your favoured learning style it indicates the following characteristics are typical of you:

- You place a great deal of importance on the outcomes, correctness or accuracy of your responses and performance.
- You often look outside the conventional "thinking box". Frequently you find yourself asking, "What happens if we do things differently?"
- You are creative, in that doing things differently is a pleasing experience for you.
- To some extent you are a natural "acceptable risk taker". When it comes to learning you are prepared to step outside your performance comfort zone and have a go at things you've never tried before.
- You don't like having to stick to just one method of assignment reporting or learning.

## 4.7   Activity 14 – Strategies Related to Learning Style: Applying Learning Style

### Directions

Once you have identified your preferred learning style attempt the tasks outlined below under the appropriate style. Then try an activity listed under your least preferred style. Discuss your responses with your mentor. Make a list of the kind of activities that are best suited to your learning style. *(The main source for the following activities is: Wayne, S. (1995), Creative and Practical Ideas For The Multiple Intelligences Classroom, Hawker Brownlow.)*

### A. The "Why/Why Not" Learning Style

- ❏ Research the Loch Ness monster. Do you think it exists? Justify your point of view.
- ❏ Create a numerical code and use it to tell a friend five interesting facts about the solar system.

### B. The "What" Learning Style

- ❏ A 1 litre milk carton can be recycled to make four pieces of A4 paper. If everyone in Europe recycled one carton per day, how many pieces of paper would this be? How much would it weigh? Try working this out for a week, a month and a year! How many trees could be saved?
- ❏ Make lists for the following animal categories: Pets, British, Spots and Stripes, and Endangered. Have at least 20 animals in each list.

### C. The "How" Learning Style

- ❏ Design a new machine that can clean up oil spills.
- ❏ A windsurfer was adapted from a surfboard to produce new technology. Change an existing piece of recreational equipment so that it becomes new technology. Choose from the following: a bicycle, a kite, a boogie board or roller blades.

### D. The "What If" Learning Style

- ❏ Create a radio advertisement for a new fishing rod that guarantees that you catch a fish every time you use it. Record it. Add some "sea music" to the beginning and end of your advertisement.
- ❏ Design a new wheelchair that enables the user to play any type of sport he or she wants.

## Case Study

### *Julie – Slow and Steady Wins The Race*

Julie was one of the quietest members of her Year 11 class. Whenever a class member was asked to give a comment about Julie they had to think for a moment just to recall who she was. She was so inconspicuous that for many of her classmates it was as if she wasn't a part of the class. This was how Julie wanted it as for many years at school she had carried a secret. Whereas the other children in the class seemed to handle their studies with few problems, Julie found it a real struggle. The main problem was that, although with most things she got there in the end, she always took much longer than her classmates. This had been the case for so long that Julie's classmates thought she was quite stupid. Julie was not unduly worried about this label – better they thought she was dumb than they know that she struggled with her reading.

Julie had battled with her reading from primary school days. She always struggled to recognise the printed words in books she was asked to read. It was O.K. if someone read the story to her – she could always answer any questions she was asked about the story. She could understand what was read to her.

For the most part Julie used her ability to guess what the printed words were saying or she asked her mum or elder sister to read the textbook information to her. Whilst this meant she made lots of mistakes and didn't get very good marks, somehow she got through. Sitting her exams, though, was another matter – there would be no mum or sister to help and guessing wouldn't work. This was very frustrating for Julie because all she had ever wanted to do when she left school was to be a nurse and this meant she needed to get a score high enough to allow her to enter a university to do her Bachelor of Nursing.

Then an event occurred that was to change Julie's life forever. She met Granny Nobes, a retired teacher and grandmother who lived in the same street as Julie. One afternoon Granny Nobes was walking in the neighbourhood park when she came across Julie who was sitting on a park bench looking forlorn and really down in the dumps. The older woman sat alongside Julie and asked if she was O.K.. Suddenly Julie was pouring her heart out and the more she did so the more Granny Nobes listened. When she stopped, Granny Nobes sat quietly for a while and then replied:

"Look love, why don't you forget about your exams this year? Instead, come to me after school and we'll see if I can teach you to read. We'll go right back to the beginning, back to the things about reading you had to learn when you were in junior primary classes. If we make good progress this year you can sit your exams next year and enter university the year after.

Granny Nobes and Julie became best friends. Twice a week come rain, hail or sunshine, Julie turned up for her lessons. Sometimes it was boring, sometimes it was frustrating but gradually things began to change. One night about three months after she started, Julie read the daily TV guide out loud to her family, then a letter from her aunty, and then an item from a newspaper.

Julie sat her exams the following year and got the required marks to enter a Bachelor of Nursing course at a university. Today Julie is a fully qualified nurse working in a public hospital.

### *Why did Julie succeed?*

Whilst she had a significant learning difficulty Julie was able to keep her self-image intact and her dreams alive. She was fortunate in that she met a very special "significant other" in Granny Nobes. It wasn't easy for her but she also had the mental-toughness and resilience that allowed the work of Granny Nobes to bear fruit.

# Chapter 5

# Self-Esteem, Ability to Socialise and Ability to Communicate Self to Others

## Contents

## Outcomes

**Readers will ...**

❏ Have a greater understanding of the relationship between self-esteem and interpersonal relationships;

❏ Have a greater awareness of the importance of the interpersonal relationship skills of showing respect, communicating with genuineness to others and displaying empathy to others;

❏ Have a greater understanding of the relationship between self-esteem and effective communication;

❏ Have a greater awareness of the skills required to be an effective communicator.

## 5.1   The Importance of Interpersonal Relationship Skills

There is nothing more frustrating for a student than to feel that they are not able to communicate what they really think or feel to their parents, teachers or friends. Many secondary school students have indicated to me that the following situations cause them most frustration:

- *Saying "yes" to someone when they really want to say "no".*
- *Giving a response to the teacher that they know the teacher expects rather than a response that truly reflects what they think.*
- *Agreeing with their peers in a group discussion even though they don't really agree.*
- *Not being able to show their parents just how they feel about certain things.*
- *Finding they say nothing because they don't want to make a fool of themselves by possibly saying something that is considered wrong.*
- *Wanting to introduce themselves to a member of the opposite sex but not knowing how to.*
- *Not knowing how to share their emotions with someone else.*
- *Continually saying the things they think people want to hear rather than what they really think.*

Many of the frustrations reported above are due to the student experiencing difficulties in communicating their "real self" to others. This, in turn, is related to them having a self-image that has a number of gaps, uncertainties and anxieties that take away their confidence to relate to others.

The healthier their self-image becomes, the easier the student will find it to communicate and relate to others. To assist them to build this confidence and ability there are a number of special skills involved in making friends with someone and interacting with other people, that they need to be familiar with. The more aware they are of these, the more likely it will be that they develop them and the healthier their social self will be.

A number of research studies *(Aspey and Roebuck, 1977; Pinner and Pinner, 1997)* demonstrate that there are three fundamental building blocks necessary for secondary school students to establish positive friendships. These are: **RESPECT GENUINENESS EMPATHY**

## 5.2   Reviewing The Image Projected To Others

Many secondary school students give little attention to the status of their relationship skills and consequently are totally unaware of the image they project to the people they are interacting with. If a student is a person who is constantly trying to please others or impress the people they interact with, there's a good chance that they are displaying interaction behaviours that don't reflect the "real them". If students are constantly trying to be the person they think others want them to be it could be causing them significant stress and, in fact, distancing them from potentially long term good friends.

If any of the following statements apply there is a good chance that students are projecting an image to others that is not the "real them".

- *I seem to make people angry with me for no good reason.*
- *I am always being misunderstood by my friends.*
- *People say I'm really shy and I don't know why they think this.*
- *I am never invited by my peers to be part of their study group.*
- *People laugh at me and I have no idea as to why.*

### 5.2.1   *Activity 15 – Do You See Yourself As Others See You?*

This activity is designed to develop your awareness of the way others, especially your friends, see you. If you are surprised by the outcome it might be a reminder for you to check the genuineness of your social interaction behaviours.

A word of caution regarding this activity – it is a fun activity rather than a psychological type measure. The result you achieve shouldn't be taken too seriously. If it is significantly different from what you expected it just might be that the survey didn't work for you.

Instructions:

* **Tick the choice for each item that best describes you.**
* **If there are no correct or incorrect answers give as honest a response as is possible.**

1. *When do you feel at "your best"?*
   - ☐ a) In the morning.
   - ☐ b) During the afternoon.
   - ☐ c) Late at night.
   - ☐ d) Don't know.

2. *Do you usually walk ...*
   - ☐ a) Fairly fast, with long raking strides?
   - ☐ b) Fairly fast, but with short quick steps?
   - ☐ c) Less fast, head up, looking the world in the face?
   - ☐ d) Less fast, head down?
   - ☐ e) Very slowly?
   - ☐ f) Don't know.

3. *When talking to people, do you ...*
   - ☐ a) Stand with your arms folded?
   - ☐ b) Have your hands clasped?
   - ☐ c) Have one or both hands on your hips?
   - ☐ d) Touch or prod the person to whom you are talking?
   - ☐ e) Fidget with your ear, touch your chin or smooth your hair?
   - ☐ f) Like to have something (e.g. a pencil) in your hands?
   - ☐ g) Don't know.

4. *When relaxing do you sit with ...*
   - ☐ a) Your knees bent neatly side by side?
   - ☐ b) Your legs crossed or twined?
   - ☐ c) Your legs stretched straight out?
   - ☐ d) One leg curled under you?
   - ☐ e) Don't know.

5. *When something really amuses you, how do you usually react? Do you give ...*
   - ☐ a) A hearty, appreciative laugh?
   - ☐ b) A laugh, but hardly a hearty one?
   - ☐ c) A quiet chuckle?
   - ☐ d) A big grin?
   - ☐ e) A slow smile?
   - ☐ f) Don't know.

6. *When you go to a party do you ...*
   - ☐ a) Make a grand, attention-getting entrance so that everyone notices you?
   - ☐ b) Make a quiet entrance, looking quickly around for someone you know?
   - ☐ c) Make the quietest possible entrance and try to stay unnoticed?
   - ☐ d) Don't know.

7. *You are working hard at an assignment and someone interrupts you. Do you ...*
   - ☐ a) Welcome the break?
   - ☐ b) Feel extremely irritated?
   - ☐ c) Vary your reaction between these two extremes?
   - ☐ d) Don't know.

8. *Which of the following do you like most?*
   - ☐ a) Red or orange?
   - ☐ b) Black?
   - ☐ c) Yellow or light blue?
   - ☐ d) Green?
   - ☐ e) Dark blue or purple?
   - ☐ f) White?
   - ☐ g) Brown, grey or violet?

9. *When you are in bed at night, in those last moments before going to sleep do you lie ...*
   - ☐ a) Stretched out on your back?
   - ☐ b) Stretched out face down on your tummy?
   - ☐ c) On your side, slightly curled?
   - ☐ d) With your head on one arm?
   - ☐ e) With your head under the blankets?
   - ☐ f) With one leg hanging outside your bed?

10. *Do you often dream that you are ...*
   - ☐ a) Falling?
   - ☐ b) Fighting or struggling?
   - ☐ c) Searching for someone or something?
   - ☐ d) Flying or floating?
   - ☐ e) Running freely through a forest or along a beach?
   - ☐ f) Or do you usually have a dreamless sleep?
   - ☐ g) Don't know.

### 5.2.2 Scoring key

| Questions | Responses | | | | | | |
|---|---|---|---|---|---|---|---|
| | a) | b) | c) | d) | e) | f) | g) |
| 1 | 2 | 4 | 6 | 3 | | | |
| 2 | 6 | 4 | 7 | 2 | 1 | 3 | |
| 3 | 4 | 2 | 5 | 7 | 6 | 1 | 3 |
| 4 | 4 | 6 | 2 | 1 | 3 | | |
| 5 | 6 | 4 | 3 | 5 | 2 | 1 | |
| 6 | 6 | 4 | 2 | 3 | | | |
| 7 | 6 | 2 | 4 | 3 | | | |
| 8 | 6 | 7 | 5 | 4 | 3 | 2 | 1 |
| 9 | 7 | 6 | 4 | 2 | 1 | 3 | |
| 10 | 4 | 2 | 3 | 5 | 7 | 6 | 1 |

### 5.2.3    Analysis: Activity 15 - Do You See Yourself As Others See You?

Calculate your total and then read through the description below that matches your total. Does the description fit your idea of the "real you"?

If not ... *could it be that you are not displaying the "real you" when interacting with other people?*

Or ... *maybe this survey just doesn't work for you.*

Talk through the outcome with your mentor and see if you can identify messages you communicate to others about yourself that don't represent the "real you".

### Total over 60:

Others see you as someone they should "handle with care"; at times you are seen to come across in a dominant manner. Others might admire you and wish they could be more like you; they are somewhat in awe of you. Some don't always trust you and hesitate to become too deeply involved with you.

### Total between 51 to 60:

Your friends see you as an exciting, outgoing, rather impulsive person. They see you as a leader, someone who is quick to make decisions. You're seen as someone who will try anything, well almost anything, once. They see you as someone who takes a chance and enjoys adventure. People enjoy being in your company because of the excitement you generate.

### Total between 41 to 50:

Others see you as fresh, lively, charming, amusing and always interesting. You are seen as someone who is constantly the centre of attraction, but sufficiently well balanced not to let it go to your head. They see you as kind, considerate and understanding, someone who will cheer them up or help them out of a difficult situation.

### Total between 31 to 40:

Your friends see you as sensible, cautious, careful and practical. They see you as clever, gifted or talented, but modest. You are seen as someone who does not make friends quickly or easily. However, once you have made a friend you are extremely loyal to them and expect the same loyalty in return.

### Total between 21 to 30:

Your friends see you as meticulous and painstaking, perhaps a bit too fussy at times, ultra- cautious and ultra-careful. It would greatly surprise your friends if you were to behave impulsively or to do something on the spur of the moment. People expect you to examine everything very carefully from every conceivable angle. Some people think at times you are a little lazy.

### Total between 15 to 20:

You are seen to be shy, nervous and indecisive, someone who needs looking after, who always leaves it to someone else to make the decisions and prefers never to get too involved with anyone or anything. Some see you as a worrier, seeing problems which often don't exist, and crossing bridges long before you come to them. You permit very few people to get close to you.

### 5.2.4    Follow up

**Activity for Developing Your Ability to Communicate the "Real You"**

This is a good activity for the student to practise with the mentor.

1. The student reviews each of the following scenarios and then communicates their response to the mentor.
2. Prior to communicating their response they write down the key feelings and views they wanted to get across to the listener.

3. The student then communicates their response to the mentor.
4. When the student concludes their response the mentor writes down the feelings and views they think the student is trying to get across.
5. The student and mentor exchange their response sheets and discuss any discrepancies:
   - Why did the mentor think x was the message when in fact the student meant it to be *y*?
   - Was there a conflict between the verbal message the student sent and the non-verbal messages they sent?
   - Was the student ambiguous in the messages they were trying to send?

### *The Scenarios*

1. Your best friend is trying to go out with someone you know. Yesterday this person told you that never in a million years would they go out with your friend because they thought your friend was really ugly and such a nerd. You want to be honest with your friend but not hurt their feelings. What would you say?
2. It is half time and your team is getting beaten. You think you have an idea that would help the team effort – you want to share this but not look as though you're challenging your captain or coach. You don't want to be seen as a "know-it-all". What would you say?
3. You are at an after-match party. Your team is celebrating a hard earned win. Someone has produced some beer. Although you are all under age the party organiser offers you a drink. You don't want to be considered a party-pooper but you don't want to drink the alcohol. What would you say?
4. You are with a group of your friends and in town looking at the shops. A homeless person approaches your group and asks for some money so he can get himself a drink. Your friends are rude to him and tell him to get lost. You feel sorry for him and want to give him a pound or Euro. You understand that your friends are entitled to their view. What do you say?

## 5.3 The Role of Respect, Genuineness and Empathy in Establishing Relationships:

### *Respect*

These are behaviours which convey to others that you think they are worthwhile, unique and valuable people. These are messages you send to a person that tell them that they are important to you.

### *Genuineness*

These are behaviours which convey to others that you trust them and they can trust you. These are behaviours which occur spontaneously and allow a person to see the "real you" not a "phoney you".

### *Empathy*

These are behaviours which convey to others that you understand where they are coming from and often understand how they are feeling at the moment. These behaviours communicate to another person "I am standing in your shoes and seeing your world through your eyes".

### *5.3.1 What behaviours can you use to show people respect, genuineness and empathy?*

❑ **Displaying respect – This is shown by the following behaviours:**
   - Using body language that shows the person you are interested in them.
   - Showing the person that you are listening to them, that you heard what they said.
   - Remembering a person's name.
   - Introducing yourself to the person in a positive way – smiling and using appropriate eye contact.
   - Showing the person basic courtesies – offering them a chair; offering them a cup of coffee; letting them walk through a door first; standing when they approach you; turning off the TV

or radio when they approach you; making sure your mobile phone is turned off when they approach you.
- Asking the person non-threatening and interesting questions.
- Avoiding making snap judgements or evaluations of the person.
- Not interrupting or talking over the person.

❐ **Displaying genuineness – This is shown by the following behaviours:**
- Not exaggerating or embellishing information you share with the person.
- Displaying a degree of humbleness, not being "too cocky" when interacting with the person.
- Responding honestly to the person's questions – if you don't know, tell them.
- Sharing your feelings appropriately with the person, in a way that doesn't overwhelm them or intimidate them.
- Avoiding being defensive with them. Don't try and be correct at all costs – be willing initially to let small things you don't agree with float by.
- Not displaying aggressive non-verbal communication behaviours. Don't stare, glare, frown at them; don't face them with folded arms, don't shake your hand or point your finger at them.
- Not pretending to be someone or something you are not in their company.

❐ **Displaying empathy – This is shown by the following behaviours:**
- Reflecting back to the person feelings they are communicating to you: "You sound very angry"; "You look very happy about that"; "You sound most upset".
- Sharing similar experiences with the person but avoiding saying: "I know exactly how you feel". The point is, you probably don't.
- Smiling when the other person smiles, frowning when they frown, etc. This is called "behavioural mirroring". You have to be careful that this is not interpreted by the other person as mocking them.
- Using "reflective listening" to show the person you have really heard them. Paraphrasing – taking a small part of their message and repeating it back to them – can also do this.

### 5.3.2   *Activity 16 - Interpersonal Relationships Survey*

This survey provides you with an opportunity to carry out a self-examination of the nature and patterns of communication in your interpersonal relationships. The outcomes of this survey should enable you to determine the relative strength of your ability to display respect, genuineness and empathy.

### *Directions*
- You should answer each question as quickly as you can, according to how you feel at the moment.
- You should not consult with anyone while completing this survey.
- The accuracy of this survey is interfered with if you keep changing your answers .
- The accuracy, and therefore value to you, of this survey is directly related to the honesty of your responses – remember there are no right or wrong answers, just your views at the time.
- The **Yes** column is to be selected when the question can be answered as happening most of the time or usually.
- The **No** column is to be selected when the question can be answered as happening seldom or never.
- The **Sometimes** column should be selected when you definitely cannot answer Yes or No. You should endeavour to use this column as little as possible.
- Read each question carefully. If you cannot give an exact answer to a question answer your best one.

## The Interpersonal Relationship Survey

| Score | Item | Yes | No | Sometimes |
|---|---|---|---|---|
| _____1. | Do your words come out the way you like them to in conversations with your friends? | □ | □ | □ |
| _____2. | When you are asked a question that is not clear, do you ask the person to explain what he or she means? | □ | □ | □ |
| _____3. | When you explain something to people do you try to impress them with your knowledge? | □ | □ | □ |
| _____4. | Do you expect that a person you are talking to should understand what you are saying without you having to explain? | □ | □ | □ |
| _____5. | Do you ever ask a person you are explaining something to how they feel about what you are saying? | □ | □ | □ |
| _____6. | Do you feel uncomfortable when talking to other people? | □ | □ | □ |
| _____7. | When you are talking with your friends do you try to make sure you talk about things that are interesting to all of you? | □ | □ | □ |
| _____8. | Do you find it difficult to express your ideas if you think they are different from those of the people you are talking with? | □ | □ | □ |
| _____9. | When talking with your friends do you ever try to stand in their shoes and see things from their viewpoint? | □ | □ | □ |
| _____10. | When you are talking with your friends do you have a tendency to do more talking than anyone else? | □ | □ | □ |
| _____11. | Are you aware of the impact that the tone of your voice can have on people when you are talking with them? | □ | □ | □ |
| _____12. | Do you stop yourself from saying something to your friends if you think it might upset their feelings? | □ | □ | □ |
| _____13. | Do you find it difficult to accept constructive criticism from your friends? | □ | □ | □ |
| _____14. | When a friend has hurt your feelings do you try and discuss this with him or her? | □ | □ | □ |
| _____15. | If you find out that you have hurt a friend's feelings do you find the opportunity to apologise to him or her? | □ | □ | □ |
| _____16. | Do you get upset when someone you are interacting with disagrees with you? | □ | □ | □ |
| _____17. | Do you find that anger stops you from thinking clearly when you are interacting with your friends? | □ | □ | □ |
| _____18. | Do you agree with your friends' views because you're frightened they might get angry with you if you disagree? | □ | □ | □ |
| _____19. | When a problem arises between you and a friend are you able to discuss it with them without getting angry or upset? | □ | □ | □ |
| _____20. | Are you able to solve conflicts that might arise between you and your friends? | □ | □ | □ |
| _____21. | Do you sulk for some time if the person you are interacting with upsets you? | □ | □ | □ |
| _____22. | Do you get embarrassed when one of your friends gives you a compliment? | □ | □ | □ |
| _____23. | Generally, do you trust your friends? | □ | □ | □ |

| Score | Item | Yes | No | Sometimes |
|---|---|---|---|---|
| _____ 24. | Do you find it difficult to praise or give a compliment to one of your friends? | ☐ | ☐ | ☐ |
| _____ 25. | Do you deliberately try to hide your faults or weaknesses from your friends? | ☐ | ☐ | ☐ |
| _____ 26. | Are you relaxed in sharing the "real you" with your friends by sharing your personal feelings with them? | ☐ | ☐ | ☐ |
| _____ 27. | Do you find it difficult to share personal information with your best friend? | ☐ | ☐ | ☐ |
| _____ 28. | Do you deliberately change the topic of conversation with your friends if you think it's heading in a sensitive direction? | ☐ | ☐ | ☐ |
| _____ 29. | When you are talking with a friend do you let them finish what they are saying before reacting to their message? | ☐ | ☐ | ☐ |
| _____ 30. | Do you often find your attention wanders when you are talking with your friends? | ☐ | ☐ | ☐ |
| _____ 31. | When you are interacting with your friends do you try to tune into the meanings behind the words they utter? | ☐ | ☐ | ☐ |
| _____ 32. | Do your friends appear as though they are really listening to you when you are talking to them? | ☐ | ☐ | ☐ |
| _____ 33. | When having a discussion with your friend are you prepared to change your view if they present convincing information? | ☐ | ☐ | ☐ |
| _____ 34. | Do you pretend you are listening to your friend's message when in fact your mind is elsewhere? | ☐ | ☐ | ☐ |
| _____ 35. | When you are interacting with your friends can you tell the difference between what a person is saying and what he or she may be feeling? | ☐ | ☐ | ☐ |
| _____ 36. | While you are talking with your friends can you tell if they are interested in what you are saying? | ☐ | ☐ | ☐ |
| _____ 37. | Do you think that your friends often wish you'd keep quiet when you are talking with them? | ☐ | ☐ | ☐ |
| _____ 38. | Do you avoid having a conflict with your friends, at all costs? | ☐ | ☐ | ☐ |
| _____ 39. | Do you try to dominate your friends? | ☐ | ☐ | ☐ |
| _____ 40. | Are you comfortable in admitting to your friends that you are wrong or have made a mistake if it has been shown that this is the case? | ☐ | ☐ | ☐ |

## Scoring

| Item | Yes | No | Sometimes | Item | Yes | No | Sometimes |
|---|---|---|---|---|---|---|---|
| 1. | 3 | 0 | 2 | 9. | 3 | 0 | 2 |
| 2. | 3 | 0 | 2 | 10. | 0 | 3 | 1 |
| 3. | 0 | 3 | 1 | 11. | 3 | 0 | 2 |
| 4. | 0 | 3 | 1 | 12. | 3 | 0 | 2 |
| 5. | 3 | 0 | 2 | 13. | 0 | 3 | 1 |
| 6. | 0 | 3 | 1 | 14. | 3 | 0 | 2 |
| 7. | 3 | 0 | 2 | 15. | 3 | 0 | 2 |
| 8. | 0 | 3 | 1 | 16. | 0 | 3 | 1 |

| Item | Yes | No | Sometimes | Item | Yes | No | Sometimes |
|------|-----|-----|-----------|------|-----|-----|-----------|
| 17. | 0 | 3 | 1 | 33. | 0 | 3 | 1 |
| 18. | 0 | 3 | 1 | 34. | 0 | 3 | 1 |
| 19. | 3 | 0 | 2 | 35. | 3 | 0 | 2 |
| 20. | 3 | 0 | 2 | 36. | 3 | 0 | 2 |
| 29. | 3 | 0 | 2 | 37. | 0 | 3 | 1 |
| 30. | 0 | 3 | 1 | 38. | 3 | 0 | 2 |
| 31. | 3 | 0 | 2 | 39. | 0 | 3 | 1 |
| 32. | 3 | 0 | 2 | 40. | 3 | 0 | 2 |

Put your score for each item in the space allocated in the left margin.

### 5.3.3   Interpretation of Activity 16 - Interpersonal Relationships Study

You can now use your survey scores to compile your own profile. This will reflect your relative strengths and weaknesses related to the key relationship elements of respect, genuineness and empathy. To do this you should record results onto the following profile sheet.

### 5.3.4   RESPECT

| Item Number: | Score: | Item Number: | Score: |
|------|------|------|------|
| 4 | _____ | 7 | _____ |
| 10 | _____ | 15 | _____ |
| 21 | _____ | 24 | _____ |
| 29 | _____ | 30 | _____ |
| 33 | _____ | 39 | _____ |

Total Score:  _____  divided by 10 = Your **Respect** mean score: _____

### 5.3.5   GENUINENESS

| Item Number: | Score: | Item Number: | Score: |
|------|------|------|------|
| 1 | _____ | 2 | _____ |
| 3 | _____ | 8 | _____ |
| 12 | _____ | 13 | _____ |
| 14 | _____ | 17 | _____ |
| 23 | _____ | 27 | _____ |
| 28 | _____ | 34 | _____ |
| 37 | _____ | 40 | _____ |

Total Score:  _____  divided by 14 = Your **Genuineness** mean score: _____

### 5.3.6   EMPATHY

| Item Number: | Score: | Item Number: | Score: |
|------|------|------|------|
| 5 | _____ | 6 | _____ |
| 9 | _____ | 11 | _____ |
| 16 | _____ | 18 | _____ |

| 19 | _____ | 20 | _____ |
| 22 | _____ | 25 | _____ |
| 26 | _____ | 31 | _____ |
| 32 | _____ | 35 | _____ |
| 36 | _____ | 38 | _____ |

Total Score: _____ divided by 16 = Your **Empathy** mean score: _____

### 5.3.7  Follow up

1. You might like to convert profile scores into a bar graph. This shows you visually what the *Interpersonal Relationship Skill Profile* looks like.
2. If you have results that surprise you, or are different from what you expected, you should discuss this with your teacher or mentor.
3. Refer to the section in Robert Bolton's book, *People Skills* (1998), related to skills for bridging the interpersonal gap (Pp. 4–60). This will provide you with back-up suggestions that you can use to further develop your skills in this area.

## 5.4  Reviewing Relationships

For many secondary school students their personal happiness, state of mind and self-esteem is significantly influenced by the kind of friendships they have or don't have.

Some students make friends easily, others don't. Some are in relationships that cause them great stress and they don't know how to get out of them. There will be many secondary school students who have excellent relationships with their parents but there are some who feel they are forever fighting with their parents.

In the main the relationships students establish with people depend first, on how skilled they are in establishing relationships and then, on how skilled they are in maintaining these relationships.

The problem is that for each individual the skills and processes needed for this differ according to their own personality, their interests, their values, standards and beliefs, their past relationship experiences and their family and cultural backgrounds.

The most important requirement is that they don't take their relationship management for granted.

This means that every now and then students should stand back and review the relationships they have. The following activity might be a first step in this process:

### 5.4.1  Activity 17 - The Student Relationship Survey

This activity is designed to develop your awareness of the kind of relationships you establish. It is designed to help you identify people you have most difficulty in establishing relationships with and those that you find it easiest to establish relationships with. You will then be in a position to reflect on those factors that make establishing and maintaining relationships easy and those that make it difficult.

### Instructions

- There are no right or wrong answers to this activity.
- Take your time in listing your responses under each of the headings.
- To maintain confidentiality requirements you should not put actual names on your survey sheet. You could lose it or a nosey person might read it. Create your own I.D. code which represents the people you are entering on the survey sheet.
- When you have exhausted your responses consider the questions in Part B of the activity. If you have a mentor, discuss these questions with them. Decide with your mentor if there are specific actions you might need to take regarding your relationships with particular people.

### Part A: The Student Relationship Response Sheet

*(Draw up an A4 sheet as below. Enter as many responses as you can under each heading.)*

| Person | Outstanding Relationship | Good Relationship | OK Relationship | Difficult Relationship | Terrible Relationship |
|--------|--------------------------|-------------------|-----------------|------------------------|-----------------------|
|        |                          |                   |                 |                        |                       |

### Part B: The School Relationship Survey

Reflect on your responses to Part A of the survey and try to answer the following questions. This is a good activity to do in the company of your mentor if you have one.

1. Of all the relationships you have recorded which one(s) do you worry most about?

   _____

2. Of all the relationships you have recorded do you have any that would fit into the "best friend" category?

   _____

3. What things do you find it difficult to talk about with the people you have rated positively in the survey? Why do you think this is so?

   _____

   _____

4. What things do you find it difficult to talk about with the people you have rated negatively in this survey? Why do you think this is so?

   _____

   _____

5. What behaviours do the people you have rated positively in the survey display that make it easy for you to like them?

   _____

6. What behaviours do the people you have rated negatively in the survey display that make it difficult for you to like them?

   _____

7. What behaviours do you display to the people you have positively rated in the survey?

   _____

8. What behaviours do you display to the people you have negatively rated in the survey?

   _____

#### 5.4.2   Interpretation and follow up

A very good book that the mentor and student can refer to if they would like to further develop skills in this area is: Johnson, D.W. (1993), *Reaching Out,* 5th Edition, Allyn and Bacon, U.S.A.

## 5.5   Developing Effective Communication Skills

The manner in which a student communicates with others reflects a great deal about the strength of their self-belief and the knowledge they have of their self-image. If they lack the ability or the confidence to communicate with others they are in danger of not being able to actualise all their potential.

As well as needing a positive attitude and confidence in communicating self with others, students' ability to communicate with others is significantly influenced by the strength of their communication skills. Sharing ideas, giving opinions, finding out important information about a topic, resolving conflicts with others, expressing their feelings, asking appropriate questions and being assertive when an occasion demands it all require them to develop competency in a range of essential communication skills.

The following activities are provided to assist students to develop their awareness of these skills and further develop their mastery of them.

### 5.5.1 Activity 18 – Sending and Receiving Behaviours Survey

There are two fundamental processes related to effective communication. These are **message sending processes** and **message receiving processes**. A secondary school student is required to display specific skills when engaged in each of these processes. The following survey will assist students to determine the strength of each of these processes.

### Instructions

Consider the following sending and receiving behaviours. After reflecting on each of them tick either the **I do this** or the **I don't do this** column, whichever applies to you.

| A: Sending Behaviour | I do this | I don't do this |
|---|---|---|
| 1. I make sure I know WHAT I want to say before I say it. | ☐ | ☐ |
| 2. I know WHEN the appropriate time is to communicate a message to someone. | ☐ | ☐ |
| 3. I know WHERE the appropriate place is to communicate with a person that I want to share a message with. | ☐ | ☐ |
| 4. I know HOW to best communicate a message to someone I want to take notice of it. | ☐ | ☐ |
| 5. I make sure I understand the MEANING of the message I wish to communicate to someone. | ☐ | ☐ |
| 6. When appropriate I know how to keep the meaning SIMPLE | ☐ | ☐ |
| 7. I make sure I deliver a message CLEARLY | ☐ | ☐ |
| 8. I try to make EYE CONTACT with the person I am communicating with. | ☐ | ☐ |
| 9. I try to MONITOR if a person has understood | ☐ | ☐ |
| 10. I attempt to make sure my NON-VERBAL communication is appropriate when sending a message to someone – I ensure what I have to say is matched by how I say it. | ☐ | ☐ |
| **B. Receiving Behaviour** | | |
| 1. I display ACTIVE LISTENING towards the person communicating to me. I show them that I'm interested in what they're saying. | ☐ | ☐ |
| 2. I show that I've ACCURATELY HEARD the message sent to me by the speaker. | ☐ | ☐ |
| 3. If I'm not sure of the meaning of the message sent to me I ask the speaker to CLARIFY it for me. | ☐ | ☐ |
| 4. I try to get rid of any "BAGGAGE" that can interfere with my interpretation of the speaker's message, i.e. my prejudices, stereotypes, biases. | ☐ | ☐ |

| B. Receiving Behaviour | *I do this* | *I don't do this* |
|---|:---:|:---:|
| **5.** I attempt to tune into the FEELINGS behind the speaker's words. | ☐ | ☐ |
| **6.** I don't INTERRUPT a speaker when they are sending me a message. | ☐ | ☐ |

### 5.5.2   Follow up

The *Sender* and *Receiver* items that you have indicated that you don't do are the communication skill areas that you need to address. You should discuss your negative responses with your teacher or mentor to see if they consider that your lack of mastery of these communication skills is interfering with your ability to communicate. The following activity will help in this area:

## Improving the Ability to Send Messages *(Adapted from: Elder, B. (1995), Communication Workshop, Macmillan Education)*

## Activity: Passing an Oral Message

1. This activity works best with a group of eight or more students.
2. Four members of the group leave the room.
3. The remaining group members compile a message that contains a number of directions, e.g. *Would you go into town and find the supermarket that is just around the corner from the station? I mean the one over the bridge around the corner from the Majestic theatre. When you get there I would like you to get 500gms of mince, 200gms of rindless bacon and half a kilo of ham. I would also like a kilo of margarine and a packet of sun-dried tomatoes. Here is £20. I want a receipt and the change.*
4. The first person from the outside group is called into the room and told that they are going to be given a message to pass onto the next person. They are not allowed to write anything down and they cannot check the information. They will be told the message only once and must remember all the details.
5. The first person leaves the room and passes the message onto one person waiting outside. This person then goes into the room and delivers the message. Having done this they go outside and deliver the message to the third person. The process is repeated until the fourth person gets to deliver the message.
6. The outside group join the inside group. The inside group then repeat the original message and share each of the outside group's delivered message. **The group discuss:** What information, if any, was correctly reported by all outside group reporters? Why do you think this was the case? What information was incorrectly reported by all outside group reporters? Why? What could have been done to make the reporting more accurate?

❏   **Activity: Describing to an Audience: Instructions**

1. The student draws a series of geometric shapes using a range of rectangles, squares and triangles. They should be placed at unusual angles to each other and the student should avoid making them standard sizes.
2. Once the shapes have been drawn, the student is required to describe them verbally to the rest of the class or group, who use the description to attempt to draw each shape.
3. The describing students are not able to use non-verbal signs or diagrams and the drawing group are not allowed to ask questions.
4. If it is possible, the student describing the objects should be placed behind a screen so that body language and eye contact cannot be interpreted.

5. Once the student's description is completed audience members display their diagrams.
6. On completion the class or group discuss:
   - Why was it difficult for the speaker to give the appropriate instructions?
   - What could the speaker have done to make the description more accurate?

## 5.6 Distinguishing Between Verbal and Non-Verbal Communication

An aspect of communication that many secondary school students have difficulty with is their ability to communicate non-verbally. Non-verbal communication is the term applied to all messages that are signalled between people, without the use of words.

90% of messages transmitted between people are communicated without the use of words. Often secondary school students are unaware that they are receiving and sending non-verbal communication messages and consequently are surprised by a person's reaction to them.

Non-verbal communication messages can be transmitted by:

- *The way we use our eyes;*
- *Our facial expressions;*
- *The gestures we display;*
- *The way we sit;*
- *The way we move;*
- *Pointing;*
- *Smiling;*
- *Raising our eyebrows;*
- *Where we sit or stand in relation to the person we are communicating with.*

### 5.6.1 Activity 19 – Reading People's Non-Verbal Communication Behaviours

The more you are able to read people's non-verbal communication behaviours, the more confident you will be with your own communication responses. This activity is designed to build your awareness of how others communicate non-verbally.

### Instructions

- *Observe people such as friends and family members, and see if you can spot them displaying any of the listed non-verbal communication behaviours.*
- *When you observe a non-verbal behaviour, alongside it on the sheet write the message you think is being communicated. (This is a "guessed message".)*
- *Having written your guessed message go and talk to the person observed and ask them what message they were communicating with their non-verbal behaviour (actual message). You need to be careful, when doing this, that you aren't seen by the observed person as "prying" or infringing on their privacy – a good reason why it is best to do this activity with people you know. Explain to them that you are trying to develop your awareness of non-verbal communication.*

| Non-verbal Behaviour | Person Observed | Guessed Message | Actual Message |
|---|---|---|---|
| Nodding of the head | | | |
| Shaking the head | | | |
| Lowering the head | | | |
| Turning the face away | | | |
| Facing you with eyes | | | |
| looking down | | | |
| Staring at you | | | |
| Glaring at you | | | |
| Looking at you with eyes wide open | | | |

| Non-verbal Behaviour | Person Observed | Guessed Message | Actual Message |
|---|---|---|---|
| Showing a slight smile | | | |
| Facing you with lips tightly closed | | | |
| Yawning whilst you are talking to them | | | |
| A person taking a deep breath | | | |
| A person sighing | | | |
| Someone showing a broad smile | | | |
| Someone waving their hand at you | | | |
| Someone facing you with closed eyes | | | |
| Someone talking to you with a shaky voice | | | |
| Someone talking to you with a loud voice | | | |
| Someone talking to you with a soft voice | | | |

### 5.6.2 Follow up to Activity 19

- When you review your responses you will notice that several meanings can be associated with a non-verbal communication behaviour.
- Careful consideration of your responses will indicate that the meaning of non-verbal behaviours is influenced by the context in which they are delivered, i.e. time, venue, people present, culture, etc.
- This should serve as a caution to you in that while you can become skilled in identifying non-verbal communication behaviours, attaching the appropriate meaning to them must be handled with extreme care.

### 5.6.3 Activity 20

### Understanding the Non-Verbal Messages Associated With Body Language

To reinforce the need for care when interpreting non-verbal communication this activity reveals that even a person's body position can reflect a wide variety of meanings.

### Instructions

Alongside each of the following non-verbal communication behaviours, situations or circumstances write what you think the non-verbal message is conveying.

Once you have responded to each of the body position items ask a friend, teacher, parent or your mentor to give their interpretation.

| Body Position Non-Verbal Behaviours | Your Interpretation | Parent/Teacher/Mentor Interpretation |
|---|---|---|
| Slumping in a chair | | |
| Sitting upright on the edge of a chair | | |
| Sitting leaning towards someone | | |
| Sitting with arms folded, legs crossed | | |
| Sitting with arms relaxed, legs slightly apart | | |
| Hands clenched tight | | |
| Hands open, arms reaching towards somebody | | |
| Pacing up and down | | |
| Standing or sitting still | | |

| Body Position Non-Verbal Behaviours | Your Interpretation | Parent/Teacher/Mentor Interpretation |
|---|---|---|
| Shrugging shoulders | | |
| Wringing hands | | |
| Fiddling with keys, pencils | | |
| Sitting still, relaxed and looking at somebody | | |
| Leaning back on chair with hands behind head | | |

### 5.6.4 Follow up to Activity 20

- Find the behaviours to which you and the second responder gave similar interpretations. Why do you think this occurred?
- Find the behaviours to which you and the second responder gave different interpretations. Why do you think this occurred?

### 5.6.5 Activity 21 – Clothes and Situations

Sometimes a person finds themselves in an uncomfortable space because the clothes they are wearing are communicating a message that contradicts their intentions.

If you have ever felt that you are being unfairly treated, misunderstood or not taken seriously when explaining something to another person, strange as it may seem, this could be the result of the clothes you are wearing. On occasion, people who you are communicating with attend more to the clothes you are wearing than the words you are speaking. They are influenced by the stereotypes, biases and values they make between people and clothes, e.g.

- Someone wearing a pinstripe suit is a banker;
- A tie is only worn by a stuffy business man;
- A suit is only worn by a female business woman;
- Students wear jeans and a t-shirt;
- Poor people wear dirty clothes in bad repair.

## This activity might clarify this phenomenon for you.

*What clothes might someone wear in the following situations?*

| Situation | Clothes |
|---|---|
| • Being relaxed | |
| • Being efficient | |
| • Acting official | |
| • Being intelligent | |
| • Acting careless | |
| • Being rebellious | |

### 5.6.6 Follow up to Activity 21

Discuss your responses with a mentor. Do they associate the same clothes that you do with the situation? If not, why do you think this is the case?

### 5.6.7 Activity 22 – Non-Verbal Communication Practice Scenarios

If possible the student, together with a parent and/or mentor, should read through the following scenarios and compare their understandings and interpretations of the non-verbal communication behaviours involved.

## Scenario One

You observe a middle-aged man wearing glasses and a pinstripe suit, white shirt and red tie and highly polished designer boots standing in the street talking to a young man with long tangled hair, wearing an earring, patched denim jeans, baggy sweater and joggers.

- What do you think they are talking about?
- What stereotypes associated with this scenario could influence the interpretations and judgements you might make?

## Scenario Two

If somebody came into your lounge room at home and you wanted to make them feel uncomfortable, how would you arrange the room?

## Scenario Three

If somebody came into your lounge room at home and you wanted them to feel welcome, how would you arrange the room?

## 5.7    Listening Skills - The Secret to Being Understood and to Understanding Others' Behaviour

It is often overlooked that the most frequently used communication skill is our listening behaviour. Students may report that they have sometimes come to the conclusion, after communicating with their teachers, family or friends that …

**"You just don't understand!"**

It is very likely that what has occurred is the person they were communicating with has listened inappropriately to their communication. In other words the student hasn't felt listened to.

If this is the situation with the "significant others" in their life it can cause students self-esteem problems. The reasoning behind this claim goes like this:

*I was sharing something really important with that person and they didn't hear me, they didn't listen. Perhaps this is because …*

- *They don't take me seriously;*
- *They don't care about me;*
- *They aren't interested in me;*
- *I've done something to upset them;*
- *I'm not important enough for them to be interested in me;*
- *They don't value the real me.*

Whatever the feeling, we do know that the consequences of not feeling listened to can result in students having unnecessary doubts about their self-image.

Further, we know that many conflicts between students and their teachers are the result of inappropriate listening behaviours.

Students may have sat down to do an assignment or some homework and come to an abrupt halt, thinking …

**"I don't know what I have to do!"** or
**"I can't remember what I have to do?"**

It's very likely that they didn't effectively listen to the instructions given to them by their teacher. Perhaps they may have experienced a situation where a friend has shared something with them and shortly after doing so has said something like …

**"I can't believe how insensitive you are!"** or
**"You just have no feelings at all!"**

Again it is likely that the student hasn't listened to (tuned in to) the feelings behind the message the speaker has shared.

For all the above reasons the ability to listen is important for the student to master. This will greatly contribute to their having a healthy self-esteem and actualising their potential.

### 5.7.1  *Important information related to listening skills*

It is very strange that a great deal of a student's time at school is spent in developing reading, writing and speaking skills but almost no time is spent in developing listening skills. The following information about listening skills might assist students' understanding of this component of communication.

### 5.7.2  *Attending, following, accepting*

Probably the most important background information students need to know is that effective listening has three competencies – **attending, following** and **accepting**.

### *Attending Competencies*

These competencies require students to:

- Check the attitude(s) they are bringing to listening situations. Do they bring very negative feelings about the person who is doing the communicating? Do they have respect for the person communicating to them? Do they place any value on the information the person is communicating? If they bring a negative attitude to the listening situation it is likely they will misinterpret or distort the messages being communicated.
- Be willing to take an interest in what the other person has to say. They should use eye contact, smiles or gestures to show the speaker that they are interested in what is being said.
- Try to avoid being distracted and ignore other people who might be in close proximity to the speaker. Don't be distracted by surrounding views or activities. Make sure the speaker feels that the listener is concentrating on what is being communicated.

### *Following Competencies*

These competencies require students to:

- Show the speaker that they are "tuned-in" to them. They do this by using appropriate verbal cues such as "uh-huh", "mm", "I see"; by using appropriate body language cues such as nodding, eye contact, smiling appropriately and by asking the speaker appropriate questions.
- Show the speaker that they are following what he/she is communicating by using open-ended questioning, i.e. questions that begin with words such as who, what, when, where, why and how and which encourage the speaker to expand on what they have been saying.
- Use paraphrasing. This is a very difficult skill to master but it is essential to becoming a competent listener. This requires students to reflect back to the speaker the feelings, key ideas or views that they have been communicating, e.g. "So what you are saying is …"; or "You are telling me that you disagree …"; or "I can see that you are angry about this".

### *Accepting Competencies:*

These competencies require students to:

- Be non-judgemental. This means that often they may have to control their cultural, spiritual and moral views. They need to be aware of the dangers that stereotyping and prejudice can cause when interpreting a speaker's message.

- Accept that feelings, opinions and views expressed by the speaker are considered by them as being valid even if the student does not agree with them.
- Be able to summarise the main points of the speaker's dialogue.

### 5.7.3   Activity 23 – The Effective Listening Quiz

*(Adapted from Pinner, D. & Pinner, D. 1999. Pp. 298-299)*
Students can determine just how competent their listening skills are by completing the following listening quiz.

**Instructions:** Tick the column that best indicates your status for each of the following situations:
**When you take part in a conversation or discussion do you …**

|  | *Always* | *Often* | *Seldom* | *Never* |
|---|---|---|---|---|
| 1. Try to have the last word? | | | | |
| 2. Try to find something that you can use? | | | | |
| 3. Try to judge the value of the message? | | | | |
| 4. Try to distinguish between the facts and opinions expressed by the speaker? | | | | |
| 5. Try to pick up on the feelings behind the speaker's message? | | | | |
| 6. Try to overcome any distractions and concentrate on what the speaker is saying? | | | | |
| 7. Try to think ahead of the speaker? | | | | |
| 8. Enjoy having to think about what is being said? | | | | |
| 9. Get impatient while you wait for a turn to say something? | | | | |
| 10. Often finish the sentence for slow speakers? | | | | |
| 11. Concentrate on getting ready to defend your viewpoint on the subject being discussed? | | | | |
| 12. Make a note of important information you have been told that you are going to do something about? | | | | |
| 13. Get irritable when a speaker gets emotional about an issue that doesn't interest you? | | | | |
| 14. Try and keep a "blank" look so that the speaker can't tell what you are thinking? | | | | |
| 15. Fire questions at the speaker trying to trap them into saying something they don't mean? | | | | |
| 16. Try and establish eye contact with the speaker and maintain it throughout the conversation? | | | | |
| 17. Frequently interrupt the speaker when you think they are wrong? | | | | |
| 18. Follow a teacher's lesson content with a flexible attitude which allows you to look for the central ideas? | | | | |
| 19. Decide from the speaker's appearance whether what they are saying is important? | | | | |
| 20. Try and put yourself into the speaker's place and try to understand what they are getting at? | | | | |

### Scoring Key

For questions: 2, 3, 4, 5, 6, 7, 8, 12, 16, 18, 20:
10 points for "Always"; 8 points for "Often"; 2 points for "Seldom"; 0 points for "Never".
For questions: 1, 9, 10, 11, 13, 14, 15, 17, 19:
10 points for "Never"; 8 points for "Seldom"; 2 points for "Often"; 0 points for "Always".

### Interpreting Your Outcomes

If your score is 180 or above, you are an excellent listener.
If your score is between 150 and 179, you listen, but not all the time.
If your score is below 150 you have some bad listening habits.

#### 5.7.4   Activity 24 – Practice Exercises to Build Student Listening Skills

**If possible, the student together with a parent and/or mentor should practise the following exercises in an informal setting:**

- Find as many opportunities as you can to practise listening for messages that lie behind the words being spoken.
- Practise maintaining eye contact with the person speaking to you.
- Practise repeating back to the speaker key things they have said to check your understanding of their message.
- Try and understand the non-verbal messages a speaker is sending.
- Practise not interrupting the speaker.
- Check that you have not used stereotypes when responding to the speaker.
- Practise giving the speaker feedback that shows them that you have accurately heard what they said.
- Practise being patient, making sure the speaker has finished delivering their message before you respond.

## 5.8   Developing Assertiveness: Communicating the Real You

One of the most empowering skills a student can develop is the ability to communicate assertively. This ability not only allows the student to confidently communicate their "real self" to others, but it also strengthens their self-belief.

#### 5.8.1   What is assertive behaviour?

The assertive person utilises methods of communication which enable them to maintain self-respect, pursue happiness and the satisfaction of their needs, and defend their rights and personal space without abusing or dominating other people. *(Bolton, R. 1993.)*

According to the standard dictionary definition, self-assertion is the action of asserting one's individuality or insisting on one's rights or claims. Simply stated, assertive behaviour means standing up for legitimate rights without violating the rights of others. It is an honest, direct and appropriate expression of feelings, wants, beliefs and opinions. Assertive people communicate an attitude of self-respect and respect for others. *(Anne Kotzman, 1989)*

#### 5.8.2   The difference between assertiveness and aggressiveness

It is imperative that a student does not confuse aggressive communication with assertive communication. An aggressive person expresses their feelings, needs and ideas at the expense of others. They often speak loudly and may be abusive, rude and sarcastic. The student who communicates aggressively attempts to get their way by dominating others, not letting them get a word in to any discussion and frequently treating other students' opinions with ridicule and scorn. They attempt to overpower their peers in any decision-making situation. The aim of their communication is to win, regardless of the consequences to the recipient.

### 5.8.3   The advantages of assertive behaviour

Communication specialists such as Pinner, D. & Pinner, D. (2000) and De Vitto, D. (1999) have argued that the ability to communicate assertively is important for:

- *Resolving conflicts;*
- *Negotiating solutions;*
- *Solving problems;*
- *Carrying out leadership roles;*
- *Engaging in discussion and debate;*
- *Participating in meetings;*
- *Being a productive team member;*
- *Being able to say "No" in a positive manner;*
- *Expressing disagreement in an acceptable manner.*

Robert Bolton (1995) tells us that one of the most striking things about assertive people is that they like themselves. A second benefit of assertive behaviour is that it fosters fulfilling relationships. Assertion makes the individual more comfortable with him or herself and therefore others find it more comfortable to be with them. One of the biggest pluses of assertive behaviour is that the individual is able to live their own life. Their chances of getting what they want out of life improve greatly when they let others know what they want, and when they stand up for their own rights and needs.

### 5.8.4   The difficulties associated with assertive behaviour

The major stumbling block about developing assertive communication skills for a secondary school student is that usually these are skills that don't come naturally or easily. For many students this communication behaviour is quite foreign to their personality and normal way of communicating. It may even cut across established communication behaviours that are practised by the family. Certainly, it is the case that a number of teachers may not encourage such communication and misinterpret it when it is used. For all these reasons students need to become as knowledgeable as they can about assertive communication and how it can help them to develop resilience.

### 5.8.5   The concept of the "I" statement

An important assertive behaviour that students can learn to use is the "I" statement. This is especially valuable when a student is annoyed or irritated by another person, or wanting to tell another person what he/she really thinks of their actions. Bruce Elder (1995) claims that the purpose of an "I" statement is to make a clear statement of an experience or incident in a way that another person will hear and not need to defend. Elder provides the following "I" statement process that students might find useful for developing this skill:

The "I" statement should be made as follows:

1. Begin with "when". Follow this with a clear statement of "when" what you are about to say applies:
   *e.g. "When ... you don't listen to what I say ..."*
2. The second part of the statement should refer to how you feel. You need to express this without blaming anyone or anything:
   *e.g. "... I feel ... you don't want to do the work."*
3. The third part of the "I" statement is to clearly indicate what it is that you want:
   *e.g. "What I'd like is to be listened to when I speak."*

If students use this process what they are stating is:

*"When you don't listen to what I say, I feel you don't want to do the work. What I'd like is to be listened to when I speak."*

The aim of this technique is to allow the student to let someone know what they are feeling without being too aggressive. If we look at the structure of these statements we note that:

- The "when" is followed by a neutral description of the event. It must simply be a statement of fact.
- The "I feel" must use a word or a few words which describe exactly the feeling the person has. It is important for the student to work out exactly how he/she feels about the situation. Are they angry, frustrated, overwhelmed, annoyed, irritated?
- The final part of the statement should describe the outcome the student wants, without demanding that the person behaves in a certain kind of way.

*(Bruce Elder, 1995, Pp. 41-42)*

### 5.8.6 *Assertiveness "rights"*

In developing assertiveness skills a number of writers have pointed to the situation that when people are trying to become more assertive, at first they don't believe that they really have the right to express their feelings, beliefs and opinions *(Anne Kotzman, 1989)*. This means that often, when they do assert themselves, they feel guilty. Everyone has personal rights and has an equal right to assert them. Understanding and accepting these assertiveness rights gives students strength to communicate the "real person" to others and builds their self belief. In exercising these rights it is very important that the tone of voice students use and the body language they display is not aggressive.

Presented on the next two pages is a table listing personal assertiveness rights that I think any secondary school student is entitled to. There may be others that mentors wish to add or there may be some that mentors disagree with. Have students reflect on these and discuss them with the mentor, and then make up their own list. Mentors could practise communicating these assertiveness rights with students. Mentor feedback will help to ensure that students exercise these rights in an appropriate manner.

## The Student's Code of Assertiveness Rights

**1** *The Right to Say "No"*

- A student who is being assertive has the right to say "No" without feeling guilty. Many students report that they have often agreed to things at school simply to please their friends or teachers or to ensure that they don't "rock the boat". You need to know that, if your genuine feeling is to say no or to disagree, then it is your right to express this feeling. However, in expressing this right you must take particular care not to do it aggressively.
- If you are struggling to say "No", or fear being reprimanded for doing so, try and think of the consequences of not saying no.
- Sometimes it is best not to say "No" straight away. In some situations you can indicate that you will think about the situation before making a decision. This not only buys time but also lets the person know that a hasty decision hasn't been made.
- You should never apologise for deciding to say "No". Don't say "I'm sorry but …". You have nothing to be sorry for, nor do you need to give a long explanation for your decision to say "No".
- Saying "No" is difficult so it needs to be practised with your mentor.

**2** *The Right Not to Get Involved*

- A student who is being assertive has the right not to get involved in other people's problems, (especially those of your friends).

- What is a crisis for someone else (a friend) does not have to become one for you.
- By being assertive you can avoid getting involved in other people's dilemmas but still show them you empathise with their plight, e.g. "I'm sorry you have that problem but I'm not able to help you solve it."

**3  *The Right Not to Answer Questions***

- A student who is being assertive has the right not to answer certain questions. This is especially the case if you think the question is infringing your privacy, is culturally insensitive, is sexist or is designed to belittle you or make you look foolish.
- If you are going to exercise this right, it is important that you make sure you fully understand the question. This might require you to ask the person to repeat the question or to clarify it before you decide not to answer it.
- Once you can justify to yourself a legitimate reason for not answering a question, inform the speaker of your decision and if appropriate give them your reason for not answering it.

**4  *The Right to Be Treated With Respect***

- A student who is being assertive has the right to be treated with respect. At times this right will require you to actively seek this, especially if a person in authority is communicating with you.
- The most effective way to ensure that you are communicated to with respect, is to inform someone who is not doing so that they are being disrespectful to you, e.g. "I feel put down by what you have just said." Or "I feel embarrassed by the questions you are asking me."
- "I" messages really work when you are exercising your right to be treated with respect.

**5  *The Right to Change Your Mind***

- A student who is being assertive has the right to change their mind. Many students feel pressured to come up with an answer or statement before they have had sufficient time to think through all the related factors. Sometimes when they do this, they quickly realise that they have a more accurate or meaningful response but they don't express it because they don't think they are allowed to change their original statement.
- This right allows you to say that you don't know the answer, or that you will need to consult a reference or expert on the matter before you respond.
- Further, in certain situations, it allows you to state that acting on advice you have been given, you wish to change your original response.

**6  *The Right to Ask For What You Want***

- A student who is being assertive has the right to ask for things he/she desires. In exercising this right you must be very clear of the difference between demanding what you want (aggressiveness) and requesting it (assertiveness).
- However, in exercising this right you need to acknowledge that the person you are requesting something from has the right to say "No".

**7  *The Right to Not to Have To Apologise All The Time***

- A student who is being assertive does not have to apologise for every mistake he/she makes. You should do so if the consequence of your error inconveniences or has a negative impact on another person.
- You have the right to state what course of action you intend taking without prefacing your comment with, "I'm sorry but …".

**8** *The Right to Express Your Feelings*

- A student who is being assertive should feel comfortable in expressing his/her feelings to another person.
- In exercising this right you need to exercise judgement to ensure you select the right time and the right place to do this.
- You also need to take care that in expressing your feelings you do not interfere with the accuracy of the message.

**9** *The Right to Make Mistakes*

- A student who is being assertive does not interpret making mistakes as failure.
- You have the right to make mistakes but are required to accept the responsibility for the consequences of these mistakes.
- You have the right to decide whether criticism directed at you for an error you have made is valid or not.
- If you find the criticism, or part of it, is valid and realistic you should acknowledge that and ask for follow-up suggestions.

**10** *The Right Not to Understand*

- It is unlikely that a student will understand everything that teachers communicate to him/her.
- A student who is being assertive has the right not to understand specific messages communicated to him/her. However, it is important that if you don't understand something you say so. It is your right to do this, so you shouldn't feel embarrassed when you express it.
- You should not be worried about what classmates might think about information or communications you don't understand. Often, such honest communication builds others' respect for you.

### 5.8.7 *Practising assertive communication* (Adapted from Bolton, R. 1998, *People Skills,* Prentice Hall. Pp. 126-128)

A student can develop their assertive communication skills by practising using them with their mentor. In this exercise students should display assertive communication to relay the key messages in the following scenarios. After each scenario the mentor can give feedback regarding the effectiveness of the student's assertive communication.

- You have gone to a movie. The people behind you have been talking non-stop throughout and it is interfering with your enjoyment of the movie.

*How would you use assertive communication to ask them to be quiet?*

- You want to explain something important to your mum. Your brother has turned the TV on and it is making it difficult for you to get your message across to your mum.

*How would you use assertive communication to ask your brother to turn the TV down or off?*

- You arrive home from school physically and emotionally drained. All you want to do is have a sleep. Your younger sister has asked you to help her with her homework.

*How would you use assertive language to explain that now is not the right time for you to do this?*

# The Ideal Image: Developing a Sense of Direction

## Contents

## Outcomes

### The reader will …

❑ Develop their awareness of the relationship between effective goal setting and healthy ideal image;

❑ Be familiar with the key processes involved in establishing realistic goals;

❑ Understand the characteristics of "personal goals";

❑ Recognise the role post-secondary school study and or career preparation plays in the establishment of a healthy ideal image.

## 6.1 The Ideal Image

The ideal image represents the collected thoughts, perceptions, ideas and knowledge of who the individual wants to be or what he or she wants to do or achieve. The ideal image represents the individual goals, dreams and expectations students have of themselves. It also includes the perceptions they have of other peoples' expectations of them. It is the ideal image that gives a sense of direction in life. It provides a focus and a target for the student's performance endeavours.

## 6.2 Effective Goal Setting – the Key to a Strong Ideal Image

Central to a healthy ideal image is the student's ability to set realistic goals and effectively monitor the expectations others have of him or her. The information and activities that follow are designed to assist with goal setting and monitoring of peoples' expectations of the student.

### 6.2.1 Key considerations for effective goal setting

Before students engage in setting themselves performance goals they should reflect on the following considerations:

- ❏ No matter how much ability and talent you have, you will never actualise it unless you first establish what it is you want to achieve and in which direction you want to head.
- ❏ Effective goals should be specific and clear. You write the goal in such a way that you know exactly what it is that you are endeavouring to achieve. If you take time to do this there will be no doubts in your mind as to whether or not you are on track for achieving it or, in fact, whether or not you have achieved your goal.
- ❏ Effective goals need to be challenging. You shouldn't make them so ambitious that they are out of sight, but rather just out of reach at the start of your endeavours. Good goals stretch you but never pull you apart.
- ❏ Effective goals must be written down. They are too important to store in your head. When you write goals down use language that is meaningful to you.
- ❏ Effective goals must have deadlines. Unless you have a date or time limit written down to achieve your goal by, you will get behind and probably lose interest and desire.
- ❏ Effective goals must be worded positively. Set goals related to things you want to do rather than things you are trying not to do.

**By setting a goal and achieving it, students will feel proud of what they have achieved and will be motivated to reach out for a higher goal. A most important outcome of this process is the strengthening of their self-esteem.**

### 6.2.2 Activity 25

*Distinguishing Between Short and Long Term Goals*

If your goals are going to provide you with a focus and sense of direction for your performance efforts you must be able to distinguish between your short and long term goals.
Here are some suggestions that will increase your ability to do this:

- In the goal planner below write down some goals that you would like to achieve over the next three years (long term). The first thing to do is to ask yourself what it is that you wish to achieve in relation to these goals. Write down whatever comes to mind – they can be changed later.
- Next write down what you would like to have achieved one year from now (medium term). These achievements should be related to your long term, three year goals.
- Now write down how you are going to achieve these one year achievement outcomes. You might need to talk this through with your mentor who might be able to identify for you any goal requirements that you have overlooked.

- The next step is to write out the things you need to do this week and today to achieve your one year outcomes. These are your short term goals.
- Remember that your goals have to be regularly reviewed. You should review your three year goals at least twice a year and your one year goals three or more times. You should review your short term goals every day.

## GOAL PLANNER

### Long Term

What would you like to achieve over the next three years?

- ........................................................................................................................
........................................................................................................................

- ........................................................................................................................
........................................................................................................................

### Medium Term

What would you like to achieve one year from now?

- ........................................................................................................................
........................................................................................................................

- ........................................................................................................................
........................................................................................................................

### Short Term

Write down the things you need to do this week and today to achieve your one year outcomes.

- ........................................................................................................................
........................................................................................................................

- ........................................................................................................................
........................................................................................................................

### 6.2.3   Activity 26

### A Four Step Plan For Goal Setting

This activity is particularly useful for those of you who have never set yourself goals. Work through the four steps in the company of your mentor who you should call upon if you have difficulties in carrying out the requirements.

### Step One

*Take some time to reflect on your current lifestyle and performance achievements. Do this by asking yourself:*

What are the things that I am doing? What do I really want to do? Are there aspects of my current performance efforts that I …
Would like to change?

Answer:...........................................................................................................................................
...........................................................................................................................................

Would like to improve?

Answer:...........................................................................................................................................
...........................................................................................................................................

Would like to increase or develop further?

Answer:...........................................................................................................................................
...........................................................................................................................................

Would like to maintain or continue in just the same way?

Answer:...........................................................................................................................................
...........................................................................................................................................

**Step Two**

Select one or two of your responses from Step One and write them down according to the following format:

- In the next few days (short term goal) I would like to (change/improve/increase/maintain?) the following behaviour, attitude or habit.

...........................................................................................................................................
...........................................................................................................................................
...........................................................................................................................................
...........................................................................................................................................

- In the next few weeks, months, year (medium term goal) I would like to (change/improve/ increase/maintain?) the following behaviour, attitude or habit.

...........................................................................................................................................
...........................................................................................................................................
...........................................................................................................................................
...........................................................................................................................................

- In the next few years (long term goal) I would like to (change/improve/increase/maintain?) the following behaviour, attitude or habit.

...........................................................................................................................................
...........................................................................................................................................
...........................................................................................................................................
...........................................................................................................................................

**Step Three**

This step requires you to add suitable criterion to your goal statements that will provide you with an indication as to how close to your goal you have moved. For example,

**Short term goal:**

*In the next four weeks I would like to increase the amount of time I spend doing my homework.*

*Criteria:*

*I will spend one and a half hours on Monday to Friday between 7 pm and 8.30 pm doing my homework.*

*Short term goal*

    Goal.............................................................................................................................

    .................................................................................................................................

    Criteria.......................................................................................................................

    .................................................................................................................................

*Medium term goal*

    Goal.............................................................................................................................

    .................................................................................................................................

    Criteria.......................................................................................................................

    .................................................................................................................................

*Long term goal*

    Goal.............................................................................................................................

    .................................................................................................................................

    Criteria.......................................................................................................................

    .................................................................................................................................

**Step Four**

Write your goal statements into your personal diary.

## 6.3   The Importance of Personal Goals

Terry Orlick (1998) in his book *Embracing Your Potential, (Human Kinetics Publications, Pp. 103-110)* argues that personal goals are required if students desire to move in the direction that they want to work on. He suggests that it is important for them not to sell themselves short in terms of personal goal possibilities. In regard to this it is O.K. to dream as dreams allow the individual to unfold new and exciting realities. Goals that cannot be imagined are rarely achieved, not because they are unachievable but because they have not been dreamed about or accepted as possible.

Orlick suggests that mentors and students need to work through the following steps in determining personal goals:

### Step One: Establish Your Dream Goal

- Spend some relaxed time with your mentor having a conversation about your dreams.
- Talk about what you would like to be or do if you were in the space of "unlimited possibility". How competent could you be? How challenged and excited could you be? Talk about dream goals that expand your horizons, stretch your limits and reach for your true potential.
- Write down these dream goals in your diary. Orlick tells us that even if you never fully attain these dreams, if you can accept that they are within your stretched potential you will remove some barriers that now limit your possibilities. What you aim at affects everything: your life, your commitment, your actions, your beliefs, how you view yourself, and what you are likely to experience.

### Step Two: Establish Your Realistic Goal

- Having discussed your dream goals with your mentor and written them in your diary you should now engage with your mentor in establishing realistic personal goals. This involves working out where you are now and your path to go further. Orlick suggests you need to spend some time in determining what is the best you can realistically attain in the short term (e.g. this term) if you really commit yourself to it.
- The really important consideration here is to understand the term "really commit yourself to it." Discuss with your mentor: "What will I have to do to really commit myself; what changes of behaviour might this require; what will I have to do differently; what will I have to do that I've never done before; what will I have to stop doing?" Write the answers to these types of questions into your personal diary.

### Step Three: Establish Your Self-Acceptance Goal

- This is the final step in setting yourself personal goals. Discuss the word "resolve" with your mentor. What does it mean; what behaviours are required to demonstrate it; who are some high profile people who demonstrate it?
- Discuss with your mentor how you can resolve to pursue your personal goals with commitment whilst accepting your "real self" and overall worth as a person.

Orlick suggests that if students fail to accomplish an important personal goal, they still must be able to accept themselves as a worthy human being. Secondary school students must not put themselves down when they experience unmet goals. If there is a lesson to be drawn from the experience of pursuing a personal goal, they need to grab it with both hands and move on.

The final word on student's personal goals is that of Orlick (p 105):

*"... The true measure of your overall worth is how you are and what you try to become as a person, not what you achieve. It is your way of travelling and not necessarily achieving a specific destination."*

## 6.4    Activity 27 – Designing a Study Success Plan

It is important that students take some time to clarify their definition of study success and then construct a study plan around this. This will involve them reviewing the values and standards they associate with study and identifying their study strengths and weaknesses. They are then in a position where they can develop a study success plan. This activity is designed to help clarify for students what secondary school study success means for them.

### Consider the following case study:

Jane is a secondary school student who has no sense of direction or no focus in her school studies. She is in Year 10 at high school, hates school and feels frustrated and demoralised by her current study programme. Jane is highly intelligent and up until this year had achieved high marks for all subjects she was studying. She has never been in trouble at school and is considered by her teachers as an exemplary student. She is popular with her peers and engages in a wide range of out of school activities.

Jane discussed her negative attitude towards her study with her mentor and as a result of these discussions she decided to construct a success chart. This appeared as follows:

### Jane's Success Chart

| AGE | SUCCESS EXPERIENCES | WHY THIS WAS A SUCCESS TO ME |
| --- | --- | --- |
| 5 to 11: | Attaining my Junior Lifesaving Certificate. | It was something I really wanted to do. It made my family very proud of me. |
| | Being appointed captain of my primary school's netball team. | I love netball and trained very hard. I enjoyed being respected by the team members. |
| 12 to 13: | Getting an A for maths in my yr 8 and 9 school report. | I really enjoy studying maths but I find it quite difficult. I didn't expect to get an A but I worked hard and am very proud of my achievement. |
| 14 to 15: | Being part of my high school's Rockfest production that got into the semi-finals of the Secondary School Nationals. | It was hard work and sometimes scary. I love performing on stage. I enjoyed the team spirit. |
| | Going white water rafting with my class on our Year 10 camp. | It was a challenge. At first I thought "No way will I ever be able to do that." I loved the feeling of pushing myself to my limits. |

### What did Jane's Success Chart reveal?

A careful examination of Jane's success chart reveals the following success patterns:

*Success Pattern One:* Jane needs to be challenged.
*Success Pattern Two:* Jane needs the opportunity to push herself to her performance limits.
*Success Pattern Three:* Jane needs the opportunity to be part of a high performance team.
*Success Pattern Four:* Jane needs the opportunity to perform in front of an audience.

### What values did Jane's Success Chart reveal?

A review of Jane's success chart reveals that her interpretation of success highlights the importance of the following performance values:

❑ Engaging in hard work: (Final primary school maths result.)
❑ Family Pride: (Surf Lifesaving Certificate.)
❑ Friendship: (White water rafting with class.)
❑ Perseverance: (Rockfest, white water rafting.)

### Jane's revised Year 11 Study Goal

After discussing her success chart outcomes with her mentor, Jane revised her goals for her forthcoming Year 11 study. Recognising her performance strengths and values Jane's goal was:

*"I will strive for a personal best mark in maths, media studies and music. I will strive to become a Year 11 Peer Tutor for a Year 9 student. I will attempt to get into the school's Rockfest group again and this time get into the national finals."*

### 6.4.1   Designing the Study Success Plan

It is suggested that the mentor should work with their student in developing a *Student Study Success Plan*. They should discuss the example given (Jane's Plan) and then the student could begin collecting data for their own chart. The following questions might assist with this process:

1 *Think back to when you were at primary school:*

- What subjects did you enjoy studying?
- What subjects did you do well at?
- What was the best report you brought home to your parents?
- What sport did you enjoy playing?
- What sport were you good at?
- Did you ever play representative sport for your school or club?
- What things out of school did you enjoy?
- What things out of school were you good at?

2 *Now think of secondary school:*

- What subjects have you enjoyed studying?
- What subjects have you got your best marks for?
- What was the best report you have brought home?
- Which teachers have you most enjoyed working with?
- What sport or out of school activity do you enjoy?
- What sport or out of school activity are you good at?
- Have you played any representative sport?
- Have you been involved in any community group work, challenges, etc.?

The student and mentor review these responses and set up a success chart using the same protocols used in Jane's success chart. Once this has been done the mentor and student can review the success plan along the same lines as was done for Jane.

### 6.4.2   A Study Success Plan - Developing a student's awareness of career possibilities

The following are a range of activities a mentor can conduct with the student to develop the student's awareness of career possibilities. They were suggested by Barbara Clark (1992) in *Growing Up Gifted,* (Merrill, Ohio. Pp. 525-529).

- Ask the student to bring along the Situations Vacant section of a major newspaper. Review these advertisements with the following questions in mind:
  - ❏ Perseverance: What kind of job opportunities exist that interest you?
  - ❏ What differences are there in job opportunities for men and for women?
  - ❏ What are the key requirements of these jobs: Age? Experience? Qualifications?
- The mentor and student can set aside one week to watch for job roles demonstrated on television. Make a list of the different jobs presented. Who were doing the jobs? What gender, qualifications, age, personalities and experience did they display?
- Write a list of job categories on a sheet of paper (e.g. agriculture, business, law, medicine, teaching, accounting, labouring, engineering, retailing, mechanic, computing, police, fire service). Ask the student to write down names of people they know who fit into these categories.; then have them describe these people in terms of age, experience, gender, qualifications, etc.
- Ask the student to make a list of advertised jobs that interest them personally and then have him/her make a list of jobs he/she is interested in that weren't advertised in the paper. Discuss with him/her why these jobs were not advertised and how he/she could go about getting more information about them.

- Discuss with the student how certain jobs no longer exist and how new career opportunities are being created all the time. Together the student and the mentor can review the Situations Vacant columns to identify jobs they think are disappearing and ones that new technology or societal pressures have recently created. They determine what sort of skills, qualifications and experiences are being sought after in the newly created jobs.

## 6.5    Preparation For a Career

For many students the question that dominates their ideal image is "What do I want to do when I leave school?" In some cases, the realisation that they have to make a decision regarding what they are going to do when they finish secondary school comes as a real wake-up call.

If students are in this situation there are a number of job-seeking skills that need to be developed. The following activities are designed to enhance an awareness of these skills. Students should discuss the outcomes of these activities with a mentor to ensure they have sufficient competence to be able to apply them.

### Activity 28 – What Do I Want From a Job?

Many students have little idea about what sort of work they wish to pursue when they leave school. Often the question foremost in mind is: "Should I go and do study at a university or FE college college or should I go straight to work?" This is a question that students may need to discuss at length with the mentor.

The following activity might assist them to clarify some choices and values related to this question.

### Directions

- ❐  Put 1 by your first choice; 2 by your second choice; 3 by your third choice and so on.
- ❐  Then, attempt to answer the questions at the end of the survey. Discuss your answers with your mentor.

*Type of job you are considering seeking:*                                          *Rating:*

1.  A job that is interesting.                                   _____

2.  A job where you are in charge.                              _____

3.  A permanent job.                                            _____

4.  A job where you develop your ideas and skills.             _____

5.  A job that is highly paid.                                  _____

6.  A job that involves helping people.                         _____

7.  A job with rapid promotional prospects.                     _____

8.  A job where you work with plenty of people.                 _____

9.  A job that is mainly outside.                               _____

10.  A job that is clean and healthy.                           _____

11.  A job that involves you making or repairing things.        _____

12.  A job that is involved with law or policing.               _____

13.  A job that gives you opportunities to travel.              _____

14.  A job that challenges you.                                 _____

15. A job that involves working with animals.  _____

16. A job that has something to do with medicine.  _____

17. A job that involves selling things.  _____

18. A job that involves agriculture.  _____

19. A job that involves working with finances.  _____

20. A job that involves government or politics.  _____

**Questions:**

1. What was your first choice? Why did you make this your first choice? _____

_____

2. Is there any pattern associated with your first three choices? _____

_____

3. What was your last choice? Why did you make this your last choice? _____

_____

## 6.6   Activity 29

### Developing Job Seeking Skill Awareness

Read through the following information. Discuss any areas of uncertainty with your mentor.

### *1. Knowing you*

A prerequisite for a student who is about to undertake job-hunting is to make sure you have developed an extensive self-awareness. This means that at the very least, prior to embarking upon job hunting, you need to be able to answer the following questions about yourself:

- Who am I? What are my performance strengths/weaknesses? What is important to me?
- What do I want or need? What would I do to achieve short term or long term after I leave school?
- What do I have to offer? What experiences have I had, what qualifications have I got, what skills have I got, and what interests do I have?

### *2. Finding out and getting help*

You need to spend time in getting to know where you can get information about post-school opportunities. Often there are people in your community that your mentor knows, who can provide you with invaluable information about these opportunities.

### *3. Going for the job*

Many of you might be able to identify a job you would like to do or a post-secondary course you would like to study, but you don't know how to go about getting it. It is likely you will have to go for a job or course interview and so you will need to be aware of all that is involved in presenting yourself for this interview. The following are a few things you need to do before applying for a job and going for an interview:

- Prepare your job application in an acceptable format.
- Know how to use the telephone when making your initial enquiries about a job or study course.
- Practise using your verbal and non-verbal communication skills to make the right impression during a job interview.

- Practise, with your mentor, answering questions you might be asked during your job interview.

### 4. Making things happen

If you just sit back and wait for a good job to fall in your lap it will never happen. You have to be **proactive** if you want to secure a good job. The things you can do to be proactive include:

- Leaving your curriculum vitae with a potential employer, even if they haven't advertised a position.
- Compiling "Why I would like to work for you" and "What I can offer your company" application letters for prospective employers.
- Planning your job-hunting strategy so that you use your time efficiently.
- Creating an "early warning" or "watchdog" system to identify potential job opportunities as soon as possible.

## Case Study: The Fat Sam Story

### The pursuit of dreams is like a game of "Snakes and Ladders"

Sam had always been big. He came into the world weighing 4365 grams and just kept getting bigger. By the time he began school he was by far the fattest kid in the class and that was the way it was to be from then on. At first it didn't matter as he played and took his place in class just like any other child.

### The nicknames

The nicknames began at about his third year at primary school – "fatso, rumble tummy, lump of lard", and so on. Soon after the nicknames came the put downs which turned to ridicule and eventually to bullying. By the time he was nine Sam hated school, and every day feared that yet again he would bare the brunt of another cruel prank. He felt lonely, afraid, humiliated and ashamed of his physical appearance.

Unbeknown to anyone Sam had a secret dream. In his dream Sam saw himself standing on a stage singing to a large audience. Ever since he was little Sam could sing beautifully. When he was eight his uncle gave him an old ukulele which he learned to play in just six months. Often at home in the solitude of his bedroom, Sam would set up a pretend microphone and imagine he was on stage facing a large audience. Off he would go strumming away on that old ukulele, singing to that imaginary crowd.

### Things come to a head

The name calling, bullying and ridicule finally got too much for Sam. It was in his last year of primary school. His class were outside doing physical education and the game they were playing was tunnel ball. The team in which Sam was a member was leading the race until it came to Sam's turn. Some how the ball bounced off his legs and by the time he'd retrieved it the team had gone from first to last. The insults flowed once again:

"For goodness sake Fatso, can't you even bend over?"

It was as if something in his head snapped. He took off, raced out of the school grounds and in tears fled home. When he got home there was no one there. His dad was at work and his mum was shopping. It didn't matter. Sam knew where the spare key was.

Inside his house, alone, Sam wept. Crazy thoughts flashed through his head:

"I hate who I am. I wish I was dead. I'm going to kill myself."

Sam knew that in the bathroom medicine cabinet was a bottle of his mum's tablets, tablets that she had told him were very powerful and that he should take particular care not to mistakenly take. Almost in a dream he rose from his bed and began to make his way to the bathroom. Just before he got there he noticed his old ukulele lying against the passage wall. Automatically Sam bent down and picked it up. He casually strummed a couple of chords and then sat in the passage and began to sing his favourite songs. In the middle of this the front door opened – mum was home. Just how prophetic the ukulele and his songs were Sam would never guess.

## The turning point

During the long summer break that came at the end of that year Sam and his family travelled to one of a popular beach resorts. Here Sam and his family were to stay for two weeks. After the first two days of sun, surfing and fishing, the terrible experiences of his final year at primary school began to fade to the back of his mind. One morning at the campsite, as Sam went to the camp supply store to get the milk and daily newspaper, he noticed on the big noticeboard outside the shop an item about the big New Year's Eve Talent Quest to be held at the campsite. There were to be prizes for an adult division and youth division as well as an overall winner.

"Just fill in the entry form inside the store and the camp manager will get in touch with you," the notice told him. Sam filled in an entry form.

He told none of his family or relations who were staying with them of his action. Come Friday evening his family and their relations took their blankets and baskets of food and drink and seated themselves in front of the big stage that had been set up for the talent quest. No one noticed that Sam took with him his trusty old ukulele. Before long the grounds in front of the stage were jam packed with spectators. On the dot of 8 pm the talent quest compere explained to the audience that the juniors would perform first and after the adults had finished the various winners would be announced. He explained that he would call out the contestant's name and he or she should then come up to the stage to perform.

## Through the self-esteem wall

Four young contestants had performed – two singers, a dancer and a pianist and they were good. Then the compere called for the fifth contestant – Sam. His dad's mouth froze open like a goldfish, his mum just smiled and all his relations turned in absolute amazement and stared at him. With his legs feeling like jelly Sam walked up to the stage. There was a lot of noise coming from the crowd and a number of insulting comments such as:

"Will you just look at that huge mess that just walked onto the stage – this will be a laugh."

Strange as it seems Sam heard nothing. What was foremost in his mind was that old dream of himself on a stage looking out at a big crowd. He nervously strummed a few chords and began his song. An incredible hush came over the crowd. As Sam's infectious voice first captured their interest and then their absolute attention he cast a special spell on them. The nerves disappeared, the hurt went away and Sam, for the first time, experienced a special sense of achievement. When he finished his song at first there was a stunned silence which soon gave way to tumultuous applause.

Sam won the junior section of the talent quest and to no one's surprise was also acclaimed as the overall winner. This is a true story and it happened in New Zealand. This marked for Sam an incredible journey that culminated in him becoming one of New Zealand's greatest ever Maori entertainers.

I met Sam when he was at the top of his career and he related the above story to me. When I asked him what the secret was to his overcoming the terrible childhood experiences he had, his reply was:

"The pursuit of my dream has been like playing the game of snakes and ladders. I would get to climb a ladder that took me closer to my dream and every now and then there'd be a bad roll of the dice and I'd slide down a snake that took me away from my dream. But what kept me going was that I knew that no matter how far I slid down the snake, there was a ladder waiting to be climbed that would get me to my dream."

# Chapter 7

# Strategies and Activites to Assist Students to Develop Resilience

## Content

## Outcomes

### Readers will ...

❐ Have a greater understanding of the phenomenon of resilience and its relationship to self-esteem;

❐ Be familiar with conflict resolution strategies that help build resilience;

❐ Be aware of negotiating behaviours that enhance resilience;

❐ Have a greater understanding of the role that motivation plays in enhancing resilience;

❐ Understand the need to manage anger to allow resilience to develop;

❐ Have a greater understanding of the role that stress-management has to play in developing resilience.

## 7.1   Explaining Resilience

Earlier in this book it was explained that self-esteem referred to a person's state of mind, whilst resilience referred to a person's mental toughness. The model explained in Chapter 1 indicated that healthy self-esteem was a prerequisite for resilience. However, it seems that there is an interesting reciprocal relationship between these two phenomena. Whilst self-esteem is a prerequisite for strong resilience, resilience can also enhance a person's self-esteem. The importance of resilience for secondary school students is a relatively new idea and so it is important to present a collection of ideas from a variety of people about what this phenomenon is.

Michael Rutter, a well known English psychologist, suggests that resilience refers to our ability to recover and move on in the face of difficult or devastating circumstances. *(Rutter, 1994)*

Many students find school performance a difficult journey and many have experienced the "gut- wrenching" experience of failing an exam or assignment. Rutter is suggesting that we need resilience to tough out the difficult journey and to overcome the gut-wrenching experiences.

The following analogy of resilience gives us a clear image of the function of this characteristic:

*Resilience is the happy knack of being able to bungee jump through the pitfalls of life. Even when hardship and adversity arise, it is as if the person has an elastic rope around them that helps them to rebound when things get low, which helps them maintain their sense of who they are as a person. (Fuller, 1998)*

Until recently many educators and psychologists have been stressing how important a healthy self-esteem is to enable a student to actualise their potential and maintain a quality lifestyle. While this claim is not being disputed, what is being suggested is that the positive state of mind that healthy self-esteem brings needs to be supplemented with a mental toughness that resilience will give, to ensure the individual moves on in the face of difficult or devastating circumstances.

The following strategies and activities, in association with the self-esteem strategies and activities previously suggested, will assist with the process of developing resilience.

## 7.2   Conflict Resolution Strategies That Help Build Resilience

An aspect of a student's journey through secondary school which often causes stress and anxiety and requires considerable resilience, is that of dealing with disagreements and conflict. From the student's perspective if they have ever found themselves in the following situation …

*"How on earth did I let that small disagreement get me in so much trouble and cause me so much stress?"*

… then it is likely that they have gone about resolving the conflict in the wrong manner. The following are a number of suggestions that have been found to help students resolve conflicts in a positive manner. They should be discussed with the mentor prior to using them to ensure full understanding of the process.

### 7.2.1   Using compromise

- This strategy requires the people involved in the conflict to make concessions so that a decision may be reached which is based on points all people involved can agree upon.
- This allows a "playing down" of those aspects on which agreement cannot be made. In carrying this out students will need to exercise their persuasion, bargaining and negotiating skills.
- Students need to exercise some caution in using compromise because these skills are not appropriate to certain conflict situations. This is particularly the case when a student feels that agreement at any price is better than spending more time arguing or debating the point. The danger of doing this is that a student might concede long term benefits for short term gains.

### 7.2.2   Using consensus

- If the student and those involved in the conflict take time to "talk out" their various views and opinions positive outcomes are often produced. Such discussion can result in the most productive form of conflict resolution – consensus.
- When using consensus to resolve conflict all people involved in the conflict must have the opportunity to put their views forward.
- Time must be provided for positive and negative feedback and constructive argument to occur, in an atmosphere that allows people to criticise others' views and accept criticism in return.
- Discussion continues until everyone has had their say and agrees upon identified issues.
- Hammering ideas out, combining the best of all the original proposals into a master solution, produces high-class decisions. Their value is proved by the fact that they have survived the debate.
- Faults in reasoning that might not be detected in an ordinary discussion are more likely to be identified in consensus debate. The decision can be modified on the spot to overcome these.
- Using consensus, if not unanimous, at least gives every person a sense of having contributed to the outcome. Participants are therefore more committed to supporting the decision and seeing it successfully implemented.
- Often as a result of a consensus discussion those who were originally against an idea may be persuaded that it really is sound, and change their stance to one of being a supporter.

### 7.2.3   Things to avoid in conflict resolution

Given the often "emotionally charged atmosphere" associated with conflict, there are a number of things a student should avoid when attempting to resolve conflicts. Again it is suggested that discussion on the conflict resolution barriers shown below should take place with the mentor.

- *Majority Rule:* This strategy can leave a significant number of people dissatisfied with the outcome. 51% in favour to 49% against means that nearly 50% of the group are not in agreement with the decision. In this instance it is better to treat such a result as "no-decision" and to continue discussions until at least a 75% majority is achieved.
- *Leader Domination:* One of the most frustrating situations students can encounter is when a meeting is called to resolve a conflict through making a group decision, but the outcome has already been decided prior to the meeting being held. A dominating leader tells students why the decision is a good one and then instructs them to vote in favour of it. The group then accepts rather than makes the decision. Students end up complying with what the group or team leader wants, regardless of what they personally think.
- *Fairy Tale Solutions:* These are quick and pleasant sounding suggestions that are either unrealistic or rely on some future event which (if it happens) will solve everything with a minimum of effort. ("... And we all lived happily ever after" type scenario – hence the term fairy tale solutions.) Resolving conflict problems means finding a practical route from where students are now to where they want to be, not an imaginary one.
- *Demanding That Someone Should Fix The Problem:* Unfortunately sometimes people in authority, out of frustration, will tell someone associated with the conflict that they must resolve the conflict and sort out the problem. They do not provide the person with any options or strategies to work, just a demand to sort it out. When this occurs usually all that results is increased stress levels and greater disorganisation amongst the people trying to resolve the conflict.
- *Ignoring The Problem:* People who have low self-esteem sometimes deny that a conflict exists. They try to put it out of their minds and do nothing, and are greatly surprised when

at a later time it resurfaces as a major problem. This situation often happens when students are put on the spot, such as being unexpectedly targeted by a teacher or coach. The student simply denies that a problem exists or claims that it is of no concern to them.

### 7.2.4 Activity 30 – A Conflict Resolution Strategy

The following strategy has been shown to provide positive outcomes for students involved in conflict situations. Discuss the steps with your mentor and then apply it to a conflict situation you have either experienced or are experiencing. The more you use it the more effective it will become for you.

#### Step One: Accurately describe the conflict situation.

Write down exactly what you think the conflict is about. Give as many details as you can.

#### Example:

*Mary and Michelle are constantly causing disruptions during our maths lessons. They call out to each other, cheek the teacher, get out of their seats and annoy the students they are sitting next to. As a result of their disruptions we are all falling further and further behind with our work and worry we will fail our end of year maths exams.*

❑ Describe your conflict:_____

_____

_____

_____

#### Step Two: Identify the emotions the conflict situation is evoking.

What are the feelings being displayed by the people involved in this conflict?

#### Example:

*The teacher gets angry and flustered and so do many students. Some students feel threatened and anxious by Mary and Michelle's behaviour. The lack of respect shown to the teacher by Mary and Michelle embarrasses some of the students. Mary and Michelle are antagonistic towards the teacher.*

❑ Identify the emotions your conflict is evoking:_____

_____

_____

_____

#### Step Three: Engage in group talk.

Get as many of the people involved in the conflict as you can to verbally state their views and feelings related to the conflict. In this session no one should be interrupted or criticised whilst they are participating. The idea is for each person to put words to the thoughts they have about the conflict and to bring them out in the open.

### *Activity 30 – A Conflict Resolution Strategy (Cont.)*

### *Example:*

*Sam, a class member: "Mary and Michelle should show more respect towards the teacher."*

*Jillian, a class member: "They need to think more about what effect the outcomes of their behaviour is having on the rest of the class." Bob, a class member: "I know there's a personality clash between them and the teacher and that the teacher previously had 'put them down'. They need to get together to talk this whole thing out."*

❏ What group talk comments were made related to your conflict?

_____

_____

_____

### *Step Four: Identify the actual behaviours that are displayed in this conflict and then write them down alongside the names of the people displaying them.*

### *Example:*

*Michelle: Constantly calls out in class.*
*Mary: Is always out of her seat moving around the class.*
*The teacher: Yells at Michelle and Mary. Refuses to continue the lesson until he is satisfied they are paying attention.*
*Class Students: Yell at Michelle and Mary to behave.*

❏ What behaviours are displayed in your conflict situation?

_____

_____

_____

### Step Five: Identify possible conflict solutions.

**Part A:** When you have completed the previous four steps you should reflect on your responses and then write down as many solutions you can think of. At this stage write down whatever comes to mind. If it is a group conflict situation make this a "brainstorming" session.

### *Example:*

*Mr. Franks is a good maths teacher and we all need to get as much from him as possible.*
*Maths is important to us all.*
*Mary and Michelle honestly think the teacher "picks on them".*
*I don't think Mary and Michelle, or Mr. Franks, know how the rest of the class feel about this situation.*
*They need to have a meeting to sort this out.*

❑ Brainstorm your conflict for solutions.

_____

_____

_____

_____

**Part B:** You should review all suggested solutions and decide what action you should take. If possible prioritise your actions.

*Example:*

1. *I will call for a class meeting to take the place of our next maths lesson.*
2. *I will ask our guidance councillor to chair the meeting.*
3. *I will prepare an agenda before the meeting and make sure all students and Mr. Franks have a copy.*
4. *I will ask the guidance councillor to draw up the meeting rules and make sure everyone has a copy before the meeting.*
5. *I will organise for someone to take detailed minutes of the meeting.*

❑ Write down your prioritised solutions.

_____

_____

_____

_____

### 7.2.5   Negotiating behaviours

A strategy alone, such as the one described here, will not resolve conflict. Some key negotiating behaviours need to be brought to the conflict resolution session. From the perspective of the students the following negotiating behaviours have been identified as being important:

- Maintain non-threatening eye contact with the person/people you are negotiating with.
- Stay on target and don't allow yourself to be sidetracked.
- Make maximum use of leading questions, e.g. "I take it we are all agreed on this?"
- When you need to explore the issues further use open-ended questions, e.g. "What possibilities can we consider?"
- Stay cool, calm and collected throughout the negotiations.
- Once the negotiating has been completed put it behind you.

---

### 7.2.6   Activity 31 – Putting Negotiating Behaviours Into Practice

For many students the art of negotiating does not come easily. It is therefore suggested that students engage in practising their negotiating skills. The following two scenarios can be used to do this. Bruce Elder, (1995) _Communication Workshop,_ (Macmillan Education, Australia. Pp. 75-82) provides a number of scenarios that can also be used for this purpose:

1. These scenarios are best done in small groups.
2. A mentor can organise and coordinate this activity.
3. This activity will involve role playing because this means that people actually have to come up with verbal and non-verbal ways of negotiating with another person.

---

4. Prior to engaging in the role play each student should work out what their character's needs, fears and behaviours might be

5. Students should try to be as real as possible but avoid playing too hard to get. Prior to undertaking the role play they should decide what issues are going to be important to them.

6. The students should use the names supplied in the scenario so that the role play doesn't become confused with the personalities of the other students in the group.

## Scenario One: The Year 12 Party

Your name is June and you are a member of a Year 11 class. It's time for the Year 11 Ball. Your friends are planning the after ball party and are discussing the issue of alcohol. You are uncomfortable about this issue and don't think there should be any alcohol. Bob Williams, another member of your class and captain of the football team, is adamant that without alcohol the party will be a "damp squid". Mary Nelson, your best friend, is torn between Bob's view, (yes, she is his girlfriend) and her parent's view which is similar to yours. Colin, the quietest member of the class, keeps reminding everyone that you will have to have parents as chaperons at the party. Jill, usually the most organised of anyone in the class, keeps asking, "Where will we have this party? Who is going to organise the music? Who is going to organise security?"

What sort of party is negotiated?

## Scenario Two: Buying A Surfboard – Negotiating the Best Deal

Your name is Kim Walker and you are in your first year of secondary school. It seems that everyone in your class is into surfing. You don't want to be the odd one out so you figure you should get into some serious surfing, too. The first major problem you have to overcome is your parents. They have been in your ear in recent weeks regarding the amount of time you spend pursuing your leisure activities and how little time you spend doing your homework. Then there is the problem of buying a surfboard and, of course, the mandatory wet suit. You have no money in the bank as your savings were spent last term on a new stereo.

Mum is dead set against this latest request of yours. No way is she going to allow you to engage in yet another thing that will distract you from your school work. As for giving you money to waste on a useless thing like a surf board just to go and mix with those yobbo kids from school, no way!

Dad is caught between a rock and a hard place over this issue. He has always loved the ocean and surfing and sees it as a good, healthy leisure pursuit. However, he knows that you have been pretty slack with your homework and work about the house. He also knows that he should support mum over this issue.

Nicole, your younger sister is really spitting tacks over this. One year younger than you she is claiming unfair treatment, discrimination, etc. if your parents give in to you. She had recently asked your parents if she could have a new iPod but had been told that it would distract her too much from her schoolwork and that she hadn't been doing enough around the house to deserve such a payment from your parents.

Negotiate a solution that at least partially meets everyone's needs.

## 7.3　Motivation and Desire

Many students have a good understanding of their self-image and their ideal image, but still feel as though they have no sense of direction or focus. If this is the case it is likely that the individual doesn't have enough of the right kind of "petrol in the performance tank". For a student to be resilient, the petrol they require is "motivation" and this petrol requires the correct blend of desire.

### 7.3.1　Important considerations related to motivation

- Motivation is a state of mind, an attitude.
- Motivation is the extent of a person's willingness to undertake a task or activity.
- As previously mentioned motivation can come from within. This kind of motivation is called **intrinsic** motivation and involves such things as a sense of pride in producing a particular performance outcome, enjoyment from doing a particular task, the thrill acquired from engaging in a challenge or the sense of elation gained from achieving a self-imposed performance goal.
- Motivation can come from an external source. This kind of motivation is called **extrinsic** motivation and is based around the rewards received for a performance outcome. Such rewards include praise from a respected person, a gift for achieving a performance outcome, a monetary reward for achieving a performance outcome or a certificate for achieving a performance outcome.
- Extrinsic motivation can be most useful when the student is beginning a task that they have previously failed at, when they are considering whether they will undertake a serious challenge, or when they are going to attempt something they have never attempted before. Extrinsic motivation is good for short, high performance bursts but in many cases won't sustain high performance effort.
- Intrinsic motivation is the major force that allows the individual to sustain high performance effort. It keeps them going when tasks become tedious or very challenging. Intrinsic motivation will help the student to set realistic performance expectations.

### 7.3.2　Important considerations related to desire

- Desire reflects the intensity of the motivation. The higher an individual's desire, the stronger their motivation and vice versa.
- The status of a student's desire determines the manner in which they begin a task. If desire is low it might take them some time before they begin the task; if the desire level is high they are impatient to start.
- Desire comes from within. Some people have referred to it as the "fire in the belly".
- A person's level of desire helps them to prioritise their performance goals. The highest priority will be given to the performance goals that create the strongest desire.

### 7.3.3　The relationship between motivation, desire and resilience

- The higher the motivation and the greater the desire, the more persistent individuals will be in pursuing their goals. Persistence is a key characteristic of resilience.
- The higher the motivation and the greater the desire, the more likely it is that the student will overcome setbacks in the pursuit of their goals. A key characteristic of resilience is the ability to interpret setbacks as opportunities, to learn something new related to current performance efforts, and to then turn them into a positive.
- The higher the motivation and the greater the desire, the more willing the individual will be to push themselves to their performance limits in pursuit of their goals. This feature of resilience allows them to undertake goals that take them outside the normal performance "comfort zone". The more time students spend outside their performance "comfort zone" in pursuit of their goals, the more rewarding will be their achievements.

### 7.3.4   Activity 32 Identifying Motivating Behaviours

Spend some time with your mentor observing role models, heroes or sports stars performing. How often do they display the following motivational behaviours? Can you add new motivational behaviours you have identified?

| Motivational Behaviours | Who displayed it? | Number of times they displayed it. |
| --- | --- | --- |
| 1. They are enthusiastic in what they are doing. | | |
| 2. They are courageous in overcoming the setbacks and barriers they meet whilst pursuing their goals. | | |
| 3. They show emotional control whilst pursuing their goal. | | |
| 4. They are competitive. Competition brings out the best in them. | | |
| Now add any new behaviours you have identified. | | |
| 5. _____ | | |
| 6. _____ | | |
| 7. _____ | | |
| 8. _____ | | |

### 7.3.5   Building confidence and self motivation

Terry Orlick *(1998, P. 58)* claims that confidence frees us to live and perform at a higher level, not because our abilities suddenly improve but because we believe in ourselves and the abilities we already have.

All of us have had the experience that when we feel good about ourselves and are engaged in satisfying activities the quality of our life and our sense of worth are enhanced.

This sense of self-confidence is an essential element of resilience and when we acquire this it results in motivation that allows us to actualise our performance potential. Whilst there is no guaranteed training programme that can give us self-confidence, Orlick provides us with a number of suggestions that mentors can refer to when engaging with their students *(Orlick, 1998, Pp. 54-63):*

- Remember to "think-and-look for the positive": Students need to remember the positive comments that others have made about them. They should think about what is possible if they simply free themselves to live and perform to their true capacity and look for real world evidence that demonstrates their value and capacity. Students should take time to remember "think-and-look for the positive" as a daily exercise.
- Use Orlick's "Why I Can" inventory. Get the student to find a quiet spot and take their time in responding to the following questions:
  - Why I can live the life I want to live (Forget about why you can't – only list why you can.)
  - Why I can achieve the performance goals that I have decided are important to me? (Forget about why you can't – list only why you can.)
  - How will I achieve these performance goals? (What will I focus on, what will I act on, what will I do to get there?)

- Why I can attain the life goals that I want to live (Forget about why you can't – list only why you can.)
- How will I live these life goals? (What will I focus on, what will I act on, what will I do to stay on that track?)

The mentor and student should reflect on the student's responses and translate this into a message the student can use to keep him/herself positive and motivated as they pursue his/her performance goals.

### 7.3.6  Activity 33 – Practising Anger Management Techniques

Like all aspects of behaviour management, the more we practise anger management techniques the more competent we become. The following suggestions drawn from Johnson, D.W. (1993) *Reaching Out, (Allyn and Bacon, U.S.A. Pp. 285-291)* are recommended for the mentor and student to use as anger management practice techniques:

**\* My Anger:** Complete the following statements. Be specific.

- ❐ I feel angry when my friends.................................................................................................
- ❐ When I'm angry at my friends, I usually..............................................................................
- ❐ After expressing my anger I feel..........................................................................................
- ❐ The way I express my anger usually makes my friends.......................................................
- ❐ When my friends express anger toward me, I feel...............................................................
- ❐ When I feel that way, I usually.............................................................................................
- ❐ I feel angry when my teacher..............................................................................................
- ❐ When I'm angry at my teacher I usually.............................................................................
- ❐ The way I act when I'm angry at my teacher makes me feel................................................
- ❐ The way I act when I'm angry at my teacher usually results in my teacher ........................... ................................................................................................................................................
- ❐ When my teacher expresses anger at me, I feel...................................................................
- ❐ After reacting to my teacher's anger I feel...........................................................................
- **Using Self Statements/Talking to Yourself:** Below are a number of statements you could say to yourself to help yourself manage anger situations effectively.

Practise saying them out loud in the company of your mentor.

- ❐ I can work out a plan for handling this.
- ❐ As long as I keep cool, I'm in control here.
- ❐ Getting upset won't help.
- ❐ It worked!
- ❐ If I find myself getting upset, I will know what to do.
- ❐ You don't need to prove yourself.
- ❐ It's not worth it to get so angry.

- ❐ I could have got more upset than it was worth.
- ❐ I actually got through that without getting angry.
- ❐ My anger is a signal that it's time to start talking to myself.
- ❐ If I start to get mad, I will just be banging my head against a brick wall, so I might as well relax.
- ❐ This could be a bad situation, but I believe in myself.
- ❐ My muscles are starting to feel tight. Time to relax and slow things down.
- ❐ I'm not going to let them get to me.
- ❐ Calm down. I can't expect people to act the way I want them to all the time.

## 7.4 The Need to Manage Anger

All students feel angry at times. Anger is one of the most powerful and common emotions. It is quite healthy to feel angry and as long as the expression of anger is managed it will not interfere with resilience. However, if the anger dominates behaviour and the student doesn't recognise its presence, it will undermine their resilience by replacing mental toughness with mental aggression. The following information and suggestions are designed to help students manage anger to avoid it interfering with their resilience.

### 7.4.1 Understanding the various forms that anger takes

There are many explanations about what anger is and the following is a small collection of these:

- ❐ **Heated anger:** Heated anger is when a person is very angry and "boiling over". People with heated anger are said to be "hot under the collar", "boiling mad" or "seeing red".
- ❐ **Hostility:** Hostile people express anger in an aggressive manner. Sometimes this is because they feel insecure, or it may be just the way that person is – it is a reflection of their personality. Hostile people intimidate others and frequently display physically aggressive actions.
- ❐ **Sour state of mind:** A sour state of mind is often associated with people who look angry. It is often expressed by glaring or scowling, looking mean at another person, sulking and not talking to someone.
- ❐ **Being unwell:** Being in ill health can cause a person to display anger. This may be due to their experiencing pain or experiencing frequent discomfort.

### 7.4.2 Recognising anger in others

It is important for a student to be able to recognise the indicators of anger in others. This will help them to determine the nature of their interaction and communication with a person. The following are key indicators of anger:

### Body Language

- This can involve someone clenching their fists and shaking them at someone.
- Glaring behaviour is often an indicator of anger.
- Obscene gestures with the hand can indicate anger.
- Pointing a finger at someone can indicate anger.
- A person screwing up their face can be displaying anger.
- Angry eyes are the most common indicator of anger.

### Behavioural Changes

- Anger is often expressed when a person displays behaviour that is out of character, e.g. if a normally quiet person is angry they might display this by suddenly slamming things around and screaming out.
- When a person displays a behaviour that is totally inappropriate for the situation they are in, it is often an indication of anger, e.g. yelling and screaming out in a library.

*Thoughts*

People's thoughts run wild when they are angry. They can think of things like hurting someone or themselves, getting revenge or thinking cruel actions against someone.

### 7.4.3 Managing behaviour

There are many anger management plans available to students but all seem to reflect the following key requirements:

- Put the anger on hold;
- Talk it out, cool down;
- Don't use violence;
- Don't scare or bully people;
- Walk away.

***These anger management principles can be implemented as follows (from the student's perspective):***

Step One:    I must stop and think about this situation.

Step Two:    I must keep calm. I need to cool down.

Step Three:  I need to take charge of myself; control my feelings.

Step Four:   I will not blame anyone or anything. There is nothing to be gained by looking for scapegoats.

Step Five:   If my anger is still boiling I need to give myself some time out. I might need to walk away for a short time or take some big breaths.

Step Six:    If my anger is under control I will proceed with what I would normally do. If it is not, I will walk away and remove myself from the situation.

## 7.5 Stress Management

A comment frequently heard from senior secondary students, especially around exam time, is:

*"I am so stressed out, my head hurts."*

Like anger, stress can erode mental toughness, and some claim that stress is the number one enemy to resilience. The thing about stress is that too much of it can cause many problems, but too little makes it almost impossible for the individual to perform to his or her maximum potential. To actualise their performance potential students need to learn how to manage their stress. This is a phenomenon that should be discussed at length with the mentor.

The secret to managing stress is for students to recognise what the optimum amount is that they require to perform to their potential. The following information and activities should help to build an awareness of stress so that this can be successfully managed.

### 7.5.1 Key facts and concepts related to stress

An important requirement in managing stress is for students to gain an understanding of some of the facts and key concepts related to stress. The following information should be discussion points between the student and the mentor.

- Stressors arise from two main sources – physical conditions that have the potential to damage the body (starvation, accidents, hypothermia, lack of oxygen) and psychological situations (intense persistent fears or prolonged unresolved conflict).
- An event or situation that is a stressor to one person (e.g. fear of sitting exams) will not necessarily be a stressor for another person.
- It is generally accepted that the primary stress response produces a common pattern of physiological reactions. These have been identified as follows:
  - An increase in heart rate and blood pressure as blood is forced to those muscle groups which may have to respond immediately to the physical threat imposed.

- Sweating, which is the way the body lowers its temperature, allowing more energy to be utilised.
- Tension throughout the body muscles in preparation for immediate response to the crisis.
- The release of glucose from the liver into the blood stream. This response provides muscle groups with a readily available source of energy.
- Shallow breathing when the diaphragm tenses. This can lead to a reduced amount of oxygen entering the brain.

- Seyle (1956) informed us that the body reacts to stress in three successive stages:

❑ **An Alarm Reaction:** Whenever the body is confronted with a stressor an alarm reaction takes place. This consists of a complicated pattern of physiological and chemical changes. One component of this general reaction is the hypothalamic stimulation of the pituitary gland. This gland releases various hormones, one of which stimulates the adrenal cortex to secrete cortin. This hormone helps the body to cope with the impact of a variety of stressors.

❑ **The Stage of Resistance:** During this stage the body reaction to stress increases. This often has the effect, especially in non-critical situations, of eliminating the source of stress. However, when the stress situation persists the body's reaction can then become too intense, e.g. cortin may be secreted at such a high rate that its supply becomes depleted.

❑ **The Stage of Exhaustion:** This occurs when the body depletes the necessary resources to deal with the stressor. Usually the stress has ended before this stage is reached. In situations when the stage of exhaustion is reached, the consequences can be disastrous, occasionally resulting in death.

### 7.5.2 Activity 34
### Identifying Stress Warnings

An important part of stress management for secondary school students is being aware of early indicators of high stress. This activity might assist you to identify stress indicators that are relevant to you. Discuss your responses with your mentor.

### Directions

In this activity you should tick the first box alongside each indicator if you have experienced it. In the second box put a **P** if you think it is a physical sign or **M** if you think it is a mental sign.

| *Stressor* | *Experienced it* | *P/M* |
|---|---|---|
| 1. Lack of appetite. | | |
| 2. Not able to sleep. | | |
| 3. Feeling constantly irritable. | | |
| 4. Not able to sit and relax. | | |
| 5. Frequently bursting into tears. | | |
| 6. Feeling bored most of the time. | | |
| 7. Frequently having headaches. | | |
| 8. Not able to enjoy a good laugh. | | |
| 9. Constantly feeling alone. | | |
| 10. Not able to concentrate. | | |
| 11. Unable to enjoy yourself. | | |
| 12. Frequently having heartburn. | | |
| 13. Frequently having diarrhoea. | | |

| *Stressor* | *Experienced it* | *P/M* |
|---|---|---|
| **14.** Feeling everything is on top of you. | | |
| **15.** Frequently having stomach pains. | | |
| **16.** Frequently feeling anxious. | | |
| **17.** Constantly feeling tired. | | |
| **18.** Putting on weight. | | |
| **19.** Not being able to talk to anyone. | | |
| **20.** Experiencing muscle spasms. | | |

**N.B.   The presence of a single indicator normally doesn't reflect significant stress. The more indicators you identify the more serious the stress.**

### 7.5.3    *The importance of relaxation for stress management*

A comment I have often heard from secondary school students, especially around exam time, is "I don't know how to relax". It is well documented that one of the key strategies available for managing stress is to use a proven relaxation strategy. There are numerous proven relaxation strategies available to you – your teacher or mentor might know of some that they can share with you. I have found the following strategy, devised by D. Lawrence (1992) to be most effective for stressed students.

### 7.5.4    *Activity 35*

Relaxation Strategy

#### Step One:

Sit comfortably:
- Ensure all your limbs are limp.
- Take off your shoes.
- Fix your eyes on a point on the wall or ceiling (don't raise your head).
- The moment you experience any discomfort close your eyes.

#### Step Two:

Breathing:
- Breathe in, slowly, until you feel this slow breathing is happening automatically.
- Focus on the breath you have in your abdomen – fill your abdomen with each intake, not just the upper part of your body.

#### Step Three:

Muscles:
- Focus on your stomach muscles – relax them.
- Relax your neck muscles in the same way.
- Focus now on each part of your body. Begin with your toes and slowly bring your attention upwards.

#### Step Four:

Visualisation:
- Bring a relaxing scene to your mind – the ocean, a mountain river, a forest or the call of a bird.
- Imagine you see a leaf or twig blowing in the wind, floating in the ocean or river, moving through the forest.

- Follow its journey down the river, across the ocean, through the forest, etc. It will take about five minutes to get to its destination.
- Now slowly, gently open your eyes.

## Case Study from Down Under: The Kids From Kwinana
### *This book will conclude as it started – with a group of secondary school students and a bikie gang.*

They were known as the Kwinana Challenge Kids. There were 20 of them to begin with and this soon dwindled to 12. They had been identified by the local high school as being students who had plenty of potential but who currently had hit a wall and were making little or no progress. There were six boys aged between 13 and 15 and six girls of similar age. They were "street-smart" and not short of answers when it came to pursuing out of school challenges. However, when it came to school and school work their greatest efforts were focused on how to avoid being there and doing any of it. They would tell you that they hated school, that many of their teachers hated them and picked on them and that there was nothing at school to interest them.

The experience I am about to recount occurred in the early 1990s. The local Rotary Club had decided that they wanted to get involved with these young people and to quote the Rotary President of the time, John Iriks: "We want to see if we can turn their lives around so that they have the opportunity to actualise their potential."

### *The Mentors*

The first part of this programme was to identify 12 members from the local Kwinana community who would volunteer to become mentors for these students for a year. They would receive no pay and would be required to undergo six × 2 hour sessions of training before they were matched with their students. Once matched they were required to meet with their student every fortnight for about one hour after school.

There were eight women and four men who volunteered to be mentors. Many of the women were mums whose children had completed their secondary schooling. All but four of the mentors were unemployed. One of the most popular of the mentors was Ralph, the local undertaker, who was forever being pestered by the kids to either take them for a spin in his hearse, have a sleep in a coffin or pop down to his shop to see a "stiff".

### *The Challenge*

After the mentoring programme had been going for approximately six months it was decided that the students, with their mentors, should undertake a challenge, to achieve something that no one would ever believe that they were capable of achieving.

A night of volatile discussions was held between the kids and their mentors but time after time they came back to the one challenge they could all agree on:

> *The Kwinana Challenge Group would stage a six hour rock concert featuring one of Australia's leading bands. They would stage it at Kwinana Beach to highlight the environmental issues that their beach was experiencing.*

### *Enter "C.C. Promotions"*

The proposal was put to the local Rotary Club and they agreed to a feasibility study being conducted. It was known that such a venture would require the support of the Kwinana Mayor and Council and that the local Member of Parliament would be required to get environmental approval for the venture from the Minister of the Environment.

A popular FM radio station was approached to determine what had to be done to stage such an event. The manager, without a moment's hesitation, informed the group that in Perth there was only one organisation that could stage such an event and that was "C.C.Promotions".

I was elected to approach these so-called rock 'n' roll entrepreneurs on behalf of the Kwinana Challenge Group. The address I was given was a central suburban location, and as I drove down the road towards it I was somewhat surprised by the large number of motorcycles that seemed to occupy every parking space along the road. As I walked to the sign-posted head office of this esteemed organisation I began to think all was not as it seemed, particularly when on the front verandah of the office, right alongside the main entrance, stood an empty coffin. The receptionist that greeted me was the most scantily clad receptionist I had ever had the good fortune to meet. With a "Wait a moment I'll get the boss!" she disappeared into another room.

I'll never forget my first meeting with Eddie, the boss. With biceps that looked like balloons, a number one haircut, and dressed in a fully "patched" jacket this guy looked at me and said:

"Are you really sure you want to do this? Do you know who we are?"

Well, as it turned out that Perth's most successful rock 'n' roll entrepreneur was none other than the notorious bikie gang, the Coffin Cheaters. I was informed by Eddie that the sort of concert we envisaged needed an up-front cash requirement of approximately $100,000 and a work force of about 100 people. However, he said with the most wicked of smiles, if I could get the Kwinana Mayor, the Kwinana Rotary, the local Member of Parliament and the parents of the kids involved to agree to C.C.Promotions staging the Challenge Concert, not only would they agree to do it, but they would put the money up as well.

### The Meeting At The Mayor's Office

The Challenge Group of parents decided that we should call a meeting at which the Kwinana Mayor, local Member of Parliament and local president of Rotary should meet with this organisation that was making such a generous offer. In organising this meeting it has to be said that very few details were given out about just who this very generous group actually were.

The meeting was timed for 8 pm in the Mayor's office. We were all seated waiting for our distinguished visitors to arrive – the mayor of Kwinana, the local Member of Parliament, the president of Kwinana Rotary and the members of the Kwinana Challenge Group. The next moment from outside came a noise that sounded like a Boeing 727 starting its engines up in your backyard.

"What the hell is that?" screamed the Mayor.

"Call the cops!" yelled the local Member of Parliament.

And then in walked Eddie and half a dozen of his gang members. To say that there was a stunned silence would be to underscore the absolute shock expressed by the distinguished hosts of the meeting.

Eventually, the meeting staggered on its way, and after a great deal of soul searching and intense discussion, approval was given for the event to proceed.

### A Rocky Ride

For the next six months the Kwinana Challenge Kids worked alongside Coffin Cheater members in preparing for the "Challenge Rock Concert". To say that this journey was a rocky ride is an understatement. First the Challenge Kids had to put up with a cynical media:

*"... Could someone tell me what a group of delinquent juveniles are doing working with members of Perth's notorious bikie gang, the Coffin Cheaters?"*

*"... Talk about the blind leading the blind!"*

... were typical of newspaper and radio talkback comments levelled at the programme.

Then there was the disappointment of losing the top billing act for the show. Originally the very popular group, Midnight Oil, had agreed in principle to perform at the concert. Discovery of an overseas commitment resulted in the "Oils" reluctantly pulling out three months before the concert. The Black Sorrows, another popular group, were then contacted and agreed to perform.

The poor local Member of Parliament was even subjected to embarrassing questions during question time in the Western Australian Parliament:

"Is it true that the honourable member for Peel has given his approval to a group of secondary school children to work alongside members of the Coffin Cheaters, and if so, how can he possibly justify this?"

The most stressful part of the journey was the long wait for environmental approval to stage the event. This was not given until just one month before the concert was due to take place. It was as if every authority at every turn was deliberately testing the resolve of the group.

During this six month period, the Kwinana Challenge Kids were not just idle spectators. Eddie, leader of C.C. Promotions, had given an undertaking to their parents and local authorities that, not only would he ensure that there would be no crime, no drugs, no alcohol involved at any stage, but that he would ensure that the Challenge students would be actively engaged in every aspect of preparation for the concert. Thus, the students learned about contracting; they learned about and engaged in advertising, marketing and merchandising; they were involved in organising security, parking and traffic control; and of course they were introduced to stage management and sound recording. Three students were selected to act as comperes for various aspects of the concert.

### The Challenge Concert Day: A DISASTER!

The beautiful morning of the Challenge Concert that faced the Challenge Kids gave no warning of the storm they would have to endure later that day. Gates opened at midday. The public began to trickle in. The first act began on time at 1 pm and through until 5 pm everything was running as it should have. A good-humoured crowd was building and they appreciated the music of the support acts. Kwinana students were handling parking and ticket sales admirably and those who had been assigned stage management tasks went about their business as if it was something they did every day.

Then came the first ominous warnings. It was 6.30 pm – the final support act, the Jets, were in full swing; cars were queued up for two kilometres and there was an expectant buzz amongst the crowd. Then … an almighty bang accompanied by a shower of sparks came from the stage. Immediately the stage plunged into darkness.

"It's O.K. folks, just one of the generators has blown up. The second generator will take over in a few minutes," the compere informed the crowd.

Sure enough in three minutes the lights were back on and ten minutes later the Jets were belting out their numbers as if nothing had happened.

Fifteen minutes before the Jets were due to conclude, there was another explosion from the stage and once again the stage plunged into darkness.

"Sorry folks another generator has blown. We do have a third as back-up and we'll be back in business in a few moments."

Well, the Jets finished their performance and there was a 60 minute break before the main act. The crowd now numbered well into the thousands but the electrical problems had caused there to be a rather apprehensive air amongst them.

"What if another generator blows?" was the feeling.

The Kwinana students went on about their business as if nothing had happened.

Fifteen minutes before the main act The Black Sorrows' support staff came out to tune the guitars and make sure everything was in ready.

Then, ten minutes into this tune-up session, you guessed it, yet another explosion, yet again the stage plunged into darkness. After a delay Eddie eventually came out onto the stage:

"Folks, I'm sorry. That's it! We have no more generators, we have no stage power. I'm afraid the concert is cancelled. Send your tickets into C.C. Promotions and we will issue a refund."

### *"Hey, Thompson!"*

The Kwinana students were instructed to report to the home of Ralph the undertaker – most appropriate I thought. How I dreaded meeting them there. I walked into Ralph's lounge with Eddie and was greeted with a surreal calm. I'm not sure whether Eddie has ever cried but I can tell you that night he came awfully close.

*"I'm sorry!" he simply said to the assembled students.*

*"I'm sorry!" I repeated and then ...*

*"Hey, Thompson!"*

It was Lance, self appointed spokesman for the Challenge group.

"Don't be sorry, don't be upset. Shit happens. We did a good job. We've had a great journey. We've learned heaps, we've made lots of friends. It didn't end quite the way it should have, but we have done things we never thought we were capable of doing."

**Endnote:** A follow up investigation into the failure of the generators found that it was just misfortune. The insurance company paid up and all overheads were met.

All of the Kwinana Challenge students continued through school for year 11. None were suspended or engaged in juvenile offending.

# References

Altman, I. & Taylor, D. (1973), _Social Penetration: The Development of Interpersonal Relationships,_ Holt. New York.

Aronowitz, S. (1992), _The Politics of Identity,_ Routledge. New York.

Argyris, C. & Schon, D. (1974), _Theory and Practice: Increasing Leadership Effectiveness,_ Jossey-Bass. San Francisco.

Babbie, E. (1998), _The Practice of Social Research,_ Wadworth Publishing Co. Westford. United States.

Baird, L. Schneier, C. & Laird, D. (Eds.) (1983), _The Training and Development Sourcebook,_ Human Resource Development Press. U.S.A.

Bandura, A. (1977), _Social Learning Theory,_ Prentice Hall. New Jersey.

Berger, C. Roloff, M. & Miller (eds.) (1987), _Interpersonal Processes: New Directions in Communication Research,_ Sage Publishers Inc. California.

Berko, R., Ronenfield, L. & Samovar, L. (1994), _Connecting: A Culture-Sensitive Approach to Interpersonal Communication Competency,_ Harcourt, Brace & Co. Orlando.

Blanck, P.D. (9th ed.), (1993), _Interpersonal Expectations: Theory, Research and Applications,_ Press Syndicate of University of Cambridge. New York.

Carter, S. & Lewis, G. (1994), _Successful Mentoring in a Week,_ Hodder & Stoughton. London.

Cohen, N.H. (1995), _Mentoring Adult Learners: A Guide for Educators and Trainees,_ Kringer Publications. Florida.

Condliffe, P. (1991), _Conflict Management, A Practical Guide,_ TAFE Publications. Australia.

Day, S. (1998), "Universality of Vocational Interest Structure Among Racial Ethnic Minorities", in, _American Psychologist,_ Vol. 53, No. 7, 728-736.

De Porter, D. (1992), _Quantum Learning: Unleashing The Genius In You,_ Dell Publishing. USA.

Dick, M. (1996), _Learning to Learn: A Study Skills Programme,_ UNITEC Publication. Auckland.

De Vito, J.A. (1992), _Essentials of Human Communication,_ Harper Collins. New York.

Douglas, T. (1991), _A Handbook of Common Group-work Problems,_ Hodder Headline. London.

Fielder, F. (1967), _A Theory of Leadership Effectiveness,_ McGraw-Hill. New York.

Fink, A. (1995), _How to Ask Survey Questions,_ Sage. California.

Fish, D. (1995), _Quality Mentoring for Student Teachers: A Principled Approach to Practice,_ David Fulton. London.

Fuller, A. (1998), _From Surviving to Thriving: Promoting mental health in young people,_ ACER Press. Victoria

Good, M. & South, C. (1988), _In the Know: 8 Keys to Successful Learning,_ BBC Books. London.

Gray, W. & Gray, M. (1990), _Mentoring International,_ Vol.4, Issue 3, pp. 27-32, The Mentoring Institute Inc. USA.

Gresham, F.M. & Elliot, S.N. (1990), _Social Skills Rating System._ American Guidance Service.

Gresham, F.M., Elliot, S.N. & Evans-Fernandez, S.E. (1993), _Student Self Concept Scale_ (SSCS). AGS.

Grotenberg, E.H. (1995), _A Guide to Promoting Resilience in Children: Strengthening the Human Spirit,_ Civitan International Research Centre. Alabama.

Hattie, J.A. (1992), _Self Concept,_ Erlbaum. USA.

Hattie, J.A. (1996), "Future Directions in Self-Concept", Paper presented at the Annual Conference of the American Association For Research in Education. New York.

Henderson, N. & Milstein, M.M. (1996), _Resiliency in Schools: Making it Happen for Students and Educators,_ Corwin Press. New York.

Hersey, P & Blanchard, K (1993), _Management Of Organizational Behaviour, Utilising Human Resources,_ Prentice-Hall. New Jersey.

Hopson, B. & Scally, M. (1986), _Lifeskills Teaching Programmes: No's 1,2,3,_ McGraw Hill, Maidenhead.

Kincher, J. (1990), _Psychology for Kids,_ Free Spirit Publishing Inc. USA.

Kolb, D.(1981), *Learning Styles and Disciplinary Differences,* The Modern American College, Josey Bass, San Francisco.

Oakley, G. (1993), *The Power of Positive Thought,* Wrightbooks Pty. Ltd. Australia.

Oppenheim, A.N. (1966), *Questionnaire Design. Interviewing and Attitude Measurement,* Printers Publishers. New York.

Orlick, T. (1988), "Embracing Your Potential. Steps to Self-Discovery, Balance and Success", in, *Sports, Work and Life,* Human Kinetics. USA.

Pike, L.T. & Thompson, L.J. (1994), *The Youth Challenge Project: A Community's Effort to Improve Peer Relations,* Edith Cowan University Research Publication.

Pike, L.T., Thompson, A. & Thompson, L.J. (1995), *Self-Esteem in At-Risk Youth: Efficacy of Measures and The Role of Mentors,* Edith Cowan University Research Publication.

Pinner, D. & Pinner, D. (1994), *Communication Skills,* Longman

Reasoner, R.W. & Dusa, G.S. (1992), *Building Self-Esteem in the Primary and Secondary Schools,* 2nd edition. CPP.

Rutter, M. (1994), "Stress research: Accomplishments and tasks ahead", in R.J. Haggerty, R.R. Sherrod, N.Garmezy & M.Rutter (Eds.), *Stress, risk, and resilience in children and adolescents: Processes, mechanisms, and interventions* (pp 354-386), Cambridge. Cambridge University Press.

Skerker, R. & McDonough, G. (1993), *Developing the Resilient Child: A Prevention Manual for Parents, Schools, Communities, and Individuals.* Northeast Regional Centre For Drug Free Schools and Communities, Sayville. New York.

Thayer, L. (1968), *Communication and Communication Systems in Organisation, Management and Interpersonal Relations,* Irwin Inc. Illinois.

Thompson, L.J. & Lowson, T. (1995), *Self-Esteem Books 1, 2, 3,* Ready-Ed Publications. Perth.

Thompson, L.J. (2010), *Self-Esteem: A Complex Phenomenon: A Manual for Mentors,* Aber Publishing, Abergele.

Vanistendael, S. (1995), *Growth in the muddle of life. Resilience: Building on other people's strengths,* ICCB Series. ERIC Document, ED387569, 47pp.

Zubrick, S.R., Silburn, S.R., Gurrin, L., Teoh, H., Shepherd, C., Carlton, J., & Lawrence, D. *Western Australian Child Health Survey: Education, Health and Competence.* Perth, Western Australia: Australian Bureau of Statistics and the TVW Institute for Child Health Research. (1997)

# Index

## Aber Publishing is a part of GLMP Ltd

*Books from Aber Publishing*

Aussie, Aussie Readers

Back to the Black

The Adult Skills Series

The Adult Numeracy Series

Hey Thompson: Developing self-esteem and resilience in secondary school students

Self Esteem: a Manual for Mentors

Contentious Issues

Life Skills: Bullying

Life Skills: Family Relationships

Life Skills: Grief, Illness and other Issues

Life Skills: Self Esteem and Values

Enhancing Self Esteem in the Adolescent

Survival Teen Island

Understanding the Numbers: The first steps in managing your money

Understanding Maths: Basic Mathematics Explained

Many more titles in development